THE MELODY OF TREES

The Melody of Trees
Ten Tales from the Forest

Helen Whistberry

Text copyright © 2022 Helen Whistberry
All Rights Reserved
www.helenwhistberry.com

All characters appearing in this work are fictitious. Any resemblance to real persons, living or dead, is purely coincidental. No part of this publication may be reproduced, distributed, or transmitted in any form or by any means, including photocopying, recording, or other electronic or mechanical methods, without the prior written permission of the author, except in the case of brief quotations for the purposes of critical reviews and certain other noncommercial uses permitted by copyright law. For permission requests, contact the author through her website at:

www.helenwhistberry.com

Eleven original illustrations by Helen Whistberry
Cover design by Fay Lane www.faylane.com
Interior formatting by Nicole Scarano www.facebook.com/groups/nsformatting

Other Works by Helen Whistberry

The Jim Malhaven Mysteries series:

The Weird Sisters

The Avenging Angel

The Ghostly Groom

Take My Hand at Midnight: A Gothic Ghost Tale

Short stories in the following collections:

Creating Cinderella

Autumn Nights: 12 Chilling Tales for Midnight

Of Cottages and Cauldrons

Villainous

Duplicitous

Ravens and Roses

Autumn Nights: 10 Sinister Stories

In Somnio

STORIES

Forest ... 1
Girl of Glass ... 9
Revenant of the High Lonesome ... 27
The Melody of Trees ... 51
An Invitation of Shadows ... 75
The Watcher ... 95
Written in the Ashes ... 117
Flora and Milo ... 135
Bad Day on the Job ... 161
A Gnashing of Teeth ... 191

Acknowledgments

Gratitude and love to
Ian, Jess, Kait, Jacob, Elizabeth,
Catherine, Liz, Kim, Cass, Annie,
Syreeta, AJ, LA, JR, GM, KF, Alex,
Eileen, Adam, Travis, Chase, Ginny,
Cassondra, Cassandra, Monique, Beth,
Agnes, Paul, Tiffany, Tara, Lexi,
Martine, Winifred, Theophanes,
Dakota, Crowe, Crystal, Michael,
and so many other Twitter
friends and supporters
who have lifted and inspired
me when I was low

and, as always,
to my beloved sister
without whom
none of this
would have
ever
happened

"And into the forest I go, to lose my mind and find my soul"

— ***JOHN MUIR***

FOREWORD

This collection of short stories is very close to my heart. Sparked by a theme suggested by a potential publisher from whom I've since parted ways amicably, the notion of crafting ten tales that all revolve in some way around a forested setting, without repeating myself was an irresistible challenge. Over the course of a year, I tried to stretch myself by embracing genres, styles, and moods I hadn't yet attempted to create this mix of happy and sad, hopeful and melancholy, serious and funny stories.

You'll find a little bit of everything here: fantasy, folklore, horror, humor, sci-fi, and western. What ties them all together is a touch of humanity even in those characters who aren't quite human; a feeling of empathy for all creatures; and the weird and sometimes whimsical beauty to be found in moments both light and dark.

And there are some dark moments ahead, so proceed with caution, but for those who venture into my forests, may you find something worth holding close to your heart.

FOREST

I am an Elder God, one that most have long forgot. When dawn comes, I roam, long strides through ether and cloud above and the stench of the rotting earth below. My roots are long and silvered. My bark shines and clicks in the silence that ascends. I survive. Keep one eldritch eye on the sky and one on the ground. Tales without number have played out before me. Triumphs and tragedies, birth and death. Things both magical and mundane. Nothing that enters the forest escapes my notice.

A MOUSE CROUCHES on the forest floor beneath a shelter of leaves shimmering in autumnal hues, shielded from a chilly drizzle that bounces from branch to branch before hitting the ground. She watches for the grey death, all feathers and talons and yellow eyes, that searches for her ceaselessly. Dozes and shivers and feels in her bones that the coming winter will be hard.

Dreams of a spindle that turns out the finest silk gathered from the bright auras of living things. Their own shine diminishes as the fibers of their being are harvested, a sad loss from which they will never fully recover. But oh, the brilliance of the cloth that is woven from it, threads shimmering like the scales of a trout in water.

She imagines tailoring a warm coat, layering it with goosedown gathered from river's edge. Threads a pine needle with the spidery silk and wears a thimble made of a seed husk. She ponders whether the garment is of the latest style or not, then decides she will set her own fashion.

A bright yellow flame dances through the night. It has escaped from a candle wick before it was doused and is out adventuring now. And why not? Why should it be confined, imprisoned? It has its own ambitions. To see something of the world, perhaps make a name for itself. It spies the mouse shivering in the cold and rain and stops to lend some of its warmth. There is always time for a kindness given freely.

The mouse awakens. She is cheered by the companionable fire but regrets that the warm coat exists only in her imagination. Minutes pass slowly, ears flattened, listening, waiting. The rain patters on the leaves, a dull kaleidoscope of sound. As the pings taper off, a ray of light pierces the gloom. Dawn is coming. Soon it will be time to move, to take a chance, to *run*.

A LARK TURNS his face to the rising sun, feels it warm his feathered cloak through and through, heat his hollow bones with divine fire. A small heart patters. Lungs burst with joy. Vibrant song echoes, awakening others of its kind.

Their voices rise in a chiming chorus. Wings stir, a murmuration takes flight. Whispers and prophecies swirl and dive in the arcane patterns they create, mesmerizing those creatures trapped on the ground, staring upward in astonishment. Despair and dread creep into their minds. We are powerless, they think. Great forces are at work in the world over which we have no control.

But then, a single fluttering bird breaks off from the flock, swoops low and shares a dance of joy and hope and the sheer exhilaration of morningtime with those below. Their souls fill with gratitude.

A SQUIRREL CATCHES the fever of thanks giving and sets off in search of her friend the crow. She scampers up a tree, tail flirting and flicking with a life all its own. His nest is empty. The crow has flown away in search of peace, an escape from the demons of strife and despair that weigh him down. The squirrel settles in to wait, curling herself into the twiggy nest and wrapping her tail around her like a blanket.

She watches clouds drift by. Imagines floating on one across the great river. What would she find on the other side? Others like herself, or beings unimaginable and strange? She seeks them out in the white puffballs rolling across the sky. A winking eye there, a coiled tail here, and a black spot that jars the spirit—it is the crow, winging back to its nest and delighted to find a visitor.

They catch up on important doings: a fat beetle that made a juicy snack for the crow, a treasure trove of forgotten acorns rediscovered by the squirrel. An owl passes by and spies the unlikely pair gossiping.

"How can a squirrel and a crow be friends?" he asks.

"We have open minds," the crow says.

"And open hearts," adds the squirrel.

"Ah," says the owl, "then it is an old and deep magic that binds you. Such a spell cannot be broken. Blessings on you both."

THERE IS a man in the forest. Most are not welcome here, but this one I don't mind. He treads gently, carefully. Means no harm. I can read his story. His woes are common: melancholy, heartbreak, a body worn by time and the mercilessly hard labor it takes to survive beyond these sacred groves.

He pauses near the shallows of the river where the waters run slow and calm. Removes his crumbling leather boots. Dunks one toe, shivers, then wades in, letting the laughing waters tickle his feet. A great heron lands nearby. They gaze upon one another, nod in understanding. Sometimes, patience is required. Time passes.

The heron cocks its head then strikes. A wriggling fish, its fate sealed, is gulped down and down. The man smiles, applauds lightly at the neat trick. The heron bows in acknowledgment. It is pleasant to have one's skill recognized.

"Would that I had such a talent," the man says. "I would dwell in the forest forever."

The heron blinks in sympathy.

"I think I'll be dead soon. Hope they bury me deep under a meadow of yarrow and poppy, harebell and thistle so these old bones can feed the soil, burst forth in bloom. I'll listen to the buzzy busy sound of bees, the soft thump, thump of a hare's warning against the earth. Know that those who walk above me are rejoicing in the warmth of a summer's day. Be at rest."

I can see his future. A pauper's grave in a muddy, forgotten pit with worm and beetle, rat and raven for company. Fine creatures all and not to be despised, but not quite what he envisions. My influence does not extend beyond this woody place to the world outside, but I can bestow a gift while he is within my ward.

A painted butterfly drifts by. Lands on the man's threadbare sleeve. He gapes down in delight. Another and another join it, more and more until he is caught in a whirlwind of fluttering and tenderly-bestowed kisses. He laughs, a rusty sound, out of practice from lack of use. His face is lit with joy. A memory to take with him through his final hours, days, minutes. A brush with enchantment to sustain him until the end.

My attention wanders down the way. Another pair I spy.

Sleek otter dives deep into the cold, clear water. Skips and slips, swims and slides. Revels in the feel of her body stretching and twisting, perfect control over every motion. She spies a pinchy crayfish, a crunchy morsel to split open, scoop out, shell discarded on the riverbed below. One life lost so another might continue. Satiated, she floats on her back in the warm sun, long tail ruddering as she watches red and gold leaves spin lazily down from the sky.

On the bank, a badger crouches among sharp-cutting reeds. Watches the nimble, carefree otter with jealous, rheumy eyes. The earth is stained red beneath his feet. A vicious fight, one last dispute over territory, but unlike so many times before, this verdict was not in his favor. He has cowered here during an endless night. Breathed in the heavy fog and despaired of seeing the morning sun or feeling its blessed rays warm him one last time.

I part the reeds, rearrange a few branches overhead, direct a beam of light to him in a final benediction. His spirit lifts. He counts his blessings. After all, he survived longer than any of his littermates. His final thoughts: *I have been a warrior. I have been true.*

MOVING DEEP WITHIN THE FOREST, I visit a dismally forgotten dwelling. Chattering jays perch on a fallen pine that splits the cottage in two. Moss and vine and creeping thyme have taken over the garden beds. A wary hare crouches beneath a boxwood gone shaggy and rogue with wildness. Nature reclaiming what was once hers and will be again.

The vine gossips of a husband's dark deed buried underground, kept secret by the clay molding itself around broken bones, holding them close as though to knit them back together if it could. Resurrect these relics to a life cut short. The rose bush that blooms nearby is sickly, diseased. Her favorite plant in all the garden. It misses her, the vine whispers with a knowing wink.

Much changed, the wife roams this place in a gown she wove, a garment of gossamer and dewdrops. It shimmers in the sun as she dances on the petal of a yellow daffodil. A blackbird stops to stare, grins with inward delight at such untrammeled joy. Its heart made light, it flaps away, performing cartwheels in the sky.

Tired of feigning a bliss she does not feel, this wife-that-was floats to the top of the tallest tree to speak with me.

"Why did he do it?" she asks.

"Why do men do anything?"

"Because they can," she answers.

A heavy sadness settles. The weight of unnecessary sorrow. Pointless cruelty.

"It is not only men. The lust for battle and strife has spread to even the humblest creatures," I say, touching her ghostly forehead with a long, silver branch. "See what I see."

We watch ant armies on parade. Bee and wasp sharpen their stings. Spiders weave sticky traps. Mosquito and tick prepare the blood banks while beetle and worm make ready to tidy away the dead. These humans have carelessly defiled their home long enough. Time for war.

I bend low to speak to them. A tiny prince of a fellow, all snapping pincers and brilliant green shell, waves his legs at me and warns me in shrill chirrups to go away and mind my own business.

"What do you hope to accomplish?" I ask. "You are all so very small."

"But we are legion."

We watch them march, black carpet and cloud deserting the trees. They leave a silence behind such as my forest has never known. What the outcome of this battle will be, for once, I cannot see and do not want to. All I sense is death, and I tremble in fear. At least I think it must be that for I have never felt it before.

The sun sinks low.

An oak stretches its long limbs in a clearing, easing the strains of the day. Small, furry creatures tickle its roots, make it chuckle. Passing birds alight now and again, wrens and nuthatches chattering of sights they have seen. Chipmunks dance a waltz round its ribs, chasing one another in play.

The tree daydreams of a time in the long ago when a young girl would come to visit. Day after day, she whispered her secrets to the tree alone. It hugged them close, jealously guarded them. But then, the girl became a bride, moved to a cottage where she tended her rose garden. Her visits grew fewer, she grew sadder and quieter, until one day, she stopped coming altogether. The oak keeps her confidences still, but to what purpose, it can no longer remember.

At its foot, a frilly fern releases a spore from one of its curled fronds. The spore flies high, caught on a zephyr that flings it wantonly along an old forest path as though it were just another hiker travelling through. An updraft strands it on the very top of a towering pine.

I can see for miles. This is the life, it thinks.

IT IS ALMOST DARK NOW. I trace out the path of an aurora in the sky with my finger. Grind up soul dust in the palm of my hand and sprinkle it liberally. Sing a hymn of twinkling starlight. Put on a show for the creatures below. I love to see their faces erupt with awe and ecstasy at my silly magic tricks. To distract them from their burdens for a moment in time. To be of service.

I AM AN ELDER GOD, one that most have long forgot. When twilight comes, I roam, long strides through ether and cloud above and the stench of the rotting earth below. My roots are long and silvered. My bark shines and clicks in the silence that descends. I survive. Keep one eldritch eye on the sky and one on the ground. Tales without number have played out before me. Triumphs and tragedies, birth and death. Things both magical and mundane. Nothing that enters the forest escapes my notice.

Not even you.

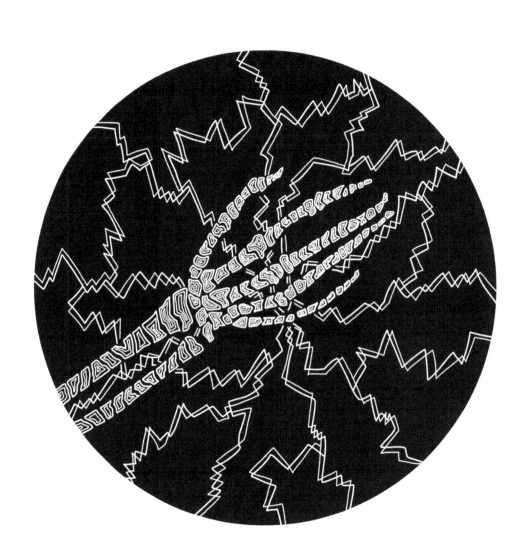

GIRL OF GLASS

"Greetings, young Ava! I saw you walking here all alone and said to myself, Barnaby, old son, there's a pretty maiden who could use some company on this fine morning. It is pure serendipity that blew us together, don't you think?"

"Or an evil wind," I muttered to myself.

Barnaby Crumb was notorious for roving eyes and hands, but not for his acute hearing. He disregarded my soft complaint and grabbed my arm to tether me to his side. "And where are you off to all alone? These woods can be a dangerous place, you know. Foxes and bears and wolves." He leered at me.

"Or wolves in sheep's clothing?" I asked, looking pointedly at Crumb's fleece-lined coat, but such wordplay was beyond him.

"You shouldn't be out here without an escort to protect you. I'm surprised at your mother allowing it."

"It was she that sent me." I displayed my wicker basket, heavy with berries and mushrooms. Any other man might have taken the hint and relieved me of my burden if he was determined to walk beside me, but Barnaby blathered on, oblivious.

"Eudora is a trusting soul, isn't she? She doesn't know the first thing about the evils that exist in this world."

I snorted. My mother was an expert in the first and last evils and all the ones in between. She was malevolence personified, though most did not see it. The mask she wore when others were around was too perfect and practiced for any to suspect. It was my privilege alone as her only child to bear witness to the vileness that was her corrupted spirit.

We were as unalike as could be. She, a blonde and blue-eyed witch, statuesque and commanding. Me, a mousy brunette, brown-eyed doll with copious curves to make up for my lack of height. I often fantasized that I was a changeling, dropped into the crib twenty years past as punishment for some sin Eudora had committed against the faerie world.

Somewhere out there, no doubt, a blonde goddess strode through a world of magic and light, more at home in that place than I would ever have been. No wonder Eudora treated me worse than the lowliest servant. I must have been a grave disappointment to her.

Barnaby rambled on, his teeth chattering in my ear as he bent down to accommodate our difference in stature, but I paid no attention. I was already dreading arriving back at the cottage and presenting my basket for inspection. No matter how successful my foraging was, Eudora always found cause for complaint. I tried to pretend I didn't care, but it was disheartening all the same.

I felt a pinch through my thick skirts. Barnaby playing fresh. Feigning surprise, I knocked into him with my basket, my aim true. I left him bent over in the lane behind our garden wall, trying to recover his breath and composure.

Verity met me at the garden gate, her long ears and perfect nose twitching in welcome. I leant down to run my fingers through her soft, white fur. Her pink eyes closed in bliss as she purred a hum of contentment. I slipped her a wild blackberry to nibble on before entering the cottage. Eudora had barred the rabbit from coming inside. With autumn weather approaching, I'd have to remember to insulate her outside pen against the harshly frigid nights.

I was barely through the door before a strident voice called out.

"Let me see." Eudora snatched the basket from my hands, sorting through my haul of mushrooms. She held one up in front of my face. "Do you mean to poison us or are you simply stupid?"

A destroying angel, most deadly of fungi. Another mistake on my part. I'd told her time and again I wasn't talented at identifying mushrooms, but she insisted I collect them all the same.

She slapped me hard across the face, first one cheek then the other. "I should feed this to that albino vermin you keep. Maybe it would teach you to be more careful."

Another threat to add to a lifetime of them. Most were never carried out, but enough were to strike fear into my heart.

"I'm sorry, Mother. I promise you I do my very best."

"The tragic thing is, I believe you. You always were a most unpromising child, and nothing changes as you grow older except the amount of food it takes to keep you. You shall skip supper tonight. It won't hurt you to miss a meal. Spend the extra time in sketching out all the dangerous mushrooms again in your journal. I'll get them into that thick head of yours one way or another." She pushed me up the stairs, great shoves against my back that would add to the collection of bruises already there.

As for my punishment, I'd eaten my fill of berries while I was picking in the forest, and I enjoyed drawing, so it was not as great a penalty as she imagined. Quite the contrary, for any time spent away from her terrifying company was a blessed relief.

Retreating to my room, I lit a candle against the gathering gloom. Opened my sketchbook to a blank page and referred to the notes Eudora had given me on fungi that I studied so often to no avail. Skullcaps and toadstools blossomed beneath my quill. I enjoyed the scritch-scratch of the sharpened nib against the rough paper. The pleasing blackness of the ink fading into grey as I blew gently to dry it before turning the page.

A toad landed on the desk, startling me into overturning the inkpot. I cursed as the liquid oozed its way across my drawing, blotting out all my hard work. But then, a strange thing. A picture formed slowly in the pool of ink. My own face, frozen in a scream of agony.

There was a sharp knock at the door. My eyes flicked away from the page. When they returned to the book, the ink was just ink again. A black nothingness. My long braid fell across my shoulder and smeared through the mess.

Another knock. It must be Eudora come to check on my progress. I tore the offending page out of the sketchbook and crumpled it in my hand, dropping it to the floor and kicking it under my bed. I flung my braid back, hoping she wouldn't notice the ink stain when I opened the door.

No one was there.

I turned to close it when a croaking noise at my feet stopped me. It was the toad from my desk, its back the color of lightly toasted bread, with dark spots that might be natural or splashes of the spilled ink. It was large in size, bigger than my two fists put together. What was it doing in the house?

As if in answer, it croaked again and hopped away down the hall, disappearing into the dark. I followed, but it was nowhere to be seen. A strange and disruptive visitor but a brief one at least.

I returned to my room and shut the door, leaning against it in sudden weariness. Caught my reflection in the ancient mirror that adorned the far wall. I'd known it from a child. Spent many an hour peering into it, hoping to see some improvement in my looks as I grew older. Equal parts defiantly proud of who I was and wishing I was anything other.

There was a gap between the mirror and the frame on one side where the carved wood had become rotten and brittle. A flash of movement drew me to the glass. An eye peered out. There was something—someone—there. Just like in a fairy tale.

"Do you need help? Are you trapped? Do you wish to be freed?" I asked.

"It is thou that is trapped," it hissed. "We pity thee."

A thrill curled round my spine. "What do you mean? I am free to come and go. As free as any maiden my age, that is."

"The witch binds thee to her. Thou are not free, but we could make thee so."

I couldn't argue. Eudora did keep me close to her, the better to beat me into submission and bend me to her will. My only escape would be through my marriage or her death, neither of which seemed imminent. The thought of a more immediate release from her iron rule was tempting.

"How?"

"First, thou must make a payment. Give us something that is precious to thee and thee alone."

I looked around my room. It was sparsely furnished. The only adornments were bits of rock and leaf, dried flowers. My wardrobe was limited and serviceable, nothing elaborate, and no jewelry to speak of except a string of cheap red beads given to me by a passing merchant.

"I have nothing precious."

"That is a lie. Look within thy heart."

An image floated before me. A white rabbit playing in a garden.

"Not Verity. She's the only friend I have."

"And what is more precious than that? Freedom comes at a price."

"It is too high."

"Very well." The eye disappeared. All was silent once more.

I was bereft. Nothing of such great import had ever happened to me before, and now it was over. I battled with instant regret, but the thought of losing Verity haunted me.

My door burst open. This time it was Eudora.

"You must be done with your task if you have time to dawdle about gazing in the mirror. Were I so unpleasing to the eye, I would not spend my time so."

She pulled me roughly to the desk, bent to examine my book. "What is this? A page has been torn out."

"I'm sorry, Mother. I knocked over the ink."

Her gimlet eye landed on my black-stained braid.

"What foolishness is this?" She grabbed my hair, jerking me painfully around to face her. "Careless might as well be your true name. Wasting ink and paper. They're expensive, girl. And now you've ruined your hair. You can't go out like that. Do you want to make me a laughingstock?"

"I'm sorry, Mother. Maybe it will wash out. I'll try in the morning."

"Don't bother." She lifted a pair of scissors from my desk and before I could protest, snipped off my waist-length braid and threw it out the window. "Take more care, or I'll throw you out next time."

I stood in shock long after she left. My head felt strangely light, untethered without the grounding weight of my hair. I turned back to the mirror, ran my hands through the roughly-chopped strands. Maybe it wasn't so bad. Maybe I could even it up. I picked up the scissors, trimmed one side and then the other, over and over and over.

Hysteria bubbled up. I couldn't stop myself until I'd cut every piece of hair so close to my head that I left a treasure map of blood crisscrossing my scalp where the sharp shears caught the skin within their merciless grasp.

I looked a freak. The eye reappeared on the mirror's edge. I could read pity in it along with a kind of contempt for one who would put up with such treatment. I stared at myself long, then padded down the stairs and out into the garden. Verity had retreated to her hutch for the night and was sleeping peacefully.

My hands trembled as I reached for her. She squirmed in my arms, snuggling close. So trusting. I couldn't do it. Then a drop of blood ran into my eye from my mangled scalp. I felt as though I was waking from a dream, a nightmare. I'd reached my limit. I couldn't face Eudora again after what she'd done. After what I'd done.

I returned to my room and offered Verity to the mirror.

"What will you do with her?" I asked.

The eye opened. "Honor her."

The rabbit disappeared from my arms. There was a low humming noise, unpleasant to the ear. The mirror trembled, shook, then shattered, spraying me with flecks of glass like needles through my skin. I watched my arms turn to silver as the shards assembled themselves into a protective shell around me, following my form in every detail. Once reflected, now I was the reflection.

A tap on my shoulder. A shadow stood there, giggled, turned and ran. I followed the twisting darkness through the house. What a flirt it was! It stopped often to look back at me. Though it had no face, I sensed a wink and a smirk in its taunting stillness. Then it raced on, sliding under doors and drifting across ceilings.

I ran, breathlessly, recklessly, down the hall and down the stairs only to come face to face with Eudora.

"Ava," she whispered, "is that you?"

She was shocked, amazed at my transformed self. Reached out to touch. The silvered bits of me cut her hand to ribbons. Shrieking, she grabbed a broom, beat at me as though she would smash me and sweep up the pieces. Tidy me away.

But my new skin was tough. She could not hurt me now. I stepped past her to the door. I had to find that shadow. Ask it what to do now that I was no longer strictly human.

Dawn was breaking, a hint of light over the tops of the trees. Eudora came to the door, moaning and wringing her bloodied hands.

"You won't survive without me," she screeched, but I barely heard it. I was listening to another sound. An eerie serenade that called to me, luring me into the woods.

I tracked the broken melody, retrieving stray notes from the brushy, quavering path as I went. The sharp notes jabbed and stabbed and cut at my armored skin, but it was the flat notes that broke my heart with their bleak, deflated, hopeless sighs. I gathered them in my hands where they glittered like stars. Of what use they would be, I could not say, but they seemed filled with meaning.

Small animals scattered at my coming. What a strange sight I must be! Dazzling and weird. My glass spoke a soft tinkling noise. I was a walking wind chime. My own alarm, warning the forest creatures to run and hide, though I would do them no harm. Perhaps they were right to be frightened. Maybe they sensed what I had done. Sacrificed up Verity without knowing what prize I would win.

What was this bargain I'd made? I supposed I was free of Eudora. She could not harm me in this form, nor keep me at home, so the mirror did not lie exactly. But like all magic, the results were never what you expected, were they? I couldn't walk into town looking like this, nor expect to lead a normal life. I would be named a monster. Put on display. The reflection of prying eyes multiplied by the hundreds on my broken skin.

And so, I followed the music for lack of a better plan. It was out of place in this wood, as out of place as I was. Perhaps whoever made it could help me, a fellow misfit.

One of the sparkling notes in my hand rose up. An insect, I thought. A firefly, but no, it spoke to me.

"Do not go farther," it advised.

"Why not? And who or what are you?"

"I am a thing that has decided to warn you. The one you follow is not to be trusted. It stalks thru the trees in a suit woven from spider silk. Dragonflies nestle in its hair and beard. Their wings will flash in the light that filters thru this high canopy of golden leaves when the sun rises. Its greatcoat brushes the ground and leaves a path of shining slime where it passes, the sign of its decaying soul."

"I suppose I should be terrified," I replied, "but it all sounds rather dramatic. What kind of man is this?"

"It is not a man."

"Not a man?"

The starry creature warbled, "It is what your kind might call fae, though we do not use that word."

How could I help but rejoice at this news? What if I, a changeling in a very different sense now, should stumble upon the faerie realm? The adventure might be worth the price of admission after all. What would this creature make of me? A jangling collection of broken glass. Perhaps it could break the spell. Fae have their own magic if the legends hold true.

"Fascinating," I said. "I must find it."

"I thought you would think so. Humans are very stupid. Look at the trouble you're in already, and now you would go in search of more. Typical."

I giggled at the thing's cynicism. "What is your name?"

"You could not pronounce it, but you may call me Mordecai."

"Well, Mordecai, I don't know if I still qualify as human. I have been turned into a girl of glass."

"Glass on the surface, but girl beneath just the same, and girls must be careful in this world, for many there are would harm you."

I could not disagree, for my whole life was proof of it.

"But I cannot go home again. And what human I met would know what to make of me? I don't have as many choices as you seem to think."

"There is always a choice, but do as you will. It matters not to us. We will depart." Mordecai rose into the air, and the other lights I held cupped in my hands followed after. A dazzling sight until they split apart into separate tiny stars, disappearing in the forest gloom.

The sun had risen higher. Above, I could see the golden canopy Mordecai spoke of, and on the ground, a shining trail of slime winding through the trees. Perhaps Mordecai was right. It was hard to think the creature who left such a track was benevolent. But slugs and snails meant no harm, did they? Besides, I was hardly one to judge, all prickly edges and severe sharpness.

Perhaps my new form was an advantage, a protection. It had deflected Eudora's raging blows. I strode along the glistening path, filled with a new confidence, a sense of invulnerability. Mirror could be shattered easily, but I was already broken. What else could be done to me now?

I'd travelled much in these woods on my foraging trips and thought I knew them well, but the farther I walked, the stranger my surroundings. The trees grew gnarled, bent over, whispering amongst themselves. The ground was littered with restless leaves and twigs that danced away from my jingling feet. Small mushrooms, pearlescent in the light, climbed weathered trunks and winked at me.

And always, my mirrored shards reflected the sunlight this way and that, a glittering kaleidoscope of rainbowed color. So, who was to say which was more strange—the forest or my shattered self?

There was always a darkness before me. One amorphous shape that avoided the flashing of my skin. No matter how far I walked, it was always there, just out of reach. My new body did not tire, no longer weakling flesh, but my patience frayed all the same.

"You there," I called. "Slow down and speak to me."

The shadow rose to a great height, split the sky in two above my head, and rushed back to earth to confront me, a grinning, mewling thing.

"What shall we say?"

"I don't know. Hello or how do you do or your name. Anything."

"Hello. How do you do? And our name is our own, Ava."

"How do you know my name?"

"Verity told us."

My heart leapt. "Have you seen her? Is she well?"

"As well as could be expected."

What was I to make of that? Was she disappointed in me for giving her up for my own freedom? Had I placed her into danger? "Where is she?"

"A careless way to treat a friend." The darkness danced closer, absorbing both my reflected light and the light from above. Its form took shape. A face of planes and angles, a long coat that pooled on the ground, hands of claw and bone. It reached out a finger and tapped my cheek. A piece of my skin tinkled to the ground and crumbled to dust. "Was it worth it, I wonder."

I shivered, setting my shards to singing a jangled tune. "I was desperate."

"Desperate indeed if this mutilated skin seems an improvement. Is a girl made of glass really a girl at all? Or something else entirely. What is to be gained by wandering this forest?"

"I don't know. I didn't know what else to do. I followed your shadow. Thought you might advise me."

The dark creature chuckled. "And why is that? Because we are also a freak?"

"We're not freaks. We're beings of magic. Unique."

"We pity thee, girl," the shadow snarled.

"You! It was you in the mirror," I cried. "You did this. Can you not undo it? Return Verity to me?"

"Why? So that thou can return to that woman? Endure, exist, expire? We've given thee a great gift. Would thou squander it so soon, ungrateful wench?"

As inured as I was to being roughly spoken to, these words bounced off my glassy skin without harm. "You promised me freedom. What is this?" I spread my arms wide, casting reflections like silvered fish in the ocean.

The darkness bowed to me. "A beauty like none other. But take care—all beauty fades in the end."

A beauty? I can't deny a part of me warmed at the description. I'd longed for someone to think me so all my life. I reached out a hand, laid it on the shadow's shoulder and was met with the deepest chill I'd ever felt in my life. I drew back, but it was too late. My hand shattered, the glass made brittle from the icy cold.

I thought to see my skin beneath the vanished armor, but there was only sinew and bone, curling and clicking as I flexed my hand.

The shadow snarled at me. "Thou are a reckless one. Perhaps thy mother was right to punish, foolish girl." It stalked away, a gleaming trail of slime slithering in its wake mixed with a black ichor I had not noticed before.

This time, I didn't follow. I collapsed on the dank and musty forest floor and wept, small slivers of glass that soon littered the ground around me. I mourned my damaged hand and transformed self, the loss of home and friend. I'd felt lonely all my life, but I'd never been this alone.

A gentle radiance illuminated the heaps of shed glass around me. I looked up to find another being, a being of light, looking down at me. Pink eyes glowed.

"Verity?" I breathed, hardly daring to hope.

"We have been changed, dear one." Their voice sang with horror and love.

I clattered to my feet and bowed my head in disgrace. "I am so sorry."

They took my skeletal hand in their own soft one. "As am I. You are damaged. Such is the way of Leviathan."

"Is that its name? The darkness?"

"That is what we call it. The caged ones and I."

"Caged?"

"Yes. I have escaped for a time, but Leviathan will find me soon or late."

"And there are others... like you?"

"There are others. All unalike and yet alike in our captivity. A menagerie it keeps. It means to lure you in and add you to its collection. Turn back. Save yourself."

"But how horrible. How many does it keep imprisoned?"

"Beyond counting. It has been accumulating specimens for millennia. It will never cease."

My soul quivered at the thought. I knew what it was to be a captive thing. To feel helpless. To know your life was not your own. "Is there nothing to be done?"

Verity smiled. Their sharp teeth gleamed. "There is a prophecy we speak of in the still hours of the night. Of an army. Creatures of bone. It is said such warriors can vanquish the darkness."

Creatures of bone. I stared at my skeletal hand. Delicate bones knitted together with tough ligament. I grasped a branch, waved it through the air, smashed it against the ground where it shattered, leaving a deep furrow in the earth.

"These bones have strength," I said, "but I am no army—just a girl."

"A girl of glass. A girl of wonder. A glittering, glorious thing. And I know where you may summon an army, but it would be at great cost. You must sacrifice your beauty, for you have no other possessions to give."

And so I was called beautiful for only the second time in my life. Pride twisted its way into my battered heart. I'd never known love, nor worth. Now I was unique and I was strong. Why shouldn't I rejoin society instead? Perhaps I would be marveled at, admired, worshipped even.

Verity mewled. A rabbity noise. I realized I was wrong. I had known love. Verity loved me for myself. Not for any magic or miracle. I had known love, and I had known sorrow, and I had made a grave mistake by giving up my one true friend.

"Show me this place," I told them. "I would free you and those others. Defeat this evil before it tricks another."

Verity grasped my ruined hand. Glided through the crooked forest. The trees grasped at us with their branches, tripped us with their roots. They answered to a different master and suspected we were enemies, but Verity paid them no mind, and they could not penetrate my glassy shell.

We left the woods behind. Came to a high, clear place. Barrows without number laid out in neat rows with ancient, weathered stones to mark the final resting place of the dead.

"There are soldiers for the taking here," Verity said, "but you must pay a price to raise them."

"What price?" I asked.

"I think you already know."

I looked down at my shining scales. They were blinding in the bright sunlight. I could only imagine I looked like a figure on fire to any who might pass and see me. Raiding a burial ground. A deed for darkness and midnight chimes surely. Was I really meant to summon an army of the dead on this crisp fall morning under a cerulean sky?

My lesson had been learned. Magic demands a sacrifice. But what had I left to give? I picked nervously at my sparkling skin with my skeleton hand. A piece broke off. It shone like a jewel.

This. This was all I had left. My broken self.

I showed it to Verity. They nodded at me, a gaze of sadness, regret, infinite pity and infinite love. I buried the shard in the earth above the nearest barrow. The ground trembled and split. A skull grinned. The skeleton pulled itself from its prison. Shook the dirt off. Bowed low to me.

This was the way. For each piece of me, one soldier was earned. I wandered the grounds, peeling glass here and there, never too many close together, trying to preserve some semblance of my girlish form. More and more eldritch warriors were born. They followed me around like puppies, interested and respectful.

"How many would it take to defeat Leviathan? How much of myself must I lose?" I asked Verity.

They only stared at me, pink eyes shining. They were a lovely, lovely thing. No longer rabbit in form but not quite human either.

"Will you still be my friend when there is nothing left of me?" I cried.

They smiled. "Always."

A thousand times I thought to stop. To say it was enough, this was plenty. But always a doubt at the back of my mind. What if we attacked and came up short? What if one more and one more and one more would have turned the tide.

In the end, I shed all my glassy self, every last twinkle and glitter and gleam. There was no difference now between me and my army. We were bone and sinew, beings of horror with nothing left to lose.

Verity led the way back into the forest. Through mossy swamp and across grassy plain. Some of my soldiers were lost along the journey. We were awkward in our boney forms. A trip, a fall, and skulls clattered, rolled, were crushed beneath marching feet. It was well we were many. I made peace with my sacrifice. We would have need of every one of us who survived.

We arrived at a cavern mouth, wide and black. I wondered how we would see in the inky dimness. Verity was a shining beacon ahead of us, but the darkness closed in on all sides. And then I noticed the shimmering light. Each of my soldiers held a piece of me, a shard of mirror. They glimmered, reflecting Verity's brightness from hand to hand, illuminating the way.

The journey was treacherous. I tripped on a stone, lost bones from my foot. Those around me suffered similar injury, but we pressed on in memory of those who had fallen. I shed one bone after another as did the others. A skeleton crew, I thought hysterically, and would have laughed if I still had lips or tongue or breath.

From deep within the catacombs, the miasma of corruption wafted to greet our ragged army. We entered chamber after chamber, lined round with silver cages. Creatures of infinite variety peered out at us in wonder. How pitiful the cries of the captives! Wings and talons, fur and scales, magnificent creatures and humble ones. So much misery mixed with dawning hope writ large across their savage, gentle, alien, familiar faces.

Verity flitted from prisoner to prisoner, calming and reassuring them as we passed. I wished to have my friend's confidence. Of what use was this tattered legion I led against a being of darkness and shadow?

It appeared at my thought as though I had summoned it, and perhaps I had. It seemed most attuned and attracted to desperation and despair.

"And what is this? Can this be my glass girl come calling? But what a change. Thou has lost the beauty we bestowed upon thee, ungrateful thing. What a rotting, repulsive wretch thou are. And these sad followers—we suppose they are the only admirers to be expected now."

It came close, breathing rank and fetid air onto my skeletal form. My bones rattled, sinews melting with fear. What was I supposed to do? I'd no weapon, no training. How was I to defeat this thing?

Then I remembered the black ichor that dripped in the forest after I touched the shadow and lost my hand. Reaching out, I gathered Leviathan in a fierce embrace. It shrieked in pain, twisting free, running from the cavern to another. I followed, my troops close at my heels. This cave was huge. Too many places for the shadow to run and hide. Except my army came and came and came. Skeleton upon skeleton crushing through the narrow opening.

Yes, I had been right to raise them all. We'd need every bone to fill up the space, to trap the darkness. There was no other exit. We poured in as Leviathan retreated until there wasn't any more room. I pressed up against the shadow, held in place by the unbearable pressure of my soldiers breaking into pieces at my back.

And yet, and yet…

There was a part of me that resisted, fought back against my fate. Braced my boney hands against the cavern wall to prevent the final push. I remembered the face I had seen in the spilled ink. My own, agonized and screaming, just as I was now except I was no longer made of flesh and blood. Was I ready to sacrifice all, to be nothing for the sake of creatures I had never met?

I could turn, order my army to retreat, make way for my exit, but what would I be then? A girl of bone, a coward, a selfish thing, an outcast. I thought of life with my mother, the uselessness, the futility of it. Here was meaning. The chance to do a great thing. I'd little left to give but give I would. I surrendered to the pressure, fell into darkness.

The shadow hissed and spat. Steam and sludge arose. It burned what was left of me until I was nothing but a blackened hulk. A far cry from the dazzling creature I had been at start of day. I felt its last thought, a peal of bitter spite, disbelief, and even grudging respect for the glittering girl who had been its undoing.

All was quiet for a long time. It was not unpleasant, collapsed there, devoid of responsibility and care and form.

Then the bones behind me began to shift. It was Verity, burrowing their way to reclaim my shattered remains. They carried me through the cavern where others, once imprisoned, were also gathering bones.

The creatures took us back through plain and swamp. Through the chastened forest, no longer bound to its dark master. A strange parade, collecting as many bones that had been dropped along the way as they could. They brought our parts to those high, lonely hills where one by one, my soldiers sunk into their barrow homes, reburying themselves in the desecrated earth.

When all were properly housed once more, Verity carried me to the cottage. It lay in ruins, crushed and burnt. Mother's beloved possessions, twisted and useless now. The flames had reached out into the back garden, withering her precious roses. All the things she loved more than her own child had been destroyed, and I couldn't help but rejoice.

And where was she? No one knew. Neighbors came and gossiped about it. No bones were found, but much speculation. That I had started the fire. That she had. That we'd moved away to start life anew elsewhere. But I knew she was gone from this realm, gone for good.

As for me, now that I had peeled my layers, I added them back on, one by one, made of anything that came to hand. Woven rye grass, spider silk, the dry leaves that rustled round my autumned self. As I worked, I thought, *I am safe, I am free, I am.*

When I finished, I lay beneath an ancient yew tree near the barrow down. Its spreading branches shelter me from storms and snow. A curious crow comes to visit, brings his mates. Barnaby Crumb passed by once whistling but stopped and shivered as though sensing my presence. He has not come this way again.

The seasons pass. Destroying angels sprout from my grave, so innocent-looking, yet deadly beneath. I watch the needles and berries dance in the harsh winds that blow in this high place during the day. At night, Mordecai and his compatriots of light twinkle among the branches. The white rabbit makes their home here, raising generations that will keep me company for all the years to come.

I have found my true self. My bones are at peace.

REVENANT OF THE HIGH LONESOME

I was born under a cursed star. Pa was already long gone and Ma didn't want me. She dropped me off in a pit of vipers. No-account grifters, men and women of ill-repute, misfits and scoundrels who sung to me a serpentine lullaby of hiss and rattle, raised me up on spit and poison, taught me the religion of do unto others before they get a chance to do unto you. The only lesson I learned from them worth knowing was never warn your enemies before striking. Ignoring that cardinal rule was my undoing.

I'D BEEN WANDERING the borderlands down south, picking up jobs here and there as a hired gun when I stumbled into Pyretown on my firedrake, Goliath. He was larger than average but then so was I, and I'd found size goes a long way toward shutting down trouble before it starts. That and my matching set of Carville pistols. I always made sure to push my duster back behind my holsters when I was new in town so everyone could see what I was packing. There's not many want to get in a quick draw contest with a mean-looking bastard pulling that kind of fire power.

Pyretown looked to be your average frontier squat. A mix of wannabe miners who'd caught wind of rumors of a new strike up in the foothills and hopeful settlers from up north looking to push the boundaries of civilization farther down into the treacherous wilderness between here and the Minsent Sea. The rest of the town was merchants and crooks looking to profit off the new chumps arriving daily by howzer-drawn wagon trains. Those enormous beasts served as transportation and food, and I could see the dust trails kicked up by the valuable herds long before I got to town.

Ranchers were the other major players in a place like this. To raise howzers, you needed land—a lot of it. And not just any land would do. You needed mossy plains rich with the flowering feng-ice that kept the herds healthy and fed. Most of the blood that was shed in these parts would be over territory and that was good for my business. There was always someone who needed extra muscle, an enforcer who wasn't too picky about what he was asked to do as long as the coin was plentiful.

It had been a while since my last job and I was running low on funds, so I was glad to find a bustling outpost. Now I needed to find a likely mark. I left Goliath on the outskirts at the firedrake pens. He was too big and ornery to tie up in town, so I paid the girl in charge of the stables extra to keep a close eye on him. She didn't look any older than thirteen or fourteen but was wiry and full of grit. I figured she'd give me a heads up if anyone started giving my steed the eye.

Rustling was a shooting offense, no questions asked, but given the fortune a good dragon could fetch on the black market, there was always the risk someone would take the gamble. I wished them luck if they tried it out. Goliath had bonded to me as a pup and wouldn't hesitate to crush anyone else trying to hitch a ride on his red and blue-scaled back.

I strolled into the town proper. Most folks gave me a wide berth. I don't have to work much on looking mean—it's my natural expression —but I've learned it's more about attitude. You gotta take up space, dare anyone to get close to you. Most people don't even try, but you want to watch out for toughs looking to prove their mettle.

Spotted one right away. Muscle-packed woman who bristled at my approach, laying her hand alongside her holster like she was thinking about it until she caught sight of the caliber of my guns. Decided it wasn't worth the trouble and turned away. Smart. I've got the aim and speed on the draw to back up the firepower, as anyone rash enough to challenge me finds out plenty quick. I've left more bodies sprawled out in dusty streets than most and only have a couple of scars to show for it.

Hearing the sound of a tinny stringhammer, I headed in the direction of the music, knowing that's where I'd find the local watering hole. Most contracts of the kind I was looking for involved a nod and a wink over a foaming glass of jubilar ale or a shot of franzed gutrot.

Found a table in a corner that gave me a good view of the room and ordered a bottle of the hard stuff from the dolly who came to check on me. It brought the gutrot out from under its mantle with one tentacle, swiped the coins I laid out for it with another, while it gave the table a cursory wipe with a grey rag clutched in a third. Always thought it would be handy having more than two hands, but I could do without the mucus-filled beak that went with it.

I wasn't planning on drinking down the gutrot by myself. I'd found a full bottle was a magnet for any habitual drunks in a place. And there's nobody better than a rotter who spends their whole life cadging drinks in a bar to get the straight-shooting lowdown on what's what in a town.

Sure enough, in no time flat, a blowzy woman with a shock of dyed yellow hair ambled over to take a look. I could tell she was tempted to ask for a share but was put off by my size and general demeanor of not caring whether the next person who talked to me lived or died. I put her out of her misery by waving the dolly back over and asking for an extra glass.

That's all the invitation she needed to plop herself down across from me.

"Mixie," she said, reaching out a grimy hand.

I declined the shake but tipped my hat in acknowledgement of her name.

"Help yourself," I advised as the dolly set a barely clean shot glass down in front of her.

I didn't have to tell her twice. She pulled the stopper out with her teeth and filled the glass in front of her to the brim with a surprisingly steady hand that made me look at her more closely. She was younger than I thought. Hadn't been at the drinking game long enough to get the permanent shakes but if she kept on that way, she'd be shivering like a leaf in a whirlwind soon enough.

"Thanks," she said, when she'd drained the glass and poured another. "I needed that today."

"What makes today special?"

"Got booted from a good paying gig. Never could learn to keep my opinions to myself."

"What's the job?"

"Why? You interested?"

"Could be."

She gave me a good going over with a pair of bright red eyes. "You look the part. Security for a howzer train heading south through the mountains."

"Sounds like an easy berth. What's the catch?"

"The catch is they're gonna take the Bernal Pass route at the start of snow season. They'll never make it and I told some of the passengers so. Boss didn't like that. Doesn't want to scare away the fresh whelps. He knows he'll probably have to turn around the train and come back, but it'll look like he made the effort—just bad luck is all. He makes them sign a pledge that he gets to keep the coin they've thrown down as a deposit whether they make it or not."

"Quite the dodge. Did the whelps believe you?"

"A few did, but he talked the rest round. Grogan's got a silver tongue on him when he wants to use it. He could sell a case of this stuff," she added, hoisting the gutrot for another round, "to an abstinence society."

"What's the pay?"

"A thousand plenar."

"Nice payday for a short trip up and down a mountain."

"Yeah, I shoulda kept my mouth shut and taken the money. It's not my fault these suckers don't know no better than to trust a gorm like Grogan. Ma always said my soft heart would get me in trouble. Maybe I'm not cut out to be a gun for hire."

"How'd you get into it?"

"Pa taught me how to shoot when I was nine. Been practicing ever since. I can pick a kernal bug off a sloped jubilar tree at two thousand paces with a long gun. Only thing I'm good at."

"That's a valuable skill, especially on the trail. Why don't you take me to see this Grogan. Maybe I can convince him to hire you back and see if he has a place for me while we're at it."

"Why would you bother?"

"I got nothing better to do."

She laughed. "Guess that's as good an answer as any. Come on then before this stuff goes to my head."

"You seem pretty straight."

"Yeah, Pa always said I could drink any ten men under the table. That's a kind of skill, too, but it ain't come in as handy as you might think."

"Being able to keep a clear head is always handy."

I rose up from the table. She seemed taken aback when she got a gander at my full height, but she led the way out of the saloon and down the main street to a building with "Sheriff's Office" written over the door.

"You turning me in?" I asked her.

"For what? Is there a bounty out on you? I could use the coin."

I grunted. Let her interpret it how she wanted.

She looked amused but didn't press it. "Just kidding. The Sheriff and Grogan are partners. Grogan gulls the Northern whelps and Sheriff Dent makes sure any complaints get filed away under insufficient evidence."

She flung open the door and ushered me in.

"Back so soon, Mixie? You're done here. Take your big mouth somewhere else."

"Thought you might be interested in some extra muscle. You were already short-handed before you gave me the boot. Maybe you could use a big guy like this, Grogan."

He was a nasty-looking piece of work. Slack skin and greased back hair. I'd seen his type plenty. Conmen without conscience. Dead behind the eyes.

"What's your name?" he barked.

"They call me Hawk."

"First name or last?"

"Does it matter?"

"Another joker, huh? I already got my fill of that today. Nice revolvers though. Must have set you back a pretty plenar. You for hire?"

"When the price is right."

"Five hundred. Easy trip. Week at most. Babysitting some new blood from the north."

"Mixie said it was a thousand."

"A thousand if I know you. Five hundred for wise-asses who are just passing through. Half in advance and half when we're done."

"Sounds like a fool's trip. Everyone knows you can't get through that pass in snow season."

"Not everyone. Besides, you never know, we might make it. Been warmer than usual. It's risky business traveling the wilderness any time of year. They all sign a waiver saying they know there's no guarantees."

I could tell this gorm was nothing but trouble. I didn't like the look of the Sheriff either. He hadn't moved a muscle, but he had a sinewy look to him like dried-out leather and intense black eyes that had kept me pinned down from the moment I entered his domain.

I'd taken a lot worse jobs though. This one sounded like easy street. An amble with Goliath through some nice scenery, keeping an eye out for danger, beasts of one kind or another being the most likely. I had a powerful long gun in my pack that was more effective at putting down that kind of problem than my Carvilles. And my dragon was a potent weapon himself. He'd give a good thrashing to anything that made it past a bullet.

"The rubes are none of my business as long as I get my coin," I said. "I'm in—if you give Mixie another chance."

"That mouthy red-eye? She already cost me two paying customers. No way."

"Sorry, it's a package deal." I turned to head out, not caring whether my gambit worked or not. There were plenty of other towns on the trail and I wasn't desperate, but I was interested to find out if he was.

"Wait."

That answered my question.

"She can come with, but the pay's same as yours and you gotta keep an eye on her."

Mixie didn't like any bit of that. "You promised me a thousand, and I'm not a lamb that needs a mother. Particularly not some whaddie drifter. No offense."

"None taken," I agreed.

"Heed my advice and leave 'em both behind, Archie." Seemed like the Sheriff finally had something to contribute. "Wouldn't be surprised if this one had warrants out for him. More trouble than he's worth."

"I wanna get on the trail though. Ain't got time to be rounding up other guns, but I will if I have to," Grogan added, lest we get the notion we were in any position to negotiate.

I shrugged. "Don't matter to me either way. I'll leave it up to Mixie here."

Her red eyes were flashing, but I guess she needed the coin 'cause she accepted with a nod. Grogan gave us orders to meet up with the wagon train at the crack of dawn the next day outside of town. No skin off my nose. I'd always been an early riser.

Mixie and I parted ways outside, and I booked into the local hotel. Shook off a few cute glossies who offered their services—I preferred to sleep alone.

Was up and saddling Goliath by the time the suns poked their pale heads over the horizon. We'd be leaving the flatlands behind and moving south into the foothills and jubilar forests. I looked forward to the shade among those towering trees. The sound of their soft bristles rustling in the wind. There's a smell up there like nothing else. Clean and sweet.

Gotta keep an eye out for critters though. Most were harmless, but gorms grew twice the size of a man and wouldn't mind taking a bite out of one if it came across you while it was foraging on the forest floor. Brinders were worse though. They were as at home up in the trees as they were on the ground so they could get the jump on you easy if you were unlucky.

I wasn't too worried for myself—not many predators will approach a full-grown firedrake—but Grogan and I were the only ones on the trip riding dragons. They're out of the price range of most folks and it had taken me a heap of jobs I'd rather forget to save up for mine. The rest of Grogan's crew were mounted on trommels, sturdy steeds and fast. You could outrun a lot on a good trommel and Mixie had a nice one. Grey and yellow stripes and a powerful jump when she asked for it.

I was more concerned about the settlers. Their heavy-laden, sluggish howzer-drawn wagons made them sitting targets for any trouble we ran into and with only Grogan and a dozen of us to protect them. I had no doubt Grogan and most of his posse would take off, leaving the whelps to their fates, if push came to shove.

I'd probably stick it out though. I hadn't been raised up right but somewhere along the way, I picked up the idea that I should finish any job I took. Hadn't welched out of one yet and didn't intend to. Even whaddies like me can have our own code of conduct. A line we won't cross.

Not that I was expecting a lot of trouble. Seemed to me four or five days of hard travel would bring us high enough into the mountains to hit the snow and ice that would turn us back. We might lose a settler or two to a brinder or gorm, but most would make it back. What I was expecting was boredom and a lot of it.

There were about thirty families making the trip. If you've never been around a wagon train of any size, you may be surprised to hear it takes hours to get them all going in approximately the right direction, and there's always stragglers you gotta go back and check on. Howzers are the toughest beasts you'll ever meet, but they ain't known for their speed.

By mid-day, I was already regretting my decision to join in. Give me a quick in-and-out job any day. This was too much like living somewhere permanent and having nosy neighbors. Every wagon Goliath and I rode by wanted to pass the time of day and find out my life story. The kids were fascinated with the dragon and shouted a million questions at us. Most of them had never seen a firedrake before except in a picture book, but I'm not big on conversation. As soon as one family figured out I wasn't going to spout, I'd moved on to the next wagon where I had to teach the same lesson all over again.

Even Mixie got in on the action, wanting to flap her lips whenever we crossed paths. Lucky for me, her trommel was shy of the big firedrake and gave her so much trouble that she'd ride off again soon enough. That ain't exactly fair though. I didn't mind her company so much, especially at night when we gathered round the campfire. Found her easier to talk to than most because she took care of most of the talking.

The first couple of days were uneventful. It was when we hit the trail up into the mountains that things started to unravel. The path had been cleared out years before, but it was hit and miss now whether we were gonna run into a roadblock around every bend. The wagons were designed to be maneuverable and howzers aren't bothered by steep climbs, but it was tough for us outriders getting around the train on the narrowing path as we rode alongside to keep an eye out for trouble.

Grogan wanted me and Goliath up front in case they needed muscle to clear debris out of the way. That left Mixie and another of Grogan's recruits alone at the back guarding the stragglers. I wasn't too worried about Mixie—I'd seen she could take care of herself—but it was a vulnerable spot to be in with no way to get help back to them fast if they needed it.

The other problem that occupied my mind was how were we gonna get this train turned around when we inevitably hit the snow and ice belt above the tree line. There were places here and there wide enough to turn a wagon, but it's not like they could go anywhere once they did with the other wagons still coming up. I figured we'd have to let the last in line get to a turnaround and start back down the trail and then back the others up until they could turn. That kind of maneuvering would take forever and wasn't without its own risks. There was a helluva steep drop-off if the howzers got spooked or took a wrong step. No man or beast would survive a fall like that.

We camped where we stood whenever night came around again. Lighting fires between wagons and edging around back and forth down the trail to keep guard. Took turns with the watches in the night with some of the settlers who seemed to have the knowhow and nerve to use a gun.

We made it through to the fourth day without much more than squabbles between some of the families who were getting sick of each other. Snow had started up to falling that morning. Not too heavy but a sign of things to come that made everyone uneasy. Goliath hated the cold and reminded me of it by threatening to buck me off whenever I let my attention wander. I was kicking myself for getting us involved in this mess when I heard a sharp cry from far down the trail.

It wasn't easy, but Grogan and I managed to edge our dragons down the path to the back of the line. Found Mixie lying on the ground at the foot of her trommel. She had a bloody thigh, and her partner was nowhere to be seen.

"Brinder," she muttered, grinding her teeth with the pain. "Pulled Mack and his mount over the side and disappeared after first giving me a bite and spitting me out. Guess I'm an acquired taste," she added with a laughing groan.

I pulled an old shirt out of my saddlebags and bound up the wound as best I could to slow down the bleeding. There was a good chunk of meat missing, but I decided not to mention that. Commandeered the last wagon and loaded her in there with her trommel tied up behind.

"We gotta get her back to town," I told Grogan.

"Nuts to that. She'd never survive the trip down. Be kinder to put her out of her misery right now. It's bad for morale having a dying gink around, and she won't last the night with that kind of wound," he said, fingering his revolver.

"Try it and you'll find yourself with a worse one." I placed my palms against my own holsters to show I meant business.

"Fine. Let her suffer, I don't care, but we ain't turning around. We're not far now from the pass. I think we're actually gonna make it over. I get paid double at the end of the line if I get them through."

"What about the rest of us?"

"You signed up for what you signed up for. A deal's a deal."

"A dirty deal is no deal at all."

"Says you. The rest of my guys seem content with their pay. It's more plenars than most of them see in a year. You can take off if you want, but you'll get nothing more outta me."

I was tempted. This wasn't my usual style of job at all, and what did I care about a bunch of dreaming whelps with more ambition than smarts? But then I thought about leaving Mixie to the mercy of this plonk. She wasn't a bad sort. Been nicer to me in her way than anyone I'd ever met. I'm the one got her back on the train, and I couldn't help but feel responsible for her now.

I grunted at Grogan. He seemed to take it for agreement 'cause he told me to guard the rear and went back up to the head of the line.

A father and two kids were riding in the back of the wagon with Mixie while the mother took the reins up front. They promised to do what they could for her wound, and I promised to see them right if they did.

Kept a sharp eye out but didn't spot any more brinders. Didn't let my guard down though. They'd been known to stalk wagon trains and pick people off one by one. The smell of the blood from Mixie's wound might attract gorms, too. More trouble we didn't need.

While we made camp for the night, Mixie drifted in and out. I knew there was no saving that leg. If we'd been in town, I'd of got a bonesetter to take it off so she might stand a chance of living. She knew it was bad, too.

She waved me over to where she was wrapped up by the fire. "It needs to come off, don't it?"

"Might be better," I agreed.

"You could do it. Get me liquored up first."

"Don't know if we could. You told me you had a hollow—" I stopped, realizing what I was about to say.

"Leg?" she finished for me. "It's true I can hold my hooch better than most, but give me enough and it'll knock me out eventually."

"I can talk to Grogan about it."

"Whatever you do, Hawk, promise you won't let him leave me behind. I don't wanna rot out here by myself. Bury me in a nice, warm grave down the mountain, preferably with some neighbors on either side to keep me company."

"Don't talk like that. We'll figure something out. You're a tough bird and I don't give up easy."

"Promise me just the same. I won't rest easy if you don't."

"I'll do my best."

"Promise."

"And I thought I was stubborn," I said with a grunt. "Okay, I solemnly promise."

"Thanks, Hawk. You're not so bad for a whaddie."

Grogan sent one of the other outriders back for me. There was another roadblock ahead and he needed all hands on deck to clear the way. I recruited a couple of settlers who'd proven they were more levelheaded than most to stay at the rear and keep an eye out for trouble from brinders or anything else.

Mixie gave me a wave and a thin smile, those red eyes dimmed to a pale pink from pain. Goliath and I threaded our way back to the front where I put his bulk to good use pushing downed jubilar trees over the side of the trail. The tremendous crashes as they fell into the abyss looming at our side echoed and cracked up and down the line, keeping everyone awake and on edge long into the night.

When I felt like we'd done our bit, I found a spot to stretch out and catch some shuteye until dawn. Grogan kicked me awake with a sharp jab to my boots. I was half buried in a pile of snow that had started falling more heavily overnight. Goliath's fiery warmth had kept the worst off him, but he did not look happy about it.

"We're moving out," Grogan snarled.

"Looks like a blizzard setting in. Maybe we should wait it out here."

"We gotta get ahead of it. Only a couple of hours to the pass. It'll be gravy getting down the other side. I've been over before. It's nothing like as rough as the climb up. Now go get those leaders moving."

My hackles rose. I'd never taken to being told what to do, but when you're a rover for hire, sometimes you gotta swallow your pride. Besides, I thought the sooner we got over, the sooner we could get help for Mixie.

I rousted out the first few wagons and began the slow process of getting the train moving again. We were kept busy at the front of the line clearing more trees and boulders that had tumbled down the mountain.

The snow didn't let up. I argued with Grogan about it, and even some of his lackeys who didn't usually complain started making noises about turning back. He assured us it would be fine, we were almost there, but by nightfall, we'd barely made any progress and certainly hadn't crested the top of the pass.

The settlers were getting restless. Their children were cold. The fires during the night weren't able to break through the chill that had settled into all our bones. I'd finally had enough.

I left my post and led Goliath back along the trail. It was tricky going in the dark, but I was determined to leave and take Mixie with me. Groban had kept putting me off when I asked after her, but I knew unless that leg came off, she wasn't gonna get any better.

When I got to the last wagon and looked in, all I saw was the frightened faces of the family I'd left in charge of Mixie.

"Where is she?"

"She's gone."

"Gone where?"

The parents exchanged glances like they were daring each other to be the one to confess all. Finally, the man spoke up.

"Grogan came and got her."

"Where… is… she?" I spit.

One of the kids spoke up then, a young girl. "He threw her over. She was asleep and he threw her over the side of the mountain."

I gritted my teeth so hard I expected them to crack like coical shells. "Asleep? Or dead?"

"We don't know," said the mother. "She'd gone very still and quiet, but I honestly don't know what to tell you. We were busy with the fire and trying to warm some food when he took her."

Flashes of crimson sparked before my eyes. I told Goliath to stay put and ran back to the front of the train as fast as I could. Almost tumbled over the side a few times myself but didn't stop. Grogan must've heard me lumbering towards him like an enraged gorm because he didn't hesitate to pull his gun.

Too late. The barrels of my Carvilles were already smoking and he had two holes where his eyes used to be before he could even thumb back the hammer on his revolver.

"Who's next?" I demanded, as his men stood staring at their boss laid out flat on the ground.

All the answer I got was them mounting up and taking off back down the trail the way we'd come. Guess they saw the writing on the wall. With the boss gone, no more coin for them and no profit in standing around in a blizzard with a madman.

"What do we do now, mister?"

It was an older man named Mitchell who'd become the unofficial leader of the settlers, chosen without a vote to speak for them when troubles arose, and boy, we had trouble now.

"Gotta get off this mountain and fast. We'll never make the pass. Tell everyone to rest up. We're heading back at first light."

He bowed his head, wise enough to know better than to argue with a brute gripping a pair of smoking pistols.

I stared down the mountain into the endless darkness below, thinking about Mixie. Had she been alive? Had she felt the horror of falling? Was it possible she'd survived and was down there somewhere even now, alone on the mountain, like she'd feared? I couldn't keep my promise, but I had avenged her in the only way a whaddie like me knew how.

Holstering my guns, I stumbled back to the end of the line. Curled up next to the firedrake's warmth and dozed until light. We started the painstaking process of backing the wagons down until we could turn them around, but it soon became obvious it was too dangerous and too slow. We almost lost two wagons over the side before I called a halt.

"We're gonna have to abandon the wagons," I told Mitchell. There was a buzz through the crowd close enough to hear me. That was all their worldly possessions packed up in those wagons. "You can stay with them and die, or leave them and get your families back down this mountain before we all freeze to death. Your choice."

Not much of a choice and they knew it. They unhitched their howzer teams. The beasts were too valuable to leave behind, and there was enough room to send them along the path beside the wagons in single file. The smaller children and weaker adults could ride on their backs while the rest of us hiked.

I sent Goliath ambling ahead, his bright blue and red scales acting as a beacon in the snow that kept us from wandering off the side of the mountain. The temperatures had dropped since the day before. There wasn't a lot of talking. Everyone kept their heads down and concentrated on keeping moving.

We lit torches and walked on through the night. I knew we had to reach a lower altitude and warmer air before we stopped again. Those riding fell asleep where they sat and those walking had to keep a sharp eye that the passengers didn't slide off and down the mountain.

We finally emerged from the snowstorm and found a wider stretch where we could tie up the howzers and start some bonfires. I allowed them a half a day's rest before prodding everyone to their feet again.

It had taken four days to get up the mountain. It took ten to get down and back to town. We lost some along the way. An older man frozen on one of the first nights. A straggler picked off by something—no one saw what and we didn't stop to investigate. A doomed newborn torn from its mother's grieving arms and left under a hasty pile of brush and stone for a grave.

On the tenth day, we marched back into Pyregate. A sorry spectacle of a parade meandering through a rough drizzle and muddied streets. The townsfolk came out to stare and whisper.

I was feeling plenty satisfied with myself. Hadn't done much to be proud of in my sorry life, but I got those soft whelps down off a mountain that would've killed them. Had to count for something.

Unfortunately, the Sheriff didn't see it that way. He was waiting with open arms, flanked by a posse of the runners who'd left us high and dry up on the mountain. I guessed they'd reported in on Grogan's fate and warned I might head back this way. I went for my guns on reflex but then thought of the crowd behind me. They'd get caught in the crossfire and by the grin on his face, the Sheriff knew it.

I'd be damned if I walked ten days when I could have ridden my dragon down in three just to see the folks I'd saved caught up in a gun battle. I put my hands up where everyone could see them.

"Something to say to me, Sheriff?"

"You're under arrest for the murder of Archibald Grogan."

Mitchell spoke up for me. "You can't do that, Sheriff. Grogan killed a woman himself."

"Put her out of her misery, I heard. Mercy killing. That's what real leaders do. Not like this whaddie trash."

"But he led us down the mountain to safety all by himself."

"Which he wouldn't have had to do if he hadn't killed Grogan and threatened these other men."

"Don't waste your breath, Mitchell," I said. "We'll tell it to the judge and jury."

The Sheriff laughed, a hollow sound that froze my bones. "You're not from around here, are you? I am the judge and jury in these parts. String him up, boys."

I did reach for my guns then but five guys rushing you will put anyone off their stride. They managed to wrestle the Carvilles away from me with only one of them getting shot in the gut in the melee. The others got my hands tied behind my back despite my best efforts to resist. If I hadn't just spent ten hard days on the trail with little to no sleep, I might've put up a better show, but I wasn't at my usual strength.

As they led me away, I heard Goliath roaring, then gunshots and silence. Didn't like to think about what that might mean.

Before I knew it, I was standing on a scaffold. Don't know if they built it special in my honor or if it got put to regular use. Didn't have time to ponder about it too much before the floor dropped out beneath me.

If I'd been lucky, my neck would've broke right off. As it was, it was a long, slow squeeze with my head feeling like it was gonna snap off of my body. Just when the pressure became unbearable, I heard a pop in my ears, then nothing at all.

Last thing I saw was the Sheriff grinning at me like it was the best show he'd seen in years.

I WAS SUFFOCATING, choking. Dirt filled my mouth. My skin crawled or something crawled on my skin. My mind was sorting through such a mixed-up bunch of scraps of scattered thoughts and bitter memories, I didn't know what was happening. Only that I was trapped in a cold, damp darkness that seemed to go on forever, except I couldn't see to know. I tried to open my eyes but couldn't. Tried to breathe but there was a weight on my chest. Tried moving my arms and legs. Nothing.

And it was quiet. So very, very quiet.

I could feel my heart booming in my chest. The vibrations resonated up through my skull, fast and panicked then slower and slower and slower. It was winding down and taking me with it. I drifted.

EONS PASSED before a red light appeared behind my closed eyelids. The weight on my chest got heavier. Earth shifted and spilled. A giant claw smacked me in the face. That got my attention.

My eyes flew open to find the questing snout of a red and blue firedrake sniffing at me. I guess he was satisfied with whatever he smelled because he moved to one side and kept digging with his webbed feet.

It was only then it occurred to me that I had been buried underground. Not too deep for Goliath to find me but deep enough for a hasty grave. Guess those townies didn't waste a lot of time and sweat digging six feet down for hanged men.

Wasn't long before the firedrake moved enough dirt for me to start helping. Having realized my predicament, I suddenly couldn't abide being in the earth for one more minute. Panic overtook me as I tore the nails from my fingers in my desperation to be free.

I crawled out of the mud with barely the strength to flop over the edge of my tomb and sprawl on the surface. A heavy rain was falling. A blessing since it had loosened the soil enough for me to escape.

I lay back and let it wash as much of the grime off as it could. Goliath nuzzled me, poking me almost hard enough in the side to crack my ribs. I'd never been so glad to see him in my life. First, because I'd thought he was dead and second, because I'd thought I was. Even now, I wasn't sure where I stood between this life and the next.

Everything was silent. I remembered the pressure of the noose. How it felt my head would explode as I hung there. Figured it had busted out my eardrums and I wouldn't hear anything ever again. That was okay. For what I had to do, I didn't need to be able to hear. What I did need was my strength back.

I lay there a good long while, lapping up some of the rain with my outstretched tongue. Felt like I'd been born again, this time bursting from the womb of the earth, full of spite and bile. I'd been bested for the first time since I'd been a man grown, but I had a second chance. Some men might have thought themselves well out of it and crawled away to fight another day, but that ain't me.

The image of the Sheriff's grinning face was stuck in my brain. I knew I wouldn't rest until either I'd wiped away his smirk or he'd done the job on me he started out to do, but properly this time.

Goliath had wandered away, thrashing around in the undergrowth nearby. He returned with an offering, a distant and much smaller cousin of his, a sandwyrm. The skin's too tough for eating but I found a sharp flint on the ground nearby and cut the rough scales away, gnawing at the soft flesh underneath. When you've been reborn a starving, mewling infant, you can't be too picky about what you eat. The dragon kept me supplied through the night and by dawn, I felt revived enough to move along.

I'd been stripped before burial of all but my britches and shirt. Didn't blame them. I'd have done the same and had plenty of times. My leather chaps and holsters, the boots on my feet, even my hat were worth something, not to mention my guns.

The only thing I owned of value they hadn't managed to take was Goliath. I'd found some deep grooves along the scales on his left side. Evidence they'd tried to take him down, but there aren't many full-grown firedrakes that'll submit unless they've a mind to. I'd raised my dragon from a hatchling and I'm the only one he'd ever bond to.

Now it was light, I could see they'd buried me at a crossroads of sorts where two trails of howzer hooves intersected on the plains. Superstitious about me rising again maybe, as well they should have been. Should've dug a deeper hole, boys. Should have dug deeper.

I could make out the town in the distance. It looked quiet and peaceful in the early morning light. It wouldn't remain so for long, but I'd never been one to go in guns blazing. Sometimes a subtle approach is called for, and I wasn't exactly outfitted for a fight, but I knew where there was plenty of goods for the taking.

I climbed aboard Goliath, grateful he'd been too cantankerous for them to strip off his saddle. It would have been a mighty uncomfortable ride without it. We gave the town a wide berth, not wanting to alert anyone to my resurrection until I was ready. It was a cold ride back up that mountain. My feet and hands turned red then blue long before we reached the wagon train. I slid off Goliath barely able to walk, but revenge is a powerful motivator.

Had to rifle through a couple of wagons to gather what I needed. Warm clothes, a pair of boots that fit well enough, some dry goods to supplement my sandwyrm diet, and a long gun, hidden under the floorboards of a wagon. Good quality too. Surprised the owner hadn't taken it with them, but then things had been a mite chaotic on our hasty retreat.

I'd have preferred a revolver, but I was a dab hand with a long gun, too. I could've taken out the Sheriff at distance with this one, but I wanted him to look me in the eye when I shot him. That was my first mistake. Never let emotion take over.

My second was giving him plenty of time to prepare by sauntering back into town on the firedrake. They would've seen his distinctive red and blue hide coming across the plains from a mile away and word like that spreads quick. Didn't even make it past the dragon pens before bullets started flying.

I scrambled off Goliath and sent him running into the open plains with a jab of the long gun to his rear. His scales were tough enough to withstand a bullet, but a lucky shot between the eyes would take him out right enough. He didn't deserve that.

Ducking behind the stables, I reconsidered my plan. It had been foolish to think the Sheriff would wait for me to challenge him and engage in a fair draw. A man like him doesn't get to where he is by doing the dirty work himself.

I had a dozen rounds in the rifle and a pocketful of extra bullets, but that meant reloading. Takes time to reload. Too much time. I decided the smart thing to do was wait it out. Figured whoever was out there would get impatient. Make a move.

Problem was, I still couldn't hear a damn thing from my busted ears. The shooters could be stampeding toward me that minute like a herd of howzers and I wouldn't have known.

Just about jumped out of my skin when I felt a light touch on my arm. Swung the gun around to find myself staring down the barrel at the stable girl who'd looked after Goliath before. She said something. I pointed to my ear and shook my head.

She caught on quick. Held up three fingers, then two pointing to the left and one pointing to the right. I got the message. Two baddies hiding out to the left, one to the right.

I nodded and growled, "Take cover."

She melted away into a hole under the stables. She'd be safe enough under there until the coast was clear. I'd have to thank her later —if there was a later.

I poked my head around the right side of the stable and took a fast looksee. A plonk was standing up in plain sight on the roof of a building a block away. Maybe he thought he was too far to make a good target or assumed I was unarmed. Bad news for him was the long gun I had was accurate at three or four times the distance. Dropped him with a single bullet through the head.

That left the two shooters on the other side and eleven rounds remaining in my gun. I had to remember to keep at least one back for the Sheriff. I took a look to the left. These guys were either smarter or they'd gotten smart real quick when they saw the first plonk drop like a rock. They knew I had a gun now—they'd be cagier.

I leaned against the stable wall thinking over my options. Stared at the pens. There were a couple of firedrakes and a dozen trommels milling around uneasily. They didn't like all the noise I reckoned. I took careful aim and blasted the gate on the dragons' pen then the trommels'. They liked that even less and stampeded out toward town like demons from hell were riding them.

Just the distraction and cover I needed. I ran with them, making sure to keep the herd between me and the shooters. Couldn't hear the noise the animals made but sure could feel the vibrations in the ground as they roared past. Found myself in the middle of town. Two guys were running toward me, revolvers blazing. I took out the first with one shot, but a bullet tearing through my arm messed up my aim on the second plonk.

It took me two more tries before I dropped him. With the rounds I'd spent opening the pens, that left me five. Should be plenty, though I debated seeking cover to reload up to a full count again. While I was thinking it over, a bullet ripped out through my chest.

Spun around to find the Sheriff grinning at me. Some would think him a coward for shooting me in the back, but I admired it. It's kill or be killed in this world. Fair play can go right out the damn window.

I fell to my knees, eyesight blurry. The Sheriff looked like he was standing on the deck of a ship in a storm the way he was dipping and diving. I got off a couple of shots before he hit me again, but both of mine went wide.

He was starting to act annoyed now, like I was wasting his time by being so stubborn about dying. That last bullet had hit my shooting arm and knocked my gun to the ground. He approached and kicked it far away from me, bending over to place the hot metal of his pistol against my forehead. I could smell the burning skin as he leant over and said something into my left ear—something mighty droll I've no doubt, though I couldn't hear it.

Besides, I was busy pulling out the knife I had hidden down my boot so I could gut him with it. Never seen a man looked so surprised in his life as the Sheriff did as he fell over and watched his insides spill out onto the dusty street.

I fell over myself and we lay there, face to face. I had the satisfaction of seeing the light leave his eyes before mine was quenched. Felt a nudge and a tug. Goliath, that loyal bastard. Somehow levered myself up into his saddle. Told him to run for the forest on the mountain. I'd a hankering to see that place one more time before I died.

THAT WAS SO many years ago now I've lost count. I spend my days roaming the high lonesome among the soaring jubilar trees. I can hear everything. The song of birds that hush when I draw near, the rustle of every leaf that falls to the forest floor in the autumn times, the harsh grunt of gorms on the hunt. I even hear the whispers of travelers when they're brave enough to venture through.

Watch out for the revenant, they say. *He'll rip out your heart and feed it to the brinders.*

But they've got it all wrong. I'm only searching for a certain set of bones. When I find them, I'll lay myself alongside and keep her warm so she won't be alone anymore in this forsaken place. Until then, I'll walk day and night, never ceasing from hunting these unhallowed grounds until I've kept my promise.

Even whaddie ghosts can have a code of conduct after all.

THE MELODY OF TREES

"What are you reading?"

"None of your business."

"Haven't heard of that one. Catchy title. What's it about?"

I give him a thin smile. I know the type. What woman doesn't? The self-assured, self-proclaimed charmer, overconfident of their attraction for the opposite sex to the point of madness. Assuming every woman sitting by herself quietly in a café is lonely and in need of company. Impeccably dressed and coiffed. Probably spends more on his appearance in a week than I do in a year. And he'd have some sort of name like Brendan or Sebastian or…

"I'm Marcus."

"Of course you are."

He raises an eyebrow at that, and I think maybe he's getting the hint, but no.

"And you are?" he asks.

"Someone who was contentedly reading until rudely interrupted."

That gets a laugh. I give him a point. Most men of his type would have reacted angrily before walking off in a huff if I was lucky.

"Sorry, that caught my eye and I thought we might have something in common."

He points straight at my chest. I have a moment of disbelief that any jerk could be so clueless as to admit he's staring at my boobs when I get that he means the t-shirt I have on.

Marcus must realize what I think he means because he hastens to enlighten me. "*Phantastic Phantoms*. I loved that show when I was a kid. Phrank was the best character naturally."

"Don't be ridiculous. Phiona was the best. She was always out there totally kicking ghost butt while Phrank cowered in the corner making lame jokes."

"That's why I liked him. I could identify with that. And he did save the day that one time, when he made Wretched Wraith laugh so hard that he fell backwards into the Pit of Plenty. Episode 28: *Phrank Makes a Phunny*."

Okay, I'm unwillingly impressed. It's rare I run across someone with in-depth knowledge of *Phantastic Phantoms*. Rare? Hell, it's never happened before. I sometimes feel like the only person in the world who remembers the obscure Saturday morning cartoon. I even tried to start a fan newsletter once and only got two subscribers, one of which I'm pretty sure was a bot.

I hesitate, a lifetime of repelling all boarders hard to overcome in a minute, but then I close my book and set it aside in tacit invitation. He sets his coffee down and takes a seat across the table from me.

"What's your favorite episode?" he asks.

"That's easy. *Phiona Phinds a Phriend*. First appearance of Phoenix the Phennec Phox."

"Those huge ears! You know, it was years before I realized fennec foxes were a real thing. I thought it was something they made up for the show."

"That's what was awesome about it. The writers were always sneaking in little science tidbits. Of course, they were also totally messing with our ability to spell things that start with an F correctly, so it balanced out."

He laughs. "Tell me about it. I failed all my spelling tests the year the show started until my mom figured out what was going on. I think she even wrote a letter to the producers complaining about it."

His brown eyes sparkle against his skin that's a few shades darker than my own light brown, and they crinkle up in a kind of adorable way when he laughs. I give myself a mental shake. *You do not fall for random guys who hit on you in coffee shops.*

I usually never even give them the time of day, but he's found a chink in my armor. It's broad daylight, there's plenty of other people around. I haven't even told him my name. Can't hurt to indulge in a little geeky fan talk, can it?

"I had my mom make Phiona's armor for me as a Halloween costume, but I used to wear it all the time at home," I confess. "Looking back, I'm amazed I never tried to wear it to school."

"Wouldn't she have stopped you?"

"Nah, she was a big believer in self-expression and letting children have free rein with their imaginations. She was always in her own dream world. It probably wouldn't have occurred to her the kind of bullying I'd have gotten if I went to school dressed like that."

"Sounds nice. My mom was pretty uptight about everything. My brothers and I were the preppy kids at school. She picked out our outfits every day right up until we went away to college. There's definitely a right way and a wrong way to dress in her mind."

"Looks like you carried on the tradition. That's a sharp-looking suit."

"Thanks. It's bespoke."

"Be what? Is that a brand?"

"No, it means custom-made. I just like the word bespoke. I get them made when I'm in Hong Kong. There's tailors there can whip one up in 24 hours. Nothing like the feel of clothes made especially for you."

Now this is getting back into territory I'm familiar with. Hadn't been sure what to make of someone who looked like this guy yet spoke with unbridled enthusiasm about a cheesy kids' show. This bragging about international travel and fancy suits is more what I expect, and it makes me feel justified in my original snap judgment.

Before I can figure out how to give him the brush off, he laughs again.

"Sounds a lot posher than the reality. I have to dress up and travel a lot for my job, and the suits I get in Hong Kong are actually cheaper than what I could get here."

"What do you do?"

"I'm a sales rep for a software firm. Specialized software for inventory control for big corporations. Means meeting with a lot of important people so I have to look sharp."

"Sounds like a dream job," I say, unable to keep the sarcastic edge out of my voice.

"I bet you don't think so, and neither do I if I'm honest. I started out on the programming end of things. That's more my style. Sitting in a dark room, staring at a screen, problem-solving and working out the logic of the code. It was more fun than this, but I get to see the world on the company's dime as a salesman. I can always go back to coding if I get tired of it. What do you do?"

"I'm a writer."

"Oh, yeah? That's cool. What kind of books have you published?"

"I'm not that kind of writer. At least, not yet. I take gigs doing technical writing, social media posts, that sort of thing. It's not exactly my dream job either."

I'm about to break into a rhapsody about the mystery novel I have all mapped out when I catch myself up short: *Who am I right now? What am I doing?* I hardly ever talk about my writing even to people I've known for years. Some of them, including my own family, have no idea about it.

"Let me guess," he says. "You've spent years world building for your fantasy trilogy and now you just need to sit down and write it."

"It's a mystery, actually, and only one book so far, though I'd like to turn it into a series. I have lots of ideas for different plots."

"I'd love to hear about it."

The weird thing is, I feel like he means it. *And after all,* I think, *what harm could it do?*

I'll probably never see him again, and it might be fun to talk about it to someone who looks like their eyes won't glaze over the minute I start outlining my ideas.

"Well, it's like this…"

He leans forward eagerly as though the better to hear me.

And that's when the world explodes.

I WAKE up slowly to a vision of white. I'm lying in an old-fashioned cast-iron bed that's been painted white, under a fluffy white comforter in a vast empty space that is white as far as I can see in any direction. I sit up, head feeling funny, not heavy enough. Reach up and run a hand across my skull. My long black hair is gone, only the bristling start of new growth marring my smooth scalp.

The silence is complete. Afraid I've lost my hearing in whatever that explosion was, I tentatively hit my fingernails against the bed frame, relieved to hear the tinny clink of the metal echoing. I ponder my surroundings, unable to make sense of the circumstances. I remember the café, the guy who stopped to talk to me—what was his name? Can't quite remember, though it's on the tip of my tongue. We talked about *Phantastic Phantoms* after he noticed my t-shirt.

I look down. The t-shirt is gone. In its place, a white, form-fitting body suit made from a material that feels slick against my skin. No shoes. My bare feet hit the chill of the floor as I swing out of bed and stand up. Feeling shaky and weak, I wobble a bit in place, consider calling out for help, but I'm somehow reluctant to break the quiet stillness with such a harsh sound.

The body suit tightens subtly around me, almost like it's providing extra support, and I feel a surge of energy and warmth. Start walking randomly out into the daunting space. It's disorienting. The room looks finite, yet the ceiling and walls are so far away that I can't tell if they're real or an optical illusion. I try my best to march in a straight line, moving for hours or minutes or days. Who can tell? Neither time nor space seem to have any meaning here.

Finally see an object off in the far distance. Excited, I break into a run. Reach it, gasping for breath, to find it's another bed. Or the same bed, maybe? It looks the same as the one I woke up in but wait—not quite. The white comforter has a black mark on it.

I look closer. A line drawn in a perfect circle. I touch it with one finger and feel an electric thrill up my arm. Gasp in shock as something hits my ankle, a perfect metal sphere about the size of the kickball we used to play with in elementary school resting at my feet.

It has a shiny stainless-steel finish. I bend over and pick it up. It has heft but isn't as heavy as it looks. Easily balances in one hand. I stare into the orb's surface and find my face staring back, bald head distorted and alien, but I'm relieved to see something, some color other than white. The ball is far from an exciting object in and of itself, but it represents difference, newness, a change in an environment that is frighteningly uniform.

Impulsively, I lean down, setting the sphere on the floor and pushing it like a bowling ball as hard as I can away from me, listening to the rough rolling sound disappearing into the distance. All is silent for a moment. Then I hear the noise again but from behind me this time. Turn around in time to see the ball approaching the bed from the other side, coming to a rest again at my feet.

"What is this?" I yell. "Some kind of sick experiment? Who's out there?"

My words echo and roil against the boundless white space. It takes a while for the angry words bouncing around to split and join and settle down into silence again. I'm tempted to scream again and keep screaming until someone answers, but the sound of my voice repeating and repeating makes my head hurt with a dull ache.

I whisper instead. "Don't give me any answers then. See if I care."

Something whaps me on the top of the skull, striking bone and skittering to the floor under the bed. My heart races as I bend over to see what it is. It's out of reach, so I get down on my hands and knees and then stomach to stretch for it. A black marker. Ordinary except it has no markings or brand name on the barrel.

"Great," I mutter. "What am I supposed to do with this?"

I sit on the bed, staring at the perfect circle drawn on the bed cover.

Uncap the pen and sketch a quick daisy, simple in outline and form. Look around. Nothing. Lay my hand on the drawing and hear a faint tinkling sound.

Following the noise, I find a flower growing from the floor, identical in shape to the one I've drawn but made of crystal, twinkling and winking as though hit by the sun and a breeze though neither of those things are present. The jingle is pleasant, like wind chimes heard from a distance.

Now I have two objects, a ball and a flower. Not terribly useful but interesting. They make me feel less alone somehow. The space is huge and empty. I have an impulse to fill it up, so I sit on the bed again and draw a simple house shape with a door and two windows, a chimney with a curl of smoke coming out. Lay my hand upon the drawing and feel the warmth passing through it to the ink.

A thunderous crash sounds. I look up to find a lopsided cabin, made of birch logs with frosted glass windows and a pebbled chimney that pumps a fine watery mist into the air. It rains down on me as I near the structure and try the door. It won't budge, as though it's locked.

Running back to the comforter, I draw a keyhole in the door and a key. Return to the cabin and find to my delight that they have been reproduced in reality—or what passes for reality in this place. I turn the key and open the door to find an empty interior.

Of course, I think. *I'll have to fill it up, but first...*

I return to the bed and smooth out the cover to give myself a flat canvas. Close my eyes to remember the last face I'd seen. Crinkly brown eyes, a lopsided smile. This time I really concentrate on the art. My body hums with adrenaline and not a little fear. Attempting to bring a living creature to life is different than a house or even a flower made of glass.

Taking my time, I add in as much shading and as many details as I can. The more I draw, the more my memory replays the encounter at the café before that world came to an end. Staring into his eyes—whatever his name was—the kind glint of interest in them as I started to tell him about my writing.

I debate whether to draw a body or not. I've been concentrating on the shoulders and face, but will that produce a disembodied head floating around? I don't think I could take that much more weirdness on top of everything else, so decide it's better to be safe than sorry and sketch in a suit and tie. I've never been good at drawing hands, so I hide them in his pant pockets. Add a pair of leather shoes, then spend a long time staring at what I've drawn, afraid to touch it, bring it to life.

The drawing isn't a bad likeness, but will it work? Or will it be an empty shell, like the house? Devoid of internal organs, hands, or anything else I haven't drawn. In short, am I creating a monster? The desire to have someone, something to talk to, to commiserate with, to help figure out what's going on is too strong. I lay a hand against his cheek and close my eyes in a kind of prayer.

I jump as a hand lands on my shoulder. Leaping from the bed, I turn around to see *him*—the guy from the coffee shop—looking at me with a puzzled expression.

"It's you!" we both cry.

I giggle hysterically. "You have hands!"

"Um, yeah, last time I looked."

"I wasn't sure if you would because I didn't draw them."

"What? Are you okay?"

"Not really, but I'm so happy to have someone to talk to—I'm sorry, I can't remember your name."

"Marcus. I don't think you ever gave me yours."

"No, I guess not. Everything happened so fast. It's Rosa."

"Nice to meet you, Rosa."

He offers a hand and I take it. It feels warm and real. I notice he isn't wearing the outfit I'd drawn for him. Instead, he has a white bodysuit and no shoes.

"So, where the hell are we?" he asks.

"I hadn't thought of it like that, but maybe this *is* hell? Maybe we're dead. Last thing I remember was some kind of explosion."

"Me, too. At the coffee shop, right? You were about to tell me about your writing."

"And instead, I ended up in this white box and conjured you up to keep me company."

"What do you mean?"

I show him his portrait on the bed. Explain how it works.

"So, what? You're saying I'm just a drawing brought to life? A figment of your imagination? Sorry to burst your bubble, but I woke up in a similar white box and have been hanging out there quite independent of you, so I don't think you can take credit for making me."

"Was it the same as this?"

"Pretty much, except mine had a wall of glass. A line of code appeared on it. A 'Hello, world' message."

"What's that?"

"It's a tradition when you're studying a new programming language. The first thing you learn is how to write a simple piece of code to make a system produce the phrase 'Hello, World.' I touched the words on the glass and they appeared on the floor. Then a marker dropped out of nowhere, hitting me on the head." He scrubs at his skull which I realize has been shaved like mine.

"Same with me," I say. "Marker from the sky."

"Not very polite, whoever's behind this, are they? Anyway, I tried writing out a line of code to spit out the current date and time. Thought it might give me some clue as to when I was, if not where. But before I could finish it, I found myself here with you."

"What does it all mean? Do you think we've been abducted by aliens? Is this some kind of science experiment?"

"Maybe the government. Weird things go on in Area 51, don't they? Or maybe I got a concussion in that blast and this is all a figment of my imagination."

"Including me?" I ask, raising an eyebrow in annoyance. "How is that possible when I'm here too?"

"I only have your word for it you're actually here. I could be having this conversation with you in my head."

"If anything, you're the figment. I drew you, remember."

"You drew me into existence? Then how do you explain what I experienced with the code wall?"

"I could have made that up in my own brain."

"Did you know about the 'Hello, World' program?"

"No, but again, that could be some detail I invented. Writers have very creative minds you know. I've only your word for it all this coding stuff is even a real thing."

"We're going around in circles here," he says. "Whether we're both real, only one of us is real, or neither of us is real, what are we going to do? We need to figure out what's going on and get out of here."

"I agree. For one thing, we're going to need food and water and um, eventually, we'll need to, you know, eliminate."

"Yeah, it's strange though. I haven't felt the need for any of those things since I've been here, have you?"

"No, now you mention it. I felt weak when I first woke up but then—"

"The body suit, right? I had the same experience. Was almost too weak to stand and then the suit kind of constricted or something and I felt a surge of strength."

I try tugging at the material. It clings to my skin like Velcro. "You think it's keeping us alive somehow?"

"Maybe. I guess we'll see. If we never get hungry or feel like we gotta pee, that'll tell us something."

"Tell us what? You're talking about a kind of technology that doesn't exist."

"Maybe not in our time. Maybe we're in the future. Too bad I couldn't check the code. It might have told me the date."

"If you could trust it. How can we trust anything that happens here?" I pull the glass daisy up from the floor and smash it. The shattered pieces melt away like water. "Everything is an illusion."

He takes my hand again. "You don't feel like an illusion to me. Maybe everything else is, but you're warm and real. Number one fan of Phantastic Phantoms. A writer."

"And you're a coder, a salesman, a traveler."

"Don't forget a terrible speller."

I smile. "You know, I'd rather think you're real and I'm not alone here, so let's go with that unless proven otherwise."

"Deal. So, what's next?" he asks, looking around. "Cute house you have there. I didn't have one of those."

I glance over at the drunken-looking cabin. "I'd have taken more care drawing it if I'd thought it was really going to work. It's empty. Just a shell."

"Maybe we can fill it up. Test the limits of our powers. Wonder if programming works here." He drops my hands and grabs the marker, writing out a quick series of words and symbols. Touches it and looks around. Nothing has changed. "Maybe it only works back at my place."

"Try drawing something," I suggest.

"I'm no artist," he laughs, "but I'll give it a try."

He sketches out a tall tree, a simple triangle shape atop a tall skinny trunk. Touches it. Nothing. On impulse, I reach out a finger to it. A whooshing noise fills the air as a dull metal tree springs from the floor, spearing the space as it climbs into the sky. Startled, I accidentally touch the drawing again and another tree springs up.

Giddy, I touch it again and again until a whole forest of metal trees surrounds us. They look comical, like a child's drawing come to life, yet the ponderously dull silver metal and their immense size gives them an uncanny majesty.

Marcus runs over to lay a hand on the nearest one, which sends it swaying against its neighbors until the whole forest is gently vibrating. An eerie noise like the sound of a thousand fingers along the rims of a thousand wine glasses fills the air. I can feel the thrum of it from the soles of my bare feet to the very top of my skull.

"They're singing to us," I whisper, but Marcus doesn't hear. He's busy jogging around touching one after another of the trees whenever they threaten to quieten as their rocking dies down.

"This is pretty rad!" he shouts. "Like a video game come to life. What else should we make?"

"An exit out of here would be pretty awesome right about now," I reply, unnerved by the strange melody.

"Try it."

"What?"

"Draw a picture of a door, mark it exit. Let's see what happens."

I draw a simple rectangle. Print the word "EXIT" in bold and touch it. Nothing happens.

"The walls are all too far away and they never get closer no matter how far you walk," I complain. "It might have appeared on one of them, but we'd never get near enough to see."

"Those aren't the only walls," Marcus says, grabbing my hand and pulling me over to the cabin and through the front door. The exit door I've drawn is reproduced on the far inside wall.

He pushes on it. "You forgot to add a doorknob."

"Wait here." I run back outside and add a knob and a keyhole and key for good measure. By the time I get back inside the cabin, Marcus has the door open and is walking through it.

"Hey, wait for me. Don't you dare leave me behind." I grab his hand as we walk through a brief tunnel of darkness before emerging into a white space with a white bed. "We're back where we started."

"No, we aren't. This is my place, see?" He points to a wall of glass beyond the bed. "There's the code I wrote." He runs over and touches it. A projection of digits starts revolving along the floor like the wheels on a slot machine at a casino. They gradually settle into a string: 0000-00-00T00:00:00.

"What does it mean?"

"Either nothing, or that my code is flawed, or that we're at the beginning of all history before the dawn of time. Take your pick."

"Not helpful then."

"Not too much but give me a minute. I wonder if..."

Marcus stands at the glass wall, scribbling a series of words and symbols that look meaningless to me, but his fierce concentration convinces me he has a plan. I sit down on the bed watching the lines of writing grow and grow.

"Here goes nothing," he says finally, looking back at me and grinning before touching the text.

A flicker under the bed and a strange chattering noise startle me. I jump off and stand next to Marcus as we lean over to take a look.

"What did you do?" I shriek.

Marcus grins at me as he holds out a hand to the thing beneath the bed. "Rosa, meet Phrank. It's okay to come out. We're friends."

A pale, shivering form slides out from under the bed. It's—Phrank's—teeth are knocking together just as I remember from the cartoon.

"Ph-ph-ph-phriends?"

"It talks!" Marcus whoops. "I wasn't sure it would be that sophisticated. I was trying to create an image as near to what I could remember as possible."

"How did you do this?"

"I was wondering if I could write some code like they do when designing characters and settings and stuff for video games. It seemed to make sense I'd been given the tools to fill up my space the way you did over in yours but with something that was more in my wheelhouse than art. I needed something fairly simple in form to program or it could have taken me days."

Phrank is definitely simple. A classic white-sheet ghost shape, he fits right into the environment. It would've been hard to see him against all the white except for his wide, frightened eyes and chittering teeth.

"Ph-phorgive me, but who are you?" he asks.

"I'm Marcus and this is Rosa."

"And who am I?"

"You're Phrank Phantom."

"A-a-a-a ghost?" Phrank slides back under the bed, looking out at us in fear. "I'm phrightened of ghosts."

"We know you are," I say, rolling my eyes. "That was a running joke on the show."

"Show?"

"It was a television show. You were the star."

"I am a star? I thought I was a ghost."

"Well, this is real helpful, isn't it?" I say to Marcus.

"Yeah, being helpful was never Phrank's strong suit, was it? I should have coded Phiona instead. She might've actually been useful. But still, it's pretty interesting, don't you think?"

"Fascinating. In fact, something I'd really be enjoying if we weren't stuck in some weird alternate universe where we can draw or code anything into existence except a way out of here."

"Don't give up. We're just experimenting. Testing out the limits of what we can do. Early days yet."

"You're one of those 'glass half full' guys, aren't you?"

"I try to be."

"That crap drives me crazy. There's nothing good about our situation."

"You got to meet your childhood hero, Phrank."

"He wasn't my hero. Phiona was."

"Right. To be honest, I thought about trying to program Phiona, but I didn't have as clear a picture in my mind of her as I did of Phrank."

"I remember everything about her. Come with me."

I drag Marcus back through the tunnel and cabin and over to my bed. I've drawn my favorite ghost hundreds if not thousands of times in my life. A habit I adopted as a child to calm myself when I'm really upset. Doesn't take long to have a fair representation of the warrior ghost inked on the comforter.

I touch a finger to it and a flash of light beams over my shoulder.

"What's the phuss about, phoolish mortals?"

There she is, strangely muscular for a ghost, dressed in her leather armor and waving her sword, Phlame, around.

Marcus hoots. "That's fabulous! Look what you did!"

Phiona waves her sword at me. "What did she do? Is she a villain? Does she need vanquishing?"

I'm struck speechless at seeing what I've conjured into existence, but Marcus comes to my rescue.

"No, we're all friends here. In fact, Phrank is in the next room."

"That sniveling phraidy-cat? He's as much use as a phrog in a phunnel phactory."

"Uh, what? That doesn't even make sense."

"None of the jokes on that show made sense," I remind him. "It's like it really is her. How is that possible?"

"Don't have the first idea, but it's pretty wicked."

I sink back on the bed and close my eyes. "This is all making my brain hurt and that weird humming from the trees isn't helping."

"I shall slay and phlay them all!"

"No!" we both shout, but it's too late.

The ghost zooms around chopping at the metal trunks with Phlame. All she succeeds in doing is amplifying the clamor of the trees a thousand-fold with every stroke. I slap my hands to my ears in a futile attempt to shut out the excruciating noise.

Marcus pulls at my arm, jerking me back toward the cabin.

"Good idea!" I yell, even though there's no way he can hear it over the din.

We run through the cabin door and the exit to Marcus's room.

"Wait for me, you phaithless phiends!"

Phiona comes barreling along behind us. As she enters the room, she crackles and sizzles like a steak on a hot grill and burns up into a crisp of white ash that falls to the floor.

Phrank stares in dismay at the pile of dust. "Oh, Phiona! What a phate!"

I can't help feeling horrified for the warrior ghost and sorry for Phrank. They aren't really alive—couldn't be—and yet they're both capable of independent thought and action. Isn't that one definition of life?

"What happened?" Marcus asks.

"My guess is the things we make can only exist in our own rooms," I answer. "If we try to move them between spaces, they're destroyed."

"I will be staying right here then, thank you very much," says Phrank, returning to huddle under the bed with clacking teeth and wide eyes.

"Poor Phiona." Marcus reaches down and touches the dust. "I almost feel like we killed her."

"How were we to know? How are we to know how any of this works? What even is this? I can't take it. We've got to get out of here."

He grabs me in a bear hug. I stand stiffly, too angry and upset to need or want the physical contact. Getting the message, he lets me go and steps back, hands raised in mute apology.

"Sorry," I mutter. "I know you're trying to be supportive, but I'm so frustrated right now."

"Maybe we need to take a break. Go back to our separate spaces for a bit. Rest."

"I'm afraid to. What if something happens and we can't get back together?"

"Nothing we've created has self-destructed yet except for Phiona, and that was probably because she moved into a different space from where she was made, like you said. Everything else seems pretty stable."

"But you don't know that for sure."

"Nothing is for sure anymore, is it? I'm running on faith at this point."

I can't deny that a little alone time is tempting. It felt so lonely before I drew Marcus, but everything that's happening is overwhelming. I long to sit quietly and think for a minute.

"Ok, but don't you go anywhere."

He laughs. "I don't think I *can* go anywhere. That's the whole problem. Don't worry. Phrank and I will be waiting for you when you come back. Maybe I'll have an idea of what we should do by then."

"Or I will," I suggest, stung he thinks it's up to him to save the day.

I return to my bed, pick up the marker, and draw an overstuffed sofa. It appears—a violent mustard color that would have driven me bonkers under any other circumstances, but I'm too relieved to have a comfy place to curl up to worry about the aesthetics of it.

It's blissfully quiet. The trees have stilled, standing and waiting in silence again. I think of the strange melody they played. It was familiar but like a song you can only remember a snippet of lyric from and can't quite recall how the music goes.

I mourn the premature demise of Phiona. Her portrait is still on the comforter. I assume I could touch it again (and again and again) and make as many copies of Phiona as I want, but I've got to admit the warrior ghost was hardly a restful companion.

It gives me an idea though. I go over to the bed and sketch out a new picture: a tiny white fox with a long bushy tail and comically oversized ears. Scratch the completed image on its head with my finger and the trees start singing but a softer sound this time. A small creature is winding its body around and around the trunks, setting them to shivering ever so slightly.

"Phoenix," I call, and it bounds over to snuggle in my arms. I settle down onto the sofa, cradling the fennec fox. It's so warm, its tiny heart beating fast beneath downy soft fur. So real and yet not.

It sniffs my face then tucks its small nose into my armpit and falls asleep. I concentrate on the movement of its chest, the gentle puffs of air under my arm. It twitches now and again as if in a dream. For the first time since this nightmare started, I feel almost relaxed, calm, at peace even.

I sit for a long time. I'm not sleepy or tired, hungry, thirsty, not even stiff from resting in the same position for so long. The body suit must have some kind of power. I can feel it pulsing slightly from time to time like it's making subtle adjustments.

Not saying it's aliens, but it has to be aliens, I think, giggling at the image of a silly meme that pops into my brain. Phoenix opens one eye to look at me then goes back to sleep.

Okay, Marcus and I have been abducted by aliens. They're studying us to see how we react and adapt to our situation. We've not been harmed except for having our heads shaved and being held prisoner. Things could be worse.

This makes me laugh again. Hysterical laughter, sure, but it still feels good. Like I'm letting go of some of my anxiety. It wakes Phoenix up and he jumps from my arms, dancing around on the floor like an overexcited Chihuahua. He runs over to the forest, brushing up against one of the trees. A low hum echoes.

I follow the fox and run a hand gently over another of the trunks. A different note, higher and more distant. Experimentation finds the slightest touch sets a tree to ringing like a tuning fork. I improvise a song of sorts, humming along. The resonance of the sound creates its own vibrations, and the symphony bounces around and off the too-distant ceiling and walls.

It's pleasant for a time, but the intensity keeps ratcheting up, becoming jarring and disjointed. I pick up Phoenix and move away from the forest, but the trees have taken on a life of their own, moving violently. Without thinking, I run back through the cabin and the exit door straight into Marcus's room.

Phoenix lives up to his name by disappearing in a flash of fire and ash in my arms.

"No!"

In my panic to escape the forest's din, I've forgotten crossing over into the other room spells doom for anything I've created. The fennec fox had been nothing more than a figment of my imagination perhaps, but it had felt real. Had lain in my arms with its little heart beating near to mine. Its destruction is the thing that finally breaks me.

I collapse to my knees, smearing the white ash over my face, tears turning it to mud. Marcus kneels in front of me and I reach out, clinging to him like I'm drowning. I feel like I am. Can't catch my breath; weeping too hard to see anything.

He rocks me in his arms like he's soothing a child, murmuring, "It's okay," over and over, even though we both know it's a lie. I remember my first impression of him as a shallow, narcissistic jerk—how wrong could I have been? He's been sweeter and more patient than any guy—anyone I've ever known.

"Im gmpgim stltchen wichoo."

"What?" he asks as I mumble against his chest.

I pull my head back, clear my throat. "I said, I'm glad I'm stuck here with you. I mean, if I had to be in this situation whatever it is, I'm glad I ended up with you and not some asswipe."

"Me, too. Can you imagine being stuck here with someone like—"

"The Wretched Wraith. He's the most ph-phearsome and phoul being on the planet."

We turn to look at Phrank, who has ventured out from under the bed. I reach out a hand to him, and he glides over and clasps it. It's a bit like trying to grip onto a bowl of firm gelatin, but it makes me smile.

"You're so right, Phrank. That would be terrible. We're very lucky, aren't we?"

"Luckier than Phiona and Phoenix."

Marcus play-scowls at him. "Way to bring down a room, Phrank. Let's stay focused on the positives, shall we?"

"Phorgive me. I'll be waiting over here if you need me." He retreats back under the bed and proceeds to hum the theme song of Phantastic Phantoms to himself.

"That's the song! I knew I recognized it," I say. "The trees are singing it to us, or variations on the theme. How weird."

"Not really, when you think about it. If everything we create is from our imagination, then even the song the trees are performing would be too. And the show was one of the last things we were talking about before we came here. It's no wonder we've been creating things related to it."

"I suppose, but there's so many other things we could have thought of. Pop culture references."

"Like what?" Marcus asks.

"Like, you know… well…"

"Can't recall anything, can you? I've been thinking about it while you were gone. Trying to remember other shows, movies, games. I got nothing."

"Like our memories have been erased? But I remember things. My mother. She was a—"

"Free spirit, right? And mine was uptight. She made my brothers dress a certain way when we were younger. But the thing is, I can't remember what she looks like, how many brothers I have, what their names are. Just the fact she picked out our clothes. Same with my job. I know I'm a salesman, I travel constantly, buy my suits tailor-made in Hong Kong but I can't remember anything else about my job or places I've visited, the people I work with."

Turning over in my head the small number of facts I know about myself, I realize he's right. I make a living as a technical writer. Have dreams of publishing a novel, a mystery, but I can't remember anything about the book, the plot, the detective. I try to picture my mother and get a vague warm and fuzzy feeling but no image at all.

It's lonely, not being able to remember. There's an emptiness, an ache. I start to panic as I chase memories around that have no intention of being caught.

"They've stolen them," I say. "I want them back."

"Me, too, but first we have to get out of here. I've been working on something else while you were away."

He pulls me to my feet and leads me over to the big glass wall. Every inch of it is covered with ink, not all of it black, though.

"What's this?" I ask, touching a rusty red section.

He looks embarrassed. "The marker ran out of ink. I pulled a sharp spring off my bed and made a makeshift pen with it."

"And the ink?"

He pulls up the sleeves of his bodysuit and shows me deep gouges in the dark skin along his forearms.

"Marcus! Your own blood?"

"I was on a roll with the code and didn't know if or when I'd be provided with another marker. I didn't want to lose my train of thought."

I examine the writing. "This must have taken you hours. How long was I gone?"

"Days? Weeks maybe? I don't know. Time seems to work differently here."

"You've written a whole program. What does it do?"

"It's a kind of exit program. Like at the end of a game. It will open a door, I hope. A door out of here. But to be honest, I'm not sure exactly what's gonna happen when I activate it. I was waiting for you to come back before I tried, but now I'm not sure if I should or not. It might be dangerous."

"Can't be worse than hanging out here for eternity, can it?"

"Tell that to Phiona and Phoenix."

I grimace. "Fair point."

"It's something to think about. So far, it seems like we're safe. We're not hungry or tired. No one or nothing has tried actively to harm us."

"Other than those trees. That vibration when they all get going is pretty intense."

"Design flaw. My fault there. I should have drawn you some nice shrubberies instead."

"Very funny. I guess this is where we're different. You're 'glass half full' guy and 'I'm glass half empty' girl. Just because we're not being actively harmed, we're still being held prisoner against our wills with no explanation. I'd rather take a chance at freedom then hang around here hoping something's gonna change. Besides, I have faith in you."

"You do? We hardly know each other. This," he says, waving at the sea of letters and numbers on the glass wall, "could be so much crap as far as you can tell."

"Is it?"

"I don't think so. I'm a pretty good programmer if I do say so myself, but this is uncharted territory. I'm trying to take what I know about building computer programs and apply it to this virtual world. Who knows if it even follows the same logic or not?"

"I think we should try it. Chances are whoever has us here will block it if they don't want us to get out, but whatever happens might give us more information to go on. Sitting around recreating characters from cheesy old kids' shows isn't getting us anywhere. No offense, Phrank."

"None taken, ph-phriend."

"So, what do you think?" I say to Marcus.

"Honestly? I'm scared. I'd almost prefer we go on as we are, at least for a while. Maybe something will happen without us forcing it."

"I don't think so. I have a feeling they're waiting for us to figure it out. Whoever they are. If you've come up with a possible solution, we should try it. If you don't trust yourself, trust me."

He looks hard at me, then walks over to the glass. Puts a trembling hand up and pushes his palm against the part of the code he's written in red.

Everything is silent and still.

"So, that was a bust, but nice try," I say.

He comes over and takes my hand. "Wait… listen…"

I don't hear anything at first but notice a funny tickling beneath my feet, like the floor is sending a message. Then it comes: the melody of the trees in the other room. Only now it's loud enough to be heard here where we've never been able to hear it before.

The vibrations in the floor increase, causing us to stagger and clutch on to each other to steady ourselves as the wall between the rooms starts to glow. An unbearable flash and then the wall vanishes.

"It worked, kind of," Marcus yells. "There's an exit, just not the one we wanted."

"Marcus, watch out, the trees!"

The enormous metal trees in the next room are swaying dangerously from side to side, bending almost double to the floor before swinging back in the opposite direction over and over. The tremendous force they are exerting on the space is profound.

"I know but look!" He points through the forest to some kind of portal-looking thing that has opened at the foot of my bed. I can make out what looks like the interior of a coffee shop, the coffee shop where we met.

"We have to go for it. This may be our only chance!" I shout.

We grasp hands and run, dodging the deadly sway of the trees. We're almost there—so close, so close—when one of the trees snaps in half, landing on Marcus's leg and dragging him down to the floor. Desperate, I try to lift the metal but it's impossibly heavy. His leg is trapped. It looks crushed.

"Go on, Rosa! Get out of here!" he screams. "Save yourself!"

"I'm not leaving here without you. No way!"

"There's nothing you can do for me. Don't throw away your chance. Go!"

I look through the portal, the coffee shop so temptingly normal, so peaceful, so sane. Then I crouch beside Marcus, draping my body over his in a futile attempt to protect him from the growing menace of the forest.

Remember the melody of the trees, the melody of the trees, the trees, I chant over and over to myself, not knowing what I even mean by it.

Neither of us sees the one that falls and smashes us into oblivion.

"What are you reading?"

I look up into an interested pair of brown eyes and a charmingly lopsided smile, then back down to where I've been doodling in the margin of the book in front of me.

It's started again. We're back in the coffee shop. Only this time, there's a difference: I remember everything that's gone before.

Clever girl, I think, running a finger over the sketch I've been working on of a forest of metal trees, a pair of ghosts, a tiny big-eared creature, and the face of one who should be a stranger to me. *Turns out there's a loophole after all.*

I ask him to join me, go through the motions of introductions and conversation, bracing myself all the while for the explosion. How many thousands of times have we repeated this? I tell myself it doesn't matter. This time I have a clear memory of the mistakes we make. This time I have a chance to save Marcus and save myself.

This time, there's hope.

An Invitation of Shadows

"Come out, come out, wherever you are."

The boy clapped his hands to his ears and burrowed deeper into the moldy leaves inside the rotting log. If he couldn't hear the voice, it couldn't find him.

"I know you're here somewhere, Figgy. You're so close by, I can smell you."

He'd known it was going to be one of the Bad Days when he heard Father sharpening the blade of his hooked sickle. The shrill whine of the metal against the grindstone. His father muttering to himself.

"Harvest time" Father called it. A time for fear, racing hearts, screams cut short.

Mother had heard the grinding too and rousted them all out of bed. Gave the baby to Hannah. Sent everyone into the woods. She always stayed behind. Father didn't consider her worthy of harvesting. He couldn't see beneath her roughened hide into the heart of her like Figgy could. Mother was all silver-dusted bones and sapphire starlight that threatened to burst from her skin. If Father could see what Figgy could see, he would split Mother open, steal her inner riches and leave the remains for the crows.

The other children called Figgy weird, touched. They didn't understand how some days, words felt too dear for him to speak. He hoarded them, close-mouthed, and none of the others could pry a syllable from him that he didn't wish to part with. It was a strange talent. One that caused suspicion and anger, but Figgy was too busy listening and watching to care. Making notes in his memory of all that was.

"What do you see?" Mother asked him once.

"Darkness. There's a shadow over them all, every movement, every word, every thought. They don't notice it, but I do. It makes it hard to pretend to be one of them. Why can't they see what I see?"

"You have the gift, Figgy. It runs in my family. My brother was one such."

"Your brother? You never told us about him."

"He... died. In the long ago." Mother hugged Figgy to her breast, near squeezing the breath out of him. "Keep it close, what you see, child. Never let the others know. And never, ever let *him* see what you can do. My heart would break to lose you. Folks don't trust those with the gift, but keep your eyes open and remember what you see. Remember us when we're gone. You'll be the only one who does."

Times were bad. The worst any could recall and had been for years. Families closed in on themselves. Did what they had to do to survive. No questions were asked, everyone too busy with their own troubles.

Mother was prolific. A new baby every year like clockwork. Too many mouths to feed said Father. And so, one day, he started harvesting.

Jonah was the first to go. One of the oldest, but unlike the other boys, he wasn't strong and fit. No use in the fields. Had a penchant for playing malicious pranks. He was barely missed at all. Almost made the shock of Father's betrayal palatable.

Others were harder to bear. Little Stella Star as they called her, with her shy smiles. Martin and Jake, the twins. Figgy thought Mother would put a stop to it. They were her children after all. Flesh of her flesh. Hard for a child to grasp the terror of a woman alone, dependent, weakened by childbirth and hard living, beaten down by a will so much stronger than her own.

Father. None of them called him that to his face. None of them spoke to him at all if they could help it. He was the monster in their midst. A giant of a man, benign, jovial even—on any day but a harvest day. He seemed not to notice how they scattered when he strode through the yard and cowered at the table when he sat down to eat.

All but the eldest of the children. Figgy could see the clouds around them darkening, turning crimson like Father's. They were being drawn in his wake. He saw the way they looked at their brothers and sisters, considering, calculating. Perhaps one day soon, they would join in the harvesting. The strongest always survived.

Figgy huddled in the rotting log. Beetles and ants and spiders scurried around and over him, impatient with the trembling obstacle in their path. Fear oozed up every inch of his body as he listened to Father calling for him. The terror explored his toes, then nibbled at his knees. The tickling round his ribs was the worst. Made him want to giggle, but once it reached his shoulders, sniffed at the back of his neck, it was all he could do to keep from crying out in terror.

The crack of a stick nearby. He peered out, caught a glimpse of a small hoof. A deer. They'd been scarce in these parts. A grunt, a squeal cut short, a thump of falling, and then blood. So much blood.

A pair of bright blue eyes peered in at Figgy. "Thought you were in there, boy. Today's your lucky day. This deer has sacrificed herself up in your place. I'll save you for another harvest. May as well come out now. Your mother'll be wondering where we're at."

After hesitating a moment too long, rough hands reached in and dragged him out into the open. "You're about useless. Least you can do is help me carry."

Figgy supported the doe's head, its staring brown eyes looking at him accusingly as its neck gaped open from the mortal wound. He stepped in the blood, leaving footprints his siblings would follow home, expecting to see one of their own. What rejoicing there'd be. He imagined Mother's relief at this blessed reprieve.

And indeed, her solemn face relaxed as she watched them from the front porch. She never smiled, but Figgy could see her aura lighten. A harvest day come and gone with no loss was a rare thing indeed. He waited until Father and some of the others carted the deer around the back of the house to the butchering tree before running to her.

She hugged him close. "Who was it? Who was spared?"

He didn't answer. Didn't need to. Father had been focusing hard looks and sighs on Figgy for weeks.

She knelt down before him, brushed the long black curls back from his face. "Figgy, meet me tonight after everyone's asleep. Be quiet. No one can hear you. No one can see. Meet me at the tree. Promise."

He nodded. No need to ask which tree. It was a massive fig tree that grew in a clearing not too far away. He'd been obsessed with it since he could first walk far enough to reach it. Fergus was his true name, but Figgy he became for his fascination with the hard bitter fruit most found too unpalatable to bother with, even on days when food was scarcer than usual.

He had never understood that. To him, the fruits tasted so soft and sweet. He got drunk on the juice, reveled in the sticky residue that coated his fingers until he licked them clean. They filled his mind with ideas, visions of better days. He thought maybe it was a part of his gift —to see and feel the worth others were blind to.

They ate well that night. Venison stew was a welcome change from the usual harvest day feast. The relief was palpable around the table, though none said a word until Father went outside to smoke his last pipe of the day, sitting on the front steps. Then jokes and laughter, pinches and playful punches abounded. Children being children, the shadow that hung over them lightening for a moment.

Only Figgy and his mother sat in solemn silence. The burden that was their life weighed on them, never lessening. Time passed quickly, too quickly, and another harvest would soon come. Figgy could read Mother's thoughts as her restless gaze roved from child to child. She was picturing them dwindling down and down until only the hardiest few remained. No wonder she rarely showed affection. The pain of getting attached, then loss after loss was too great for anyone to bear.

Everyone was late to bed, the exuberance of being spared lending a renewed energy, a restlessness that was slow to wind down. Figgy waited patiently until all was still. Heard his mother creeping out the door and followed after.

They walked in silence until they reached the fig tree, only then feeling far enough away to safely speak. Mother lit a lantern and dropped to her knees at the base of the tree by a knotted root and began digging with her hands. "Help me."

Figgy found a shallow rock, scoop-shaped, and dug with her. Trust implicit, he felt no need to question. They made steady progress until Figgy's rock hit something hard in the earth. Mother cleared the rest of the dirt carefully and tugged a wooden box from the ground with a grunt of effort.

Figgy watched in fascination as she brushed at the surface revealing intricately carved symbols. He ran his finger over one and a shock burst through his body. He jumped back, sucking on the finger as though burnt.

Mother inserted a small silver key into the lock and opened it up. Inside was a book, its leather cover dusty and crumbling from rot. She clucked and opened the pages hastily, seeming relieved to find them intact and covered in close writing that crisscrossed the page in every direction.

"This belonged to Ferret. My brother."

"Ferret?"

"That's what we called him. Sly and slippery, the others said. His real name was Fergus. I named you for him. His gift was great. He saw and heard many things and wrote them here. It may be of use to you."

Figgy took the book his mother offered him. She'd taught him to read. The only one of the children who'd shown any interest. Something else to set him apart from the others, make them suspicious. What use was such a skill when survival was on the line day to day? He held the lantern over a page and thought he might be able to make out the strange, crabbed hand if he studied it.

Mother took the book back and closed it. Stuffed it into a worn knapsack she produced from behind the tree. "I've put in a little bread and some of the venison. You should gather figs to take with you too.

There's a cup for catching water. You'll have to look for streams or gather up rain."

He stared at her, uncomprehending.

She fit the knapsack to his back and grasped his shoulders with hands that trembled. "You must go, Figgy. Leave this place. There is nothing but death for you here. He has his eye on you. Today was a blessing and a sign. I cannot save all my children, but by the goddess, I will save you."

She reached into the unearthed box and pulled out an empty ink bottle and pen, adding them to the supplies in his bag. "The ink is long gone, but you may find a way to make your own. Perhaps there is a recipe in the book. Fergus knew so many things. Foresaw so many things. Everything but the most important one." She lay a hand gently on one of the great roots of the fig tree. "It's too late for him, but not for you. Add your own story to his if you can. That way, I'll know he isn't forgotten."

His mother's aura had never shone as brightly. Figgy saw the hope in her eyes, something he'd never seen before. He was young in age, no more than nine or ten, he thought, though birthdays were one of those things paid no notice in the family, and he was small, raised on a sparse diet amid constant terror, but his soul felt as ancient as any god.

He pushed down his fears, cupped his mother's face in his hands. "I will add to the story. I will live. And I will come back for you."

"No, that you must never do. Promise me."

"I can't. Don't ask me. What rest will I have knowing you're still here?"

She saw the determination in his face. Dropped a fervent last kiss among his dark curls and ran away into the night without a glance back.

He gathered some figs, picking those on the edge of ripeness, but not too many—the fragile fruit wouldn't last long. Then he set out in a random direction, no destination in his mind other than *away*.

It was an eerie feeling being alone. He'd never been by himself for more than a few minutes in his whole life. At first, he was filled with the pleasant pressure of excitement, as though he'd swallowed a stone of possibility as big as the sea. It was comforting to be so full, no room for worry or doubt, no need. But as he walked, the stone wore down and down until it rattled around like a pebble, a hollow feeling that let in a thousand other thoughts, none of them good.

He was a coward to abandon the others to their fate. His mother. How could she bear it? He should have insisted she come too. They could have looked after each other. But she wouldn't abandon the others, and Father would never let her go. Figgy doubted he'd be bothered to set out to fetch back his strangest child, but Mother was a different story. Her husband viewed her as a possession and a valuable enough one so long as she kept producing more fodder for the harvest. She was right to send Figgy off on his own, but what a lonely feeling.

He kept his head down, watching his feet. Mother had taken the lantern back with her, but there was a moon. Not full, but sufficient to keep from tripping and sprawling until he was far enough away that it felt safe to nestle into the roots of a spreading oak and doze until first light.

Lucky the weather was warm. Those first days of high summer when the chill at night is quickly dismissed by the rising sun. He kept as close an eye on that yellow disk as he could through the trees, trying to head due east. Didn't want to wander around in a circle back to the house and undo his mother's last hope. He'd no shoes, but his soles were tough as leather from a lifetime of running barefoot. He ate sparingly of his small hoard at midday, taking a rest under a soaring pine near the thin trickle of a stream and flipping through the strange book.

It was a heavy thing. Weighed down his pack, but he would have no more thought of discarding it to lighten his load than tunneling to the center of the world. A precious object. He grazed here and there, quickly becoming accustomed to the crimped writing and crisscross pattern meant to save paper. The early pages were full of observations of the natural world. Gradually, visions and portents crept in as his uncle's gift emerged and grew strong:

"Perhaps you must walk through fire to reveal the core of what is real but oh, the scars that grin in the night. The dreams that unlock stubborn thought. I have forgotten a thousand happy memories but

those that stick are full of a bitter taste I cannot spit out and the nightmare begins again. Always the same. Searching and searching for what can't be found, only felt along the rotting bones of my spine. I am become one with the mist. A thing of horror for those with eyes to see. But they look right through me always..."

Figgy marveled at this voice from his past. A man he'd never known. Or a boy. Had he grown to manhood? Maybe the book would say. It would take long to decipher the whole thing, but Figgy felt he had all the time in the world now.

Every step away from home broke another tether, invisible bonds that had imprisoned him since birth. His soul lightened, and he felt all the world must see it. He smiled and then he laughed. Not a booming one to be sure, more of a nervous giggle, but then the sound of it set him to roaring—a lifetime of tension and terror expelled in the raucous noise.

Distracted, he tripped and tumbled down a ravine made slippery by fallen pine needles that got stuck in his curls as he slid. He landed in a tangled heap, staring at a rabbit that was caught startled and frozen by this abrupt arrival. They shared a moment of communion before the rabbit came to its senses and bolted. This struck Figgy as very funny as well, particularly since he wasn't harmed by his accident.

"What a to-do," said a craggy voice, silencing Figgy's mirth all in a moment.

There was a figure peering down into the trench at him, wrapped up in a black cloak even though the day was warm. Whether it was a man or a woman, Figgy couldn't decide. Perhaps neither, perhaps both. But their aura—what a sight! He'd never seen one like it. Golden as the sunlight with streaks of lavender that flashed and darted like the shining scales of fish in a shallow brook. Whatever this being was, it meant him no harm. Of that, he was sure.

They reached a hand down to him and helped him to his feet. "Quite a young lad to be out here on your own. We are far from field or town in this part of the forest."

"Good," said Figgy. There was nothing he'd rather hear. He'd had enough of farm and people if they were anything like his own.

They laughed at him. "A forthright lad, I see. And if I am not mistaken, and I never am, a special one." One hand gnarled with age gently took hold of Figgy's chin and another smoothed his ruffled curls, picking out the stray pine straws. "What is your name?"

"Figgy. That is, it's Fergus really, but folks call me Figgy."

"Fergus." They laid back the hood of their cloak and revealed a craggy face, much lined, with faded blue eyes. Their hair was sparse and silvered and floated about in the breeze. "I knew a Fergus once. You have the look of him."

"My uncle, I think. He had the…" Figgy trailed off, his mother's word of warning to let no one know his secret ringing in his ears.

"He had the gift of sight as you do and I."

"You?"

"Yes, I've not seen an aura such as yours in many moons. As blue as a cloudless sky with nary a bit of corruption. I pray you keep it that way. Life has a way of adding in its own colors, often not to the good. It is an honor to meet you, young Fergus. You may call me Whent. I am a caretaker of sorts to the forest and those that dwell here. What brings you out this way?"

How to explain? A shameful thing. A father culling his own children. The horror of it struck him anew now that he was distant in space if not in time.

"Ah, I see, I see." Whent rested a hand on Figgy's shoulder. "A darkness has driven you from your home. It is not easy being one such as us. The others do not understand, and what they do not understand frightens them. Anger follows soon after. Come with me."

Whent stalked ahead, black cloak flying as though it was a creature with a mind all its own. Figgy stumbled after, elation and guilt at his escape wrapped up together into a great weight that was a burden to carry for one who was still a child.

Before long, a clearing appeared with an antic wooden dwelling as its centerpiece. A stone chimney rose impossibly high into the air and leaned so far from the house, it seemed it must surely tumble over and crumble into dust at any moment. Frowning attic windows appeared disappointed in all they saw, and eerie sighs creaked and groaned from the ancient wood.

Figgy would have thought it abandoned if not for the puffs of smoke that indicated a fire in the hearth and the neat rows of daisies and bluebells and hellebores that spoke of a loving, attentive gardener. An enormous orange tabby leapt down from the roof and wound its way around his legs as though in welcome. He'd never seen a cat before in his life, but the gentle thrum it emitted was soothing.

"Gavin likes you. He enjoys having his head rubbed, like this." Whent demonstrated, and Figgy tentatively imitated the motions, the cat's deep purr of appreciation bringing a smile to his solemn face.

Whent led the way into the strange abode. The inside was a sharp contrast to the exuberant exterior. A single, large, dirt-floored room that was bare of anything other than an iron cauldron bubbling merrily over the fire in the hearth.

Figgy looked around in amazement. Even his poor family had a table and chairs, straw mattresses for sleeping, rude plates and implements for eating.

Whent let out a throaty, crusty laugh. "I spend most of my time outdoors where I never feel crowded and do not own a thing I see, and so I have made my home the same. As wide open a space as you can get, but then I am not used to company. You will have to forgive my lack of amenities."

Crossing to the fireplace, Whent used a corner of their cloak to lift the hot cauldron out and place it on the floor, settling down beside it cross-legged. "We shall have to share the ladle."

Figgy sat and shyly pulled the cup his mother had given him from his bag. "I can use this."

"Prepared for any eventuality, I see!" Whent chortled, dipping the cup full of the rich-looking stew from the pot.

"My mother packed it for me. I have these too." Figgy produced the venison and bread and figs.

Whent's eyes sparkled as they picked up one of the hard fruits. "I've not seen these in years. Not since the other Fergus. They are quite the delicacy as I remember."

"Perhaps he wrote about you?" Figgy dragged the heavy book out and flipped through the pages until a name leapt out at him. He read aloud:

"Met an extraordinary new friend today name of Whent. I believe they are older and wiser than any I've ever known. They are the first I've met who share the gift. What a joy to speak to one who knows."

"How about that? Although I don't know that I would describe myself as extraordinary, but it was extraordinarily kind of him to say so. That is a treasure you have there, indeed."

"What was he like? I never knew him."

"A kind young man, but sad. He had seen hard things as you have. He wished to see justice done. Became obsessed with it."

"Is that a bad thing?" Figgy asked, thinking of his own thirst to rescue his mother and end his father's reign of terror.

"Obsessions of any kind can be destructive, even when their author has good intentions. There is a balance one must find if one does not wish to become what one despises."

"Is it... is it bad to kill if it saves others?"

Whent contemplated this question while Figgy sipped the broth of his cup of stew, fishing out large chunks of meaty root vegetables and mushrooms with his fingers.

"Killing always calls shadows down upon the killer. Shadows that cannot be cured or banished by any means I know of. They eat away at your mind. It is a heavy price to pay. Would not any other remedy be better?"

"But if there were none," Figgy persisted. "If it was a choice between someone you cared about and a... a monster..."

"A monster? In whose eyes?"

"Everyone's."

"Not in its own, I would imagine. An unsettled mind, one overcome by shadows. Perhaps we should pity it."

Figgy's entire being revolted at the idea. Pity his father? He remembered the screams, the blood, the butchering, then turgid meat eaten for days with desperate, reluctant hunger.

Whent reached out and touched a point above Figgy's shoulder. "I see you do not agree. There is the faintest shadow here I had not noticed in your beautiful blue. A small grey speck. Be careful, lad. You are inviting shadows. That never ends well. It did not for your uncle."

Sighing, Whent lay their hand on the book. "Read this. See how his thoughts darken. When he left here, the cloud around him was so black, I could barely see his figure as he walked away. It was a failure for me that I could not prevent it, but all must follow their own path. Bide here with me awhile. Rest and spare time for careful thought. Some decisions cannot be unmade."

Figgy nodded. Saw the wisdom in waiting. The venison at home would last a while through the careful rationing Mother employed with all but his father, who ate his fill. There was time before next harvest day.

His own stomach comfortably full of vegetable stew, Figgy retreated outside to a tree with gnarled roots that served as an impromptu chair. Gavin followed and settled down beside him, curled in an orange ball made blinding bright by a sunspot illuminating him.

Figgy opened the book and read here and there. Whent was right. He could see the pages darkening to a dirty grey as the agony of his uncle's words invited shadows to linger:

"I've run out of ink, so I fill my pen with mud. The letters that emerge take on a different feeling, filthy with despair and the rotten stink of decay. My story takes a darker turn. I try blood instead, and now the words scream across the page and my marrow sings to me. Soft, tinny sounds only I can hear. Ditties of despair and melodies of madness. The ragged rhythm at the hidden core of me grows louder. If a stranger were to see the look in my eyes, they would run away. Cross themselves. Evil has passed me by, they'd think, by turns horrified and relieved at their narrow escape..."

Figgy shuddered as he ran his finger over the red ink, deepened into a rusty brown by time. How desperate must a writer be to tell his story to resort to such a trick? There were blank pages toward the back. Maybe he should fill them as his mother wished, but he was far too used to hoarding his own thoughts close and quiet. The idea of spilling them out onto the page where any might see disturbed him.

He turned to his uncle's final entry which looked bereft and lonely on an otherwise empty page:

"I am finished."

Figgy pondered. Finished with what? His journal? Or... Figgy didn't like to think about the or.

Whent prepared them a supper of thick hearth cakes by turning over the cauldron and using its broad bottom as a griddle. Figgy discovered his host was not as bare of resources as it had first seemed. The cloak they never took off had a multitude of pockets from which a useful variety of objects could be fetched. A folding knife for chopping, the end of a candle for lighting the way to bed, which would be nothing more than whatever piece of the dirt floor they claimed as their own for the night.

They even produced a pair of spectacles, something Figgy had never seen, and showed how the glass magnified the writing in the book. Whent tsked and sighed as they read out a passage:

"Built a cauldron of river mud and hawthorn twigs today. Filled it with the high clear cries of a hawk on the hunt, the rustle and bustle of a mouse hiding beneath fallen leaves, the low mourning of wind thru trees bared to winter's wrath. A potent brew that will suffice for my mission.

I smear thick paint across my face like a mask. Violet and goldenrod, periwinkle and rose. The colors and pattern call out to the old, old gods. The gods of thorn and hedge and musky earth. They come as summoned. I will be avenged tonight..."

"Such darkness. Such sadness there is here. What do you make of it, young sir?"

"Is it true what he writes? Is there a ritual for calling on the gods? My mother often spoke of a goddess who has dominion over the beasts and the trees of the forest. Would she help me?"

"There are such beings in the world, but they are capricious and even savage. They are as likely to destroy you as assist you depending on their mood."

"Wouldn't it be worth the risk to save someone you love?"

Whent bent forward and lay a skeletal hand on Figgy's shoulder.

"The grey is spreading in your blue. A shadow upon your soul. How would this someone you love feel about that?"

Figgy couldn't say the words aloud, but he knew. Mother wouldn't want him to suffer for her sake. She'd sent him away to save him, not so that he could return with help. Had even pleaded for him not to. But he couldn't get the images out of his mind of what they'd endured and endured still. Father loomed over all, towering and formidable, savage and relentless. It seemed impossible any but a god could topple him.

Retreating outside to catch the last light of the day and escape from Whent's too-knowing gaze, Figgy read on in his uncle's journal:

"The deed is done. What strange meat is this before me? I pluck the tendons like strings on a harp. A baritone thrum not audible to most, but then I am not most, am I? A meaty melody such as this is much to my taste, but it is not the only thing here to my taste today. A symphony of suffering. Though I must admit, I thought revenge would have a sweeter flavor..."

The words brought bile up into Figgy's throat. What vengeance had his uncle wrought in such a gruesome manner and on who? Must one become a monster to defeat a monster? Gavin padded over softly, batted his head against the book as though to say it was high past time to close it and go to bed. Figgy ran his hand over the cat's soft fur. The light was fading.

Less than a full day since he'd left his mother. Already she seemed as distant as the stars coming out to play above. He went inside Whent's house, curled up by the weakening embers of the fire, wondering what consequences, if any, his father had laid upon Mother when he was discovered missing. His eyes heavy, he whispered to himself there was nothing to be done, at least until morning, and slept.

Daybreak came. After a breakfast of thick porridge sweetened with honey, Figgy returned to his perch outside to study his uncle's book:

"My thoughts bedevil me. I bury them deep in the ground beneath layers of clay and earth, gravel and rocks. Set a stone guardian, gargoyle-like, atop it all. But when I return home, they are waiting for me, muddied and bedraggled, but grinning. Always grinning. Then the floor speaks to me in creaks and groans: 'Boy, you'll never amount to

anything.' But I just smile and don't answer back like Da taught me. He's gone, only his bones left beneath the floorboards. They can't hurt me anymore. And yet..."

Figgy shivered, the words hitting too close. He'd never asked his mother about her parents, and she never spoke of them. Had she left behind one tyrant for another when she married? He could imagine her being grateful for the opportunity to escape, not realizing her danger. Father could be charming when he cared enough to be. He'd lured in more than one traveler passing through that way. Figgy had felt sorry for them, but it meant that much longer until the next harvest day.

Times were hard. Of that, there was no doubt. Maybe his father only had the courage to do what others didn't. To take care of his family the best way he knew how. They might all have starved otherwise. Thoughts tangled up in Figgy's head of wrong and right, evil and good, and where one left off and another began. It made his brain feel buzzy and light, like the bee Gavin was chasing around the garden.

He shut his eyes against the dizziness, felt the morning sun against his face, the light red and blinding even behind closed lids. He had escaped but felt far from free. How could he ever be free knowing that the others, that his mother were not?

Whent emerged from the cottage. They seemed different today. Taller, wider, pulsating with an energy Figgy could see as flashes around the black cloak like lightning illuminating the sky at night. They scowled in his direction, no longer the genial, sympathetic host. They were dark and wyrd and ancient, Figgy thought, and a chill arose within him.

"Your aura is grey, boy. You've chased the blue away despite my warnings. None of you ever listen. I don't know why I bother. You'll never rest until you've exacted revenge. Don't argue. I can see your thoughts. You would sacrifice your own soul for others. I suppose you think that's noble. Evil begets evil begets evil begets evil. None are ever willing to put an end to the cycle."

Figgy wanted to deny it but knew Whent was right. He had to go back, do something, even if it meant subverting his own nature. But how was he to fight his father? He was only a small boy. It would be years, if ever, before he was strong enough to have a chance. By then, how many of his siblings would be dead? Would Mother be?

Whent frowned. "I might as well help you and be rid of you. You are all nuisances when it comes right down to it. Gavin has more sense in his shortest whisker than all of you lot put together. Here, take this."

Figgy held out his hand to receive Whent's gift. It was a fig like the one from the tree.

"When you are near to your enemy, eat this down as fast as you can and do what you must. Now, begone. Your doom awaits." Whent threw Figgy's bag to him and laughed, a high, strangled sound that caused every hair on Figgy's body to stand on end.

Figgy gathered his pack, thrusting the book and fig inside and backing away slowly toward home, more frightened than he'd ever been in his life. Whent stared after him, arms outstretched, cloak and hair writhing in an invisible maelstrom. There was contempt written across their face tempered by the barest hint of pity.

Overcome, Figgy turned and fled, running and running until his lungs ached. Was nowhere safe? Was no one kind? He'd thought he had found a friend, a haven. Nothing in this life was ever what it seemed. In his despair, he concentrated his thoughts on Mother. Tried to recall every feature of her face, memory dimmed even in this short time away. It couldn't be wrong to save her, could it? She had given him life. Didn't he owe her his in return?

He stumbled to a stop, panting. Tried to take his bearings, gauge his direction by the sun. He had headed away east, west should take him home. He wandered half the day, grew hungry. Looked in his pack to find three figs, two left over from home and the one Whent had given him, but which was which? Afraid to take a chance, he drank as much water as he could from a stream to dampen his stomach pangs.

It was near nightfall when he smelt smoke, heard voices. It was Father. He was hollering at someone. Figgy flinched as he heard the crack of leather against skin, his father's preferred method of punishment. He'd recognize the sound anywhere, having been on the receiving end of it more than any of the others.

He crept close. It was Mother, facing away, hands tied around one of the posts on the front porch. Her faded dress was torn from where the belt had slashed through the fabric. His brothers and sisters were gathered in the yard. The younger ones cried and wailed, but the oldest stood by impassively, some even with evidence of pleasure on their faces. As long as they weren't today's victim, what did they care?

Mother flinched as the belt landed again and again, but never cried out. Perhaps she had no voice left, thought Figgy, or just didn't want to give Father the satisfaction.

Blood was flowing, creeping down her back and spreading stains along the ruined dress, one of the only two she owned. Figgy bled with her, watching her beautiful aura flickering and fading away.

Father raised his arm. "Answer my question, woman! Where is he? Where is that idiot boy?"

Time to act. Figgy pulled out the three pieces of fruit. Ate the first, felt nothing. The second, same. It was only with the third that the change came. A seed had been planted deep within him. It sprouted and grew, tickling and entwining round his organs. Pushed at the boundaries of his skin until it was taut, then broke through. His body split and molted in an agony of pain. A crust formed, smooth, grey bark, branches twining. Figgy's black curls turned green and leafy.

He shot into the sky, a throbbing tower of rage and spite. His family stared up in wonder at this tree that had appeared from nowhere and... and... *walked.*

The children scattered, screaming as Figgy's roots uncoiled and thumped, shaking the ground as they pulled him close to the house. Mother twisted frantically, unable to see the cause of her reprieve. And Father? Father smirked and grabbed his axe from out the wood-splitting stump. Pawed at the ground with his outsized boots, like a bull announcing its intention to charge, and did.

The axe bit into one of Figgy's roots, chopping clean through it. Red sap flowed. The man retrieved his axe and got in another blow, a mighty one that sunk deep into the trunk before Figgy embraced his father for the first and only time. When he was done, there was a thing of gore and crush and shattered bone at the foot of him.

Mother had worked herself loose from her restraints. She stared in astonishment and horror. "Figgy?"

The tree recognized the name. Tried to reply, but all it could do was rustle its leaves and wave its branches.

She shrunk back from it and wailed. "What have you done? What have you done? What will become of us now? Who will take care of us?"

The tree trembled before the naked grief on his mother's face, then turned and stomped away. Found the clearing with the fig tree. Buried its roots deep into the earth. Pulled a book from out a knothole with a twiggy hand. Opened a page and absorbed the words before the gift of knowing left it:

"I started a chronicle written in tears and bitterness. Somewhere along the way, it was translated into a language that is foreign to me. Although I cannot understand the words, the rhythm of the sounds speaks of a fluttering of wings on a warm summer morning. I like it.

Ravens swoop and dive, weave silver strands of silk into a web around my soul. I watch idly as they capture it and bear it away with them into trembling skies. I could have stopped them if I had lifted one finger, but I don't really need it anymore…"

This seemed very wise and somehow important, thought the tree. Something to ponder on hard and long in the years to come.

THE WATCHER

Henry Featherstone had long outlived his usefulness to others and to himself. It was a waiting game now. Mind or body? Which would wind down completely first? He sat swathed in blankets on the stone patio, enjoying a rare moment of privacy, of being truly alone.

That was the worst of it at the nursing home. Always there was a member of staff hovering, some more solicitously than others. Or worse, one of the other residents crowding close, desperate for conversation, to prove they were still someone, that they mattered.

Old fools, Henry thought, *we are nothing but a burden on the state and our families. A nuisance that must be tended to until our expiration date.*

He escaped to this quiet place whenever he could. The other inmates eschewed it, a weak autumn sun insufficient to tempt them outdoors, but the staff had grown weary of arguing with Henry about the dangers of the frosty air. Knowing he would throw a temper tantrum if they resisted, they swaddled him up like a baby and pushed his wheelchair to the farthest edge of the paving stones so he could watch.

The Watcher. That's how he thought of himself. Keeping an eye on the neglected gardens and lawn and the great forest beyond. His eyesight was still keen, the only part of him that was. When he was in a more generous mood, he gave thanks for that small blessing among so many losses. His hearing was shot, and his tongue had lost the talent for forming words. He could see them in his mind's eye, but they were garbled in translation before his lips could make the sounds.

A few of the staff were skilled at guessing his meaning, but most offered patronizing "Is that right, Henry?" responses. The careless use of his given name was another indignity, a familiarity he would never have allowed before. Oh, how he had railed and fought against those small humiliations when Maddie first brought him here, but the days of open rebellion were long past.

Now there were only quiet moments of defiance. A refusal to eat until hunger pangs became too great. Turning his back on the jolly entertainments provided for residents. Ridiculous sing-alongs and endless craft projects to decorate their rooms. His was stark and bare. Maddie tried bringing in nice things at first, but after he had trashed them one too many times in anger, she stopped bothering.

Her visits were fewer and fewer as well. He wished she would give them up altogether. They brought no joy to either of them. Only served as painful reminders of the past and how much had been lost. But she'd always been a dutiful child. The responsible one. His other children relied on her to keep up appearances, using the excuse of distance to avoid their own part in the farce. He didn't blame them. He'd never made time for them, why should they sacrifice their time to him now?

So, watching was his one remaining pleasure, if you could term it pleasure. It felt more like an absence of self for a while. Blessed relief from the agony of his imprisonment in a mind and body no longer under his control. He sat, keeping watch for as long as he was allowed until an officious staff member came to wheel him back inside, tsking about the cold.

The grounds were much neglected. A few of the more mobile residents made feeble attempts to neaten the flower beds but staff had no time for such, and management wouldn't waste their pennies on hiring a gardening firm to do anything other than mow the lawns. The wildlife loved the unkempt landscape though, and Henry loved all the creatures he spotted, as much as he could be said to love anything.

A flinty sort, his acquaintances would describe him. Astute businessman, the Midas touch. All his wealth and success had not saved him from this fate of endless waiting. He felt keenly the absence of friends he failed to make along the way and the thought of the morbid delight of the enemies he cultivated who had lived to see him humbled. But when he kept watch, those stings faded away.

The fallow deer were his favorite. A small herd crossed the lawn most afternoons as the light grew dim. They nibbled nervously at the wild grasses that encroached upon the weedy garden plots and expansive lawn. He'd seen this year's crop of fawns growing and gaining independence. They shed their summer colors and morphed into the darker coat of winter.

Mostly females and young in the herd but there was one buck, a stag with antlers of startling size. They looked too heavy for his delicate head, but he bore them proudly as the sign of his dominance. It often stopped to stare at Henry, perhaps assessing whether the man was a threat, perhaps simply curious about the strange creature sitting turtle-like, straining his neck to see as far as he could.

There were other subjects of Henry's interest. Rabbit and fox, mole and hedgehog, and one very grumpy badger, rarely seen but always spoiling for a fight it would seem from its many wounds and scars. There were a multitude of insects he supposed, but he could not get near enough to the garden to appreciate more than the stray butterfly that fluttered past his grey self on its way to a more colorful landing spot.

Birds of every variety were always busy. He clutched the one useful gift Maddie had brought him, a pair of binoculars, in gnarled hands and attempted to follow their hectic flight patterns and chattering conversations.

This day, there was a long-eared owl taking refuge near the top of an oak tree at the edge of the forest. It was well-hidden in the shadows, but Henry caught sight of its yellow eyes from time to time when they peeked from out its sleepy daytime doze.

The forest was decked in fall finery. The fiery reds and glowing oranges filled Henry with a quiet satisfaction. It was a painting that changed from day to day, even hour to hour as the sunlight struck here and there. Clouds racing across the sky threw their shadowed patterns down below. It was the only show on earth that he had never tired of.

Henry was shaken from his reverie by the sudden flight of the owl in a hasty beating of long-feathered wings. *Startled by something, but what?* he wondered. He trained his binoculars on the forest, scanning for movement.

There. Something just… there. He pulled the glasses down. A dark shadow moving along the forest line. The fallow stag perhaps? It looked like antlers or—no, it was too human-like. Upright and stealthy. As if it didn't wish to be noticed, but it noticed Henry. Stopped still. Was it watching him?

Henry found a strange delight in the notion. Two creatures, two watchers, locked in an old-fashioned staring contest across the lawn. There was a definite thrill in being noticed. He had become all but invisible except to the staff who were forced to deal with him. Even the other residents had learned to ignore him, for he gave them no pleasure when they tried to engage.

He raised his binoculars again, but by the time he focused on the right spot, the shadow was gone. Disappointed and aggrieved not to get a closer look, he rested the glasses in his lap and speculated.

A hiker, most likely. Ramblers often cut along the edge of the forest on their way to visit the ruins of Duledin, an ancient castle that drew the curious with its tales of ghosts and demons that haunted the grounds. *So much poppycock*, Henry thought. *Gullible fools.* But it was rare to see a lone walker. They tended to travel at least in pairs.

He kept watch on the forest until an attendant came to wheel him in for lunch. She turned the chair too sharply and the binoculars went flying from his lap to the pavement.

"Idiot!"

"Very sorry, Mr. Featherstone. I didn't see them sitting there. I'm afraid the lens is broken but maybe they can be mended."

"Maddie buy more. You pay, idiot!" He would have liked to expand on his wrath, but his words were no longer up to the task of a true Featherstone tongue lashing.

The woman rolled her eyes behind his back. They were all used to Henry's "little ways" as his daughter called them when she was desperate to placate disgruntled staff. They knew Maddie was terrified her father would be kicked out of this home the way he was from his last one, but the owner was much too greedy to be so rash. He was milking Maddie for three times the rate any other resident's family paid and reminded staff often that they were to put up with any of Mr. Featherstone's eccentricities if they wanted to keep their jobs.

Maddie ran a new pair of field glasses out to her father that same afternoon. She was still terrified of him although he had no real power left to harm her, but the habits of a lifetime were difficult to overcome.

The weather had turned harsh after lunch, with a steady, cold rain. Henry sat and fumed by one of the large windows in the common room. There was a view to the woods here, but it was too far away to watch as closely as he preferred.

He dozed off, dreamt of a great stag, far larger than any he'd ever seen. It stared at him with eyes a malevolent ruddy color. There was a sneer to its mouth and its horns were enormous. They formed a complicated design that looked familiar to him, but the word for it was just out of reach of speaking, the same as his struggles when he was awake.

The stag lowered its head and paced toward him. Sharp and deadly, the antlers approached so, so languidly. There was plenty of time to back away, but Henry was stuck in his chair and no one answered his cries for help. He felt the point of one sharp horn penetrate the skin of his chest. Agonizingly slowly, he was pierced to the heart. He felt the thrum of its frantic beating, beating, and then... nothing.

"I am dead!" he screamed, waking himself up. The other residents in the room were alarmed, upset. Some of them started to cry or screamed out themselves. Staff wandered in to calm and chide, soothe them all down again like restless toddlers. Henry, they wheeled away to his room, making light of the nightmare he tried to describe.

His words would not come as he would have liked. "The stag... the stag... kill me," the best he could do.

The man who transferred him into bed patted his shoulder reassuringly. "The deer around here are no threat. They run a mile whenever they catch sight of us. Only a bad dream, Henry. Look at your book a bit until you're sleepy again."

The man handed him a well-thumbed wildlife guide. Henry's ability to read had not left him yet. He spent hours looking at the pictures and memorizing the habits of local animals. To be a good watcher, you must do your research after all. Many of them had rough cross marks next to the names, indicating an animal or bird he had seen in the garden or forest's edge.

With difficulty and a trembling hand, he turned the pages to the section on deer. There were several species native to the area, with the fallow deer being by far the most common. He turned the page and saw a picture of a red deer stag. A large beast, noble looking. It was similar to the creature in his dream. It comforted him to know his brain had pulled the image from somewhere. Being at heart an unimaginative man, he shrugged off the nightmare and slept well.

By the following morning, the rain had cleared, so he retook his watching post after breakfast. As the aide parked his wheelchair, Henry was amazed to see an enormous alder tree rising from the middle of the lawn where none had been before. It must have cost a fortune to plant. Why on earth would the management spend money to install a tree that large when they wouldn't even pay a gardener to tidy up the flower beds?

"Tree?" he asked, pointing.

"That's right, Henry. Very good. It's a tree," his aide said, setting the brakes on the wheelchair and patting him on the shoulder. "You enjoy the view out here. Nice sunshine this morning."

Henry fumed about being congratulated like a child who'd just learned a new word, unable to form the question he wanted to ask about why the tree had been planted. He'd spent his life barking orders and giving speeches and now he was unable to command the respect of the lowliest of the low in this prison.

He focused his ire on the tree. What a waste! And it blocked the best part of his view into the woods. He focused his binoculars on the brilliant golden leaves that rustled and shook in the breeze.

There was something odd there. A sinewy shadow coiled up in the innermost branches. A pair of eyes that flashed as the something moved. Too big and long for even the largest owl, what could it be? It looked almost serpent-like, but there were no native snakes that large. He supposed it could be some exotic pet that had escaped its captivity.

Henry watched it all morning in fascination. The thing seemed to be watching him back. It was exhilarating. Something new, something different to occupy his mind and help pass the endless hours. He almost regretted not accepting Maddie's offer to buy him a camera to photograph the wildlife he saw. He was no good with technology, and his arms were weak and trembled so much, it had seemed pointless, but what he wouldn't give to get a picture of whatever that thing was.

The same aide returned to bring him in for lunch, and Henry pointed again.

"In tree," he managed, hoping to bring the man's attention to the strange creature.

"That's right, Henry, a tree. We talked about it earlier, didn't we? You like that yellow color? There's Yorkshire pudding on the menu today. Your favorite, isn't it?"

The man prattled on as he pushed Henry back inside, but Henry did not try to protest further. On reflection, he enjoyed having a secret. It was something he had reveled in all his life. Hoarding up information and gossip that might be put to good use pressuring a business partner or embarrassing a rival. There weren't many opportunities for secrets now. He decided to hug this one to himself. Everyone else at the home had eyes. If they couldn't be bothered to use them, that wasn't his problem.

He was mildly disappointed to find the creature had gone from the tree after lunch, but the deer herd wandered by shortly after he had retaken his watchful position. They circled the alder, sniffing at it and starting, uneasy and nervous. Henry figured they were as puzzled as he was by the need to import a brand-new tree onto the lawn when there were plenty a few hundred feet away in the forest.

The stag appeared and snorted, rearing and pawing at the tree trunk. He shook his great antlers, backing away and then running full tilt into the alder with a mighty bang. Henry shivered, remembering the feel of the horns in his dream.

The buck staggered and dropped to one knee. Its antler had been damaged, a piece of the bone dangling down where it had splintered but not broken off. The other deer gathered around and sniffed the stag. Then, as if of one mind, the herd leapt away, scattering into the forest and disappearing beyond Henry's sight.

He trained his binoculars on the fallen buck. It seemed stunned and slumped over onto its side. A dark shadow fell over it. Henry looked up to see a lone grey cloud passing over the sun. When he looked back down, the stag was gone.

Strange. He thought he would have seen its movement as it ran off, if only from the corner of his eye. All that remained was a great gash in the trunk of the tree where the antlers had slashed. Dark sap flowed from the gaping wound and the leaves were still, so very still. As though they were holding their breath in pain.

Henry had much to think about that night. The most interesting day he'd had in all the many months he'd spent in this place. The new tree, the serpent creature, the stag. For the first time in as long as he could remember, he looked forward to the next day, hoping for further developments. The last thing he expected to find was another tree on the lawn.

This one was an oak. Enormous. It shook him. He'd certainly heard of large trees being transplanted but never a full-grown spreading oak. They must weigh thousands of pounds and were as common as dirt. Why on earth would anyone go to the trouble and expense of replanting such an ancient one even if it was possible?

After he got over his shock, he noticed other smaller trees had also been planted out in advance of the forest's edge. None as large as the alder or oak but not small saplings either. What was management playing at? His blood boiled when he thought of the exorbitant fees being paid to keep him here, and this was what they chose to spend money on?

It made no sense at all. If they were trying to reduce the size of the lawn, they could simply stop mowing. The weeds and woods would start to reclaim it at no expense. And how were they installing these giants without him hearing the noise or seeing any heavy-duty construction equipment? The lawn looked undisturbed. Surely there would be signs, ruts and disturbance in the grass?

It made him very uneasy. He'd prided himself all his life on his keen intelligence and sense of order. He was no fan of uncertainty or mysteries. How frustrating not to be able to ask simple questions of his caretakers. He was surprised they hadn't mentioned the trees. They usually gossiped and complained endlessly about everything that went on about the place, as though their patients were all deaf, but no one had mentioned this new landscaping gambit.

He focused the binoculars restlessly over the gardens and lawn searching for any other changes. Movement around a yew hedgerow caught his attention. Another shadow, slinking low. He could see the long grasses moving and parting as the thing traversed the weedy ground, giving tantalizing glimpses of the shape within. It was skirting the garden's edge and approaching the patio where Henry sat watching.

His heart began to beat faster with a fear such as he had never known in his breast. He was no coward, was contemptuous of men who quailed before danger or disaster, so this was a new emotion for him, and he did not like it one bit.

Pull yourself together, man. Get a grip, he thought. *It's simply a cat or some other low creature. What harm could it do to you?*

But he could not shake the feeling of terror as he followed the thing's relentless approach. A miasma of scent filled his nose. A stench of death and despair and other things too dark to name. He reached down for the wheels of his chair. Fought with the brakes and loosened them. He had never tried to move himself before, hands and arms too weakened to be effective, but a surge of adrenaline, a determination not to be caught here alone by whatever that was, motivated him.

Yanking at the wheels, he succeeded in moving back a few inches. This retreat seemed to intrigue the shape in the grass. It quickened its approach. Panicked, Henry twisted in an attempt to turn the wheelchair around, overbalanced, and was unceremoniously ejected onto the rough patio stones. The last thing he saw before darkness descended was a round face of indescribable malevolence, grinning at him.

He awoke back in his bed, automatically felt for the buzzer, and mashed it frantically.

A nurse appeared. "You gave us a scare, Henry. How are you feeling now?"

"Thing… thing…"

"Hm? Are you having any pain? You took quite a tumble, but the doctor came and checked you out and decided not to transport you to hospital. Nothing broken, but I bet you're sore and your head may be aching. Gave yourself a mild concussion. Lucky one of the other residents saw what happened from the window and we got you up off that cold pavement quickly, or things might have been worse. Whatever were you trying to do?"

Henry grasped at her hands. "Thing!"

"What thing?"

"Thing… grass…"

"Did you see something in the grass? A snake maybe? Probably harmless, but I know lots of people who are frightened to death of snakes."

"No! Idiot!" Henry clenched his hands in frustration.

"Now, Henry. Don't work yourself into a state. Get some rest."

She bustled out. Henry heard her talking to someone in the hallway. "Poor thing. Can't help but feel sorry for them when they're so helpless, can you? But he's his normal charming self, so I don't think there's any real harm done."

Low laughter followed by Maddie's entrance only enraged Henry further. How dare they talk about him like that? Like he was an infant. Someone to be pitied, joked about.

"How are you, Dad?"

Henry just glared at her, willing her to go away, but she stayed a dutiful half-hour, wheezing on about her children and their antics, as though he could possibly be interested, and scolding him for being so careless as to fall. He wondered if this was a subtle revenge of hers.

Talking and talking, knowing he no longer had the words or power to stop her. He hoped so. He admired all forms of pettiness and payback and felt something akin to paternal fondness at the notion she might have taken after him in some way after all.

He spent the next few days in bed, bruised and not a little shaken by the fall, but more so by its cause. The face rarely left his mind. A putrid green thing with pus-like eyes and a red hole of a mouth that smacked together in a toothless smile. He flipped through his collection of nature books, looking for anything that vaguely resembled the creature in the grass, knowing deep down he would never find it. It was too monstrous to be among nature's works of art.

By the third day, he was bored of being confined to his room and had raked the embers of his failing courage back to life. His aide got him dressed and wheeled him outdoors after breakfast only because he threw a fit when she tried to dissuade him. With many admonitions to be more careful, she parked him on the patio, locking his brakes pointedly with a firm hand.

Henry paid no attention to her words or actions. He was busy focusing on the view. There were at least twenty more trees since he was last here. The lawn was still visible among and between, but it was getting crowded out by these arboreal transplants.

"They're walking."

He jerked his head around to find he had company. An elegant older woman who held her head with its crown of coiled white hair proudly and stood tall in a stylish crimson wool coat with oversized horn buttons. Henry was used to assessing people's worth at a glance and this one reeked of money and privilege.

"Who?" he tried to ask, though it came out more like "Huh?" but she caught his meaning.

"The trees of the forest. They are on the move. I've been watching them come closer day by day. Something is calling to them or whispering marching orders in their ears. It's a marvelous thing to witness, isn't it, Henry?"

"Know... me?"

"Of course, Henry. Although we've never formally met. We all know the great Henry Featherstone. You're famous where I come from."

Henry preened a bit. His renown had not completely faded from the world. A twinge of his old power and pride roared through his fragile bones at the thought.

"You?" he spit out, curious to know who his admirer was.

"You may call me Edina, or at least think of me that way. I know the cat of aging has got your tongue in its grasp, but I am very intuitive at picking up meaning, the things left unsaid. I hope you will find me a restful companion."

"V- V…" Henry gasped in frustration.

"Visiting?" she guessed. "Yes, you could call me a visitor, I suppose. Or perhaps an inspector would be a better choice. A watcher, like yourself. Oh, yes, I know you like to watch the creatures of the woods and air and other things when you get the chance."

"Things."

"Yes, things. A word that can encompass so much and so little at the same time, can't it? The trees are on the move and so are things."

"What?"

"Ah, which what, Henry? What are the things? Or what is making the trees move? As a watcher, you should know the answers. But don't worry, if you don't know now, you will sooner or later. All questions get answered if you wait long enough. Or perhaps they just become irrelevant."

Normally, Henry would be enraged by this type of wordplay and foolery, but he enjoyed hearing the woman's voice. It had a soothing quality, like cold milk after the irritation of a heavily spiced curry. His cantankerous spirit felt gentled and smoothed out by her round tones.

That didn't mean he believed her. Trees don't walk. Life wasn't like one of those ridiculous fantasy films people wasted their time on. Not that he had a better explanation. He felt an unusual agitation as he wrestled with the problem, studying the new trees and the lawn through his binoculars.

If trees don't move, then someone moved them. But there were too many of them and they were too large to have been shifted without a major operation. Bulldozers and cranes, workers and disruption. Maybe they worked at night to avoid disturbing the residents? He couldn't hear as well as he used to. It was possible he missed the noise.

Even as he thought it, he knew it was absurd. Such a large operation would leave signs, would excite comment and speculation from the residents and staff. He had not heard one other person mention the encroaching forest. No one except Edina.

He lowered his glasses and glanced over. She was gone. He hadn't heard her leave and couldn't help feeling annoyed she hadn't bothered to say goodbye. She'd been the first worthwhile person he'd met since being warehoused here.

Noticing a shadow circling lazily on the paving stones where she had been standing, he looked up. High, high above, a black speck in the sky. Some type of bird, large enough to be a raptor or vulture certainly. He craned his neck and did his best to focus the glasses, but it was an awkward angle. All he caught before it disappeared were extended tail feathers that curled and twisted sinuously like a dragon's tail.

He snorted to himself at the fanciful notion. Walking trees. Dragons. What next? Elves and magicians? A sinister thought crept in between the folds of his scornful mind. He was losing it. First it had been his body that had grown weak and frail. Then his speech had abandoned him. Now he was seeing things, experiencing things that couldn't possibly be real.

Bitter tears flooded his eyes. Frustration and anger rather than melancholy. That he, the great Henry Featherstone, who had spread fear and envy wherever he roamed, should be reduced to this. He sat grinding his teeth until an aide came to wheel him in for lunch. While he choked down the vile food, he made a resolution to give up his favorite pastime. What good was watching when you could no longer trust the evidence of your own eyes?

He sulked in the common room after lunch, resisted efforts to join in the activities and shouted "No!" when someone offered to wheel him back outside into the afternoon sun. How grey his life had been before. Now it seemed unendurable. When a watcher gave up watching, what was he? Nothing.

His stubborn resolve lasted only two days before he gave in and painstakingly made his desire to be taken outside after lunch known. It was an overcast day. Even with an extra blanket, he felt an inner chill as soon as the aide settled him. The view didn't help.

The new forest had advanced halfway across the lawn and filled in with smaller trees and scrubby bushes and underbrush, but it was strangely lifeless. No birds called or flew, no small creatures scurried. All was still and quiet.

"It's preparing."

Henry's heart jumped. He peered shyly over like a nervous suitor to see Edina standing as she had before in the same crimson coat with its oversized buttons.

"Trees?"

"Yes, Henry. The trees. The forest. It is gathering its breath, its force."

"For?"

"That's the big question, isn't it? What does it want? What will it do? Quite exciting. We must watch and wait to find out. I think it will not be long. There is a certain something building in the atmosphere. Do you feel it?"

Henry closed his eyes and concentrated. There was a hum, a low, throbbing sound. It radiated against his face like sleet pellets hitting the ground. Sharp pinpricks of spite, questing, searching, exploring, seeking answers, to know him, to wrest from him his deepest thoughts.

He gasped, opening his eyes in dismay. No one knew him. Not like that. There were too many secrets he had buried deeper than deep. They were never meant to be seen by any but himself.

"No. No!"

"Why, Henry, you've gone a funny color. Shall I summon help? Perhaps it is all too much for you, though I had hoped you were made of sterner stuff. A man of your stature and accomplishments."

That stung. Henry prided himself on his strength. He'd never given in, never folded in the face of any challenge. If this woman could withstand the scrutiny of the forest, then he certainly could.

"Fine," he spit out.

"Good. I'm relieved to hear it. You and I can take such an inspection in stride, can't we? That makes us very special. Most people are so weak and easily cowed."

He *was* special. He'd always known that, even as a child, but it gratified him to have someone appreciate the fact without his having to go to any great trouble to impress his superiority upon them. He was filled with a warmth for this woman such as he had never known. Certainly not for his wife, a sniveling, whining ninny whose striking looks when she was young had been her only saving grace.

But this woman. Edina. She had style and substance, and most importantly, understood his worth even though he was no longer the eloquent Henry of old. What a fine partner she would have made. They might even have had children together that he could be proud of. Who wouldn't have sold the company he had built up from nothing.

That was the blow that stung the most. He'd known none of them shared his ruthless business sense or passion, but he'd never imagined they'd be so shortsighted as to give it away for half what it was worth and to his bitterest rival.

"They didn't appreciate what you'd done. All you'd accomplished."

Henry looked up, surprised to see Edina leaning over, peering into his face with wide brown eyes.

"Sharper than a serpent's tooth, eh, Henry? Ungrateful children. Shakespeare understood the human heart better than most, don't you think? Or no, I forgot. You hadn't much time for plays and books, but you can take my word for it. I wouldn't steer you wrong."

She smiled, her breath in his face filled with the scent of wood smoke and ash. He wanted to look away but dared not. It was she that turned away with a laugh.

"I'm in a rather silly mood today, I'm afraid. Something festive about. Making me giddy. Never mind. All you need to worry about now is keeping watch. You wouldn't want to miss it."

"What?"

"Your opportunity. It knocks but once is what they say, and I've found that to be very true. I'm sure you had many occasions in your life when you spotted a good thing and had to pounce on it to make sure it didn't get away, even if that meant shoving others aside. That's what I admire most about you, Henry. Strong men take action. Without remorse or hesitation. Your scope is more limited now, of course, but never be afraid to act."

"Yes."

Henry agreed with this sentiment wholeheartedly. What a woman. What he would give to have met her in his youth. He felt they might have conquered the whole world together. A rare sense of regret filled his soul. This was a loss that couldn't be mended. It was too late, too late.

"It's never too late, Henry."

Edina winked at him. At *him*, a mere husk of the man he once was. He bowed his head, blushing for the first and only time in his life. When he looked up, she was gone again.

An awful thought occurred to him. She was simply a figment of his imagination. Like the trees, the weird shadows. His brain cells were misfiring, pinging off fragments of memories like a pinball machine, creating crazy patterns that seemed real but were not. His body flushed hot with the fear of it.

His aide approached. Henry fought desperately to form the word, frantic to know.

"E-dee-nah."

"What's that, Henry?"

"E-dee-nah."

"I'm sorry, sweetie, are you asking about your dinner? That's where I'm taking you now. Roast chicken and potatoes. That's your favorite, isn't it?"

Henry fumed but gave up the attempt. He was surrounded by fools. Even if he could ask the question properly, they were unlikely to know who he was talking about.

If Edina was real, she wasn't a resident. Of that, he was sure. She retained the power of her body and her mind. It emanated from her in an unmistakable contrast to the capitulation of spirit, the resignation his fellow inmates radiated. And if she wasn't real, the staff would only look at him with that sickening pity, shaking their heads at this further proof of a shattered mind.

He filed her away in his memory. Another secret for his miles-high stash, but this one more treasured than most. Did it really matter if she was real or not? When everything you once possessed has been stripped away, you should accept such a gift as this without questioning too closely.

He awoke the next morning, impatient and eager to go outside, but a small tragedy had struck in the night. An early snowfall. Not enough to discourage him, but enough excuse for his keepers to refuse to let him out. They parked him in front of one of the windows where he peered eagerly, hoping for a glimpse of a crimson coat. If she came, perhaps he could knock on the window, attract her attention, invite her in.

Wouldn't the others be amazed that such a woman would come to visit him? He pictured the envy on the old men's faces, the catty speculation among the women. This fantasy amused him for a time, but a creeping gloom overcame him. He watched the trees. So calm again. If there was a breeze or wind, the snow covering their branches would be falling off or blowing away, but it was as stagnant and stiff as one of those landscape portraits decorators buy by the dozen to hang in office buildings.

He'd had the same one for years on the wall across from his desk. The ruins of a castle with one tower still standing set back amidst desolate hills. The bleakness of the image had pleased him. He'd often stared at it while on the phone, manipulating, lying, wheedling, threatening.

He suddenly remembered a fancy he'd gotten one day that there was a figure in the highest window of the tower, staring back at him. Hadn't thought about that in a long time, but it returned to him now as he looked out across the lawn buried in white. The giant oak he'd noticed on the second day of the trees' march had moved to the front of the line. Its branches arched out in impressive splendor and strength beneath the weight of the heavy snow.

Something flashed red. He leaned forward excitedly. Was it her? But no. It was a pair of eyes, wide set, glowering at him. Gaping. Henry was overcome with revulsion. A need to look away, to move away. He grunted, flailed, succeeded in attracting an attendant. Managed to make his wishes known. He was wheeled away to his room, relieved. He was safe now. Those eyes couldn't see him here.

He cowered there the rest of the day, the staff bringing his meals when he made a fuss about coming to the dining room. The next day, he stayed in bed, refusing to get up. Afraid to watch, of what he might see.

That night, he dreamt of her. Edina of the crimson coat and smiling eyes. She beckoned to him, striding away among the trees. Playing a slow game of hide and seek as he followed, young again and free. Edina was young too, her crown of white transformed into a deep, rich brown to match her eyes.

"Come, Henry, I've something to show you."

"Wait for me, my dear," he called, his voice sure, his words at the ready. "I will follow you anywhere."

She stopped in a clearing and knelt down, crimson coat against a red stain that was spreading across the pristine snow. The stag, the one from his dream, not from life. Its throat had been slit, head nearly separated from the body. Edina reached down and twisted the great antlers off with a grunt, setting the severed finery over her own smooth brow.

"What do you think?"

"Beautiful," breathed Henry, for indeed she was, standing bathed in starlight and reflected snow. Slow drops of red rolled down her radiant face from the borrowed crown. A queen, a monarch. All should bow before such power and bold delight, and so he did.

"You shouldn't grovel to me or anyone, Henry. It will only make us think the less of you. You are ruler here. Watch."

As he looked, the antlers snaked and entwined to form a figure. His own. He was filled with pride for a moment to see himself mirrored there so nobly. But the sculpture was a living thing that was not done twisting and growing. Now the figure took on an expression so warped by a malice unspeakable that he was loath to claim it as his.

"No!"

Edina laughed. "But it is your crown, my liege."

So saying, she lifted the antlers from her head and drove them point down onto his own with such force that they sliced him through to the soles of his feet and pinned him to the earth where he writhed in agony. In this dream state, death would not come to relieve him.

"What would you have, my king?"

"Release me."

"That is not my decision."

"Then whose? Whose?"

He was still shouting when he was shaken awake.

"Dad? Are you okay? You were having a bad dream."

Maddie hung over the bed as he panted, unable to set aside the terror of his nightmare. It had felt so real. More real than this moment, here in the bed, his daughter patting him gingerly on the shoulder, frightened even now of him.

He knocked her hand away impatiently. She had no power to help him, and Edina had failed him, betrayed him. He would have to save himself as usual. Bitterness and bile at the incompetence of people rose in his throat, choking him, making him cough and gasp for air. Maddie's attempts to help him by offering a glass of water only maddened him further.

"Out!" he shouted, striking her hand so hard the glass shattered, slicing her palm.

"You hateful, nasty old man!" she shrieked. "I hope you die miserable and alone. It's what you deserve."

Clutching a wad of hastily gathered tissues to her wound, she pushed past the aide who had entered the room wide-eyed and curious.

Henry watched his daughter go without regret. He hoped it was the last he saw of her. *Useless, useless fools all,* he thought, as the aide fussed over the broken glass and wet covers, but he screwed down his fury and bade himself wait in patience. He had no choice but to depend on others if he wanted to watch again.

The day passed with a steady rain that relentlessly washed away the thin coating of snow. By the next day, Henry was seated again on the patio. He was focused on the oak tree. It had approached so close, he could reach out and touch the tip of one of its spreading branches. It sent a spark through his hand, like static electricity.

He bent sideways awkwardly to peer under the canopy at the wide tree trunk. There were two large knots in the wood there, souvenirs of branches lost in some earlier season. The marks twirled and swirled, side by side, like two great eyes that stared back at him.

"Who is the watcher and who is being watched?"

Edina was back. His disappointment at her dream-self vanished in an instant. She was dressed differently today. A floor-length black woolen dress, long-sleeved, high-necked. It brushed the ground with a modest train as she approached him, the swish-swish of the thick fabric against the stones pleasant to hear.

"Had a nasty dream? A common complaint but no less disturbing when they are one's own."

He smiled up at her as she came to stand by his side.

"But you didn't answer my question, Henry. Who is the watcher and who is being watched?"

"I... I... watch."

"You do indeed. You have been a watcher your whole life, haven't you? Would you like to see this old beauty more closely?"

He thought at first she was referring to herself, but then she swept one hand toward the oak. He was hypnotized by its knots, its eyes. They seemed alive. He was overcome with a desire to touch them, explore their depths.

"Yes."

"Your wish is my command, my liege."

She lifted him from his chair as though he weighed nothing and carried him under the massive canopy. He looked up through the tangle of branches to the cloudless blue of sky. It made him dizzy.

Edina set him on his feet at the base of the tree. He teetered, almost fell, reached out and grabbed the pitted knots. Warmth flowed through him, strength.

"Pull," she suggested.

He pulled. A hidden door opened in the trunk, accompanied by a sulfurous smell underlined with the musk of excitement, the unknown.

His words found tongue.

"What is it?"

"An opportunity, of course."

"Where does it lead?"

"To the repose you merit from the life you have lived. You will be revered there. A paragon of all they honor and value."

Henry preened. Finally, a place where his worth would be appreciated. He'd always known he was special.

"Go," Edina advised, kissing him lightly on the forehead, a searing heat that burned his skin while it lit his soul on fire. "I will follow."

"You will?"

"Of course. I live there. I was only visiting here. An inspection of sorts. We have to make sure only the right kind are invited in, you know."

Henry smiled in smug delight and stepped through the door. A grinning shadow slipped in behind him and slammed it shut.

TWO OF THE staff found Henry's lifeless body sprawled in the middle of the treeless lawn. No sign of how he got there. They looked around furtively. No one had seen yet. They carried him back to his wheelchair on the terrace. Arranged the body carefully. Better this way. Fewer questions.

The only thing that would be hard to explain away was the look of complete terror frozen onto his face, but it wasn't like his family would raise a fuss. The passing of Henry Featherstone would be a relief to all who knew him. The only kindness he ever performed in his long and spiteful life.

WRITTEN IN THE ASHES

A figure sorts through the ashes with one long bony finger. There is a tale to be read here for those with the gift of seeing. A high, far-off place. The bitter taste and sting of smoke. A frightened face with haunted eyes. It is my own story, the figure thinks. A story written in death.

YOU GAZE at the heavy iron key in the palm of your hand with a thrill of excitement. It fits the lock of your new home, a small stone cottage, one of a row of six along a narrow lane that leads into the nearby village center if you follow it long enough. The cottages all have postage stamp-sized gardens in the front but lovely views out the back of open fields that border an old-growth forest preserved by a local trust from development. You have plans to take long walks through those trees every day, reclaim your peace in the quiet busyness of nature.

The old-fashioned key turns smoothly in the lock, and you step inside. Furniture was delivered and placed the day before. Only a few more belongings to bring in from the car and loads of unpacking to do, but there's no rush. You've all the time in the world.

The cottage is modest. A large open room on the main floor with modern kitchen fittings tucked into one corner. A small oak table with two chairs squeeze into the space to make an informal dining area. An overstuffed and over-flowered sofa and comfortable armchair with ottoman fit perfectly across from the large fireplace. Up a cramped stone staircase is a bedroom with another fireplace and a bathroom that retains the retro charm of its last renovation sometime mid-previous century.

There's a surprisingly large closet in the bedroom. You notice a small door at the back of it that's only half the height of a normal one. Such an interesting feature of this charming old property. The wood is carved with geometric patterns and warm to the touch. Faded red and blue paint flakes off as you run your fingers over it. You'd have to crawl through the tiny opening on hands and knees, but first, you'll need to figure out how to open it. It's either jammed or locked, and the estate agent hasn't left any other keys but the iron one for the front door. You send off a letter of inquiry to the agent. Perhaps they'll know more about it.

In the meantime, you enjoy your new surroundings. The forest proves as delightful as you'd hoped. A cool, private place where you rarely see anyone else, though the paths that crisscross the mossy floor speak of other explorers. You're careful not to stray too far at first but grow bolder as you become familiar with the local landmarks. A bent tree that seems to be bowing in greeting; an outcropping of granite that looks like the head of a troll; an old, abandoned hut, roof fallen in and overgrown with green vines. You peer into the ruin once, but a peculiar smell puts you off from further exploration.

The sights and sounds among the towering trees, the low ferns, mushrooms, and wildflowers soothe your soul. You catch sight of birds without number, of rabbits and squirrels, stoats and chipmunks, and one memorable day, a grumpy badger that hisses at you and waddles away into the underbrush. There's a burbling stream where you spend hours watching frogs and silvery fish, listen to the soothing sound of running water. A place of peace and renewal.

Then a note arrives from the estate agent: *Ask Mrs. Jensen at number 5 about the key to the door in the closet.*

Number 5. The cottage across the way. You hadn't realized anyone was living there. Seen no signs of life since you've moved in. Curiosity piqued, you walk over and knock. No answer at first, but then the doorknob starts to turn ever so slowly. A wary face looks out, much lined and worn with age.

"Mrs. Jensen?" you ask.

"Yes."

"I'm your neighbor at number 6. Forgive me for bothering you, but my estate agent said I should talk to you about a key to a door in the closet of my bedroom. Does that make any sense to you?"

A frown followed by a begrudging "You'd best come in then, I suppose."

You step through the door to see a space very much like your own, except the kitchen area is far from updated, with a stove that looks like a holdover from the 1800s. The lounge area is furnished with a faded plaid sofa set that has seen better days.

Your eye is drawn to the fireplace hearth where a magnificent golden cat is curled into a basket. The sound of mewling precedes four small kittens who tumble around and out of the bed, scrambling around the hearth after their tails and each other.

"May I hold one?" you ask.

The woman nods. "They need to be handled so they aren't afraid of people."

The mother cat looks on with benign pride as you cuddle one of her offspring. The kitten thrums with a purr that seems far too large and loud for her tiny body. You cradle her close to your chest, smiling at the enthusiastic sound of contentment, relishing the soft fur and the feel of the rapid heartbeat against the palm of your hand.

"She's chosen you," Mrs. Jensen observes. "You may have to take her home."

The woman stares at you in a way that is as unnerving as her next words. "I have the curse of seeing into people's futures without being able to change the course of events. You have a true soul and have been lost once and will be again, I'm afraid. In the meantime, you might do worse than adopt a cat or even two."

You're unsure of how to react to such a strange pronouncement. Fortunately, the woman reminds you of your mission.

"You came over about the key. That's a good example of what I was saying. I can see this key will lead you into peril. I could just not hand it over. Pretend I had lost it or never received it, but I know it will do no good. You will open that door one way or another. Might as well give it to you."

She crosses over to a credenza standing against the wall and opens a small drawer. "Here it is. Right where I put it when it was given to me by Edith's daughter. Edith owned the house before the people you bought it from. Funny, they never asked about the door, but then I suppose it was not their fate to ask."

You decide to speak up for yourself. "Are you trying to upset me with all this talk about fate? You can't really believe if I open the door, I'll be doomed."

"I cannot see what precisely will happen, and it wouldn't matter if I could. You will open it. Edith did, though I warned her not to, and she vanished. Her daughter found that key with a note to give it to me for safekeeping until someone asked for it. No one ever has, until now. You will go through the door. What will happen then I cannot say, but that much I know."

Mrs. Jensen hands you the key. A shiver runs up your spine as you grasp the cold metal. You don't believe any of this nonsense, but it is eerie to think a previous owner of the cottage had simply disappeared without a trace.

"What if I promised never to go through the door," you suggest. "Would it ease your mind?"

"Don't make a promise you can't keep, but do have a think about the kittens. No matter what may befall us in life, it is never made worse by owning a cat."

You return to your cottage, shaken but determined not to let it ruin your enjoyment of your home. You're tempted to open the door at once, yet strangely repulsed at the idea at the same time. Instead, you thrust the key to the bottom of the junk drawer in the kitchen and attempt to forget about it.

But ignoring it is not so easy as that. Every time you go to pull out a sweater or root through your jumble of shoes, the small door is there, staring at you, mocking you. You go so far as to rearrange your clothes so you can't easily see it but still, you know it's there. Can feel the heat that radiates from it at the back of the stuffy closet.

Distraction arrives in the form of two tiny terrors. Sammy is a black kitten, laid back and independent, content to spend time alone sleeping in the sun or chasing bugs in the back garden. Franny, a grey tabby, sticks to you like glue, a needy little madam. It's equal parts sweet and annoying, but when the two fuzzballs curl up beside you on an extra pillow at night, it's comforting to hear their soft sighs and dreamy mews.

Comforting until the night they both start hissing and spitting, waking you up out of a sound sleep. You flip on the bedside light, adrenaline racing, wondering what has them so upset. Then you hear it. The sound of running feet overhead, gentle and fleet.

You comfort the kittens. "A squirrel or a rat. Nothing to be afraid of. They're up in the attic and likely to stay there. If not, I'll protect you, don't worry."

They cock their heads at you for all the world like they're trying to understand what you're saying. Provoked to giggles at their quizzical expressions, you settle back down to sleep.

The same routine repeats the next night and the next. The kittens wake you with hissing and spitting, the rollicking footsteps are heard, and sleep is hopeless. It's time to take action. You jump out of bed in your pajamas, run down to the kitchen and yank open the junk drawer, rooting around to find the key. With any luck, the small door provides access to the attic, and you can at least catch sight of whatever is plaguing your peace and quiet.

You push aside the clothes in the closet and kneel before the small opening. The key fits into the lock but is hard to turn. You struggle with it for a minute before finally hearing the sharp snick of success.

Now you hesitate. A superstitious thrill of uncanny anticipation runs down your spine. Mrs. Jensen's strange prognostication echoes in your mind. Is this a mistake? The return of the scrabbling footsteps overhead decides you. You push on the door, swinging it open to a rush of hot, unpleasantly musty air.

Just as you'd hoped, there's a small unfinished space with a rough ladder leading up to the attic. The mundanity of it makes you feel foolish for being afraid. You crawl forward through the short entrance but once inside are able to stand almost upright as you put one bare foot on the ladder. It looks ancient but sturdy enough. You climb up into a dark, cool space, then curse yourself for not thinking to bring a flashlight.

You resign yourself to climbing down again to fetch a light, but as soon as your foot hits the first rung of the ladder, it slips. The rest of you follows, landing heavily and hard enough to force the air from your lungs. You close your eyes, struggling to regain your lost breath. Long minutes pass before the shock of the fall begins to wear off.

When you open your eyes again, the view has changed. Instead of the narrow wooden ladder, you're staring at the underside of a thatched roof. You sit up gingerly and look around, amazed to find yourself in an unfamiliar, dimly lit room. Impossible. Your head throbs from pain and bewilderment. Maybe a concussion, you think, running your hands over your head to check for bruising or bumps.

A movement catches your eye. You're not alone. There's a dark figure stooping over a fireplace.

"Hello," you call, head spinning, but you're ignored.

You roll over onto your hands and knees and use the nearby wall to steady yourself as you climb to your feet. Give yourself a moment to regain your balance, then you walk over to the person. It's a woman, dressed in an old-fashioned black dress with white cuffs and collar. Iron-grey hair as stiff as wire is roughly contained in a loose bun that looks in danger of unravelling. The woman is bent over, stirring the ashes in the fireplace with a long, thin fingernail at the end of a long, thin finger.

She mutters to herself. "The future and the past, the past and the future. They are one and the same. I am here and there. And there is nothing, nothing to be done."

Creepy, but you need to get her attention. You reach out but your hand burns when it touches the scratchy black wool of the woman's sleeve. You back away, but it's too late. Your body feels like it's on fire. You try to scream but no sound comes. Overwhelmed by the pain, you feel yourself slam to the ground as you escape into the bliss of unconsciousness.

YOU AWAKE. See leafless trees swaying above your head, feel the earth at your spine. Breathe in the fresh air. It is tinged with the acrid taste of smoke. Horrified, you lift your hands, thankful to find them unburned.

It was all some kind of delusion, a hallucination, you think. *I must have a head injury. I need to call emergency services. Get checked out.*

You sit up and look around. There's a landmark that's familiar to you—the derelict hut in the forest. Except it isn't derelict now. The roof and the door have been replaced. You rise and approach the hut slowly, open the door and peer inside. It's furnished, roughly and sparsely with rustic wooden antiques, but clean and neat. Strange, you'd walked by here only yesterday. How had someone managed to tidy it all so quickly?

Never mind, you think. *At least I know where I am now.*

If you follow the path by the hut, you'll reach home and can call for help. You pass the troll rock and the bent tree, but there the path ends. Thick overgrowth and fallen trees block your way.

Feeling dizzy, you sit on a grey boulder, try to collect your thoughts. It is so very, very quiet. You can't even hear the nearly endless bird calls that would usually be evident. No wind stirs the air. The silence is unnatural and more disturbing than anything else that has yet happened. A cold sweat rises on your skin, and you feel clammy and ill as time comes to a standstill.

A sudden rustle of leaves behind you. Jumping up in surprise, you turn to find the grey-haired woman in the black old-fashioned dress staring at you.

"You must come with me," she says.

"Who are you?"

"No one you know, but I am the only one here to help you."

"I'm hurt, I think. My head. I've been trying to find my way home."

"It is too late for that. You'll have to come with me."

"What do you mean, too late? And why should I trust you?"

"There is no one else. I will take you where you must go. You have no choice."

"You sound like my crazy neighbor. There are always choices, and I'm sure I can find my own way home, thanks very much. The path I normally take is blocked, but I know of others."

"Do as you will. I shall be waiting for you by the hearth when you return," the woman replies, turning away and heading back down the path that leads to the hut in the woods.

How maddening, you think. *I wonder if she's friends with Mrs. Jensen. They seem to have destiny on the brain.*

You take a deep breath to try and clear your head. Gather your waning strength and walk down the path to another turning you are sure leads home. It's longer than the other route but will get you there. You concentrate on placing one foot carefully in front of the other, still shaky and unbalanced from the fall. Head round a bend to find the way blocked again.

It's okay, you reassure yourself. *There are other paths.*

Hours pass and you are still walking. Your bare feet are scratched and aching. Every direction only leads to disappointment. What's happened to all the timeworn paths? Now, there's only unruly wilderness everywhere. Frustrated, you find yourself back on the path to the hut in the forest again. It seems to be the only destination you can reach, and it's getting dark. At least there is shelter there where you can spend the night out of the elements and figure out what to do next.

You hesitate at the door to the hut, unwilling to give the woman within the satisfaction of being right. *Don't be childish*, you think and enter.

The woman is stooping where you first saw her, stirring the cold ashes on the hearth.

"You are back," she says, without looking up. "I've been waiting for you."

"Yes, you were right. I can't seem to find a path home."

"I will show you the path. In the morning."

"Why didn't you show it to me earlier if you know it?"

"You didn't want to come then, did you? Had to find out for yourself. It is as it was meant to be. I've no food to share. A warm bed will have to suffice."

Your stomach complains at the mention of food. You've been too distracted to think about it, but you realize you haven't had a thing to eat since the night before. Shaky and weak, you sink into a chair at a rough wooden table and watch the woman at the hearth.

"What are you doing?" you ask.

"Reading the ashes. For those with eyes to see, there is a story here. It is always the same, but I read it as often as I can, in case it should ever show me a different ending."

"An ending to what?"

"This story. It is a sad tale that cannot be changed, but it is hard to give up hope it could turn out better. But you must be very tired. Come." The woman turns from the fireplace and indicates a rude wooden cot with a grey blanket in one corner of the hut.

Overcome with fatigue, you collapse on to a mattress stuffed with straw that pokes you in the back and makes you itch. It would keep you awake if you weren't so exhausted. The last thing you see as you close your eyes is the woman stooping back over the ashes and stirring them with one long fingernail.

You wake in the morning with a clearer head but weak from hunger and dehydration. The woman is nowhere to be seen in the small space. You search, sure there must be some morsel to eat or drink somewhere. Otherwise, what did the woman live on?

A thorough hunt turns up nothing, so you step outside, delighted to find it's raining. Turning your face up to the skies, you wet parched tongue and lips. Swallow down as much of the blissfully cool water as you can. It takes the edge off hunger for the moment, but now you're soaked through and shivering in your thin pajamas.

The door to the hut opens, and the woman appears from inside. "You'd better come in. You'll catch your death."

You stare at her in shock. There's only one door to the place and nowhere to hide. How did the woman get back inside the hut without passing you?

I suppose I'll have to learn to believe six impossible things before breakfast, you think, feeling Alice's adventures have nothing on your own strange experience.

Inside, there's a roaring fire in the fireplace that was cold and empty of everything but ashes just a short time before. Yet another mystery to add to the list.

You crouch by the fire as steam rises from you, but before you have a chance to get thoroughly dry and warm or ask for a change of clothes, the woman grabs you by the arm. She is surprisingly strong.

"We must go."

"What's the rush?" you ask.

"The sooner we get it over with, the better. Since things cannot be changed, best to go ahead and get them out of the way."

"What about some dry clothes or at least some food? I don't know how much longer I can go without a decent meal."

"There will be remedy for all your wants when we get there."

"I'm for that. Let's go if you're so determined. I'll have to trust you since I'm stumped about how to get out of this damn forest."

"Do not curse the forest. It listens and has the power to make things worse for you."

Too discouraged to argue, you follow the woman out the door and down a path behind the hut that you hadn't noticed before. Kicking yourself for not finding it when searching for ways out of the forest, you dutifully trod along. Your bare feet are blistered and sore, and you're alarmed to see your toes are turning blue in the cold. You're not the praying kind, but you find yourself pleading for some relief, some release from this misery.

The path curves and climbs. Soon your legs are protesting from the effort. Your shaking hands and stomach pangs remind you with every step of your growing hunger. Your focus narrows down to the back of your solemn and silent guide. You memorize the lines of the black dress in front of you, the messy pile of stiff grey hair, the black leather shoes. You notice the stitching has worked loose on the right one, a long black thread snaking down the heel that bobs and dances with every step the woman takes. It is hypnotic. You drag your eyes away from it again and again, but they're always drawn back.

The rain stops but it is bone-chillingly cold, the bare forest trees shivering in a bitter wind. You don't have the energy to question why you must travel up and up when the cottages are down in the valley. You've learned the futility of asking questions and can't handle one more enigmatic answer from your maddening guide.

The slope gets steeper, and your feet struggle to find traction. At one point, you slip and slide into a shallow crevasse to the side of the path. Grunting and reaching out a hand, you expect the woman to take it and help pull you up. Instead, she searches for a fallen branch and holds that out to you. You grab it and manage to regain your footing.

You remember when you first awoke at the hut and touched the woman, the burning sensation in your hands and body. It occurs to you the woman doesn't want you to touch her or be touched by her. What does it all mean? Vague ideas of mysticism and magic float through your weary brain, but that's absurd. Isn't it?

This is all a dream, you think. *I'm lying at the bottom of the attic stairs, unconscious, roaming around in my own addled brain, putting together random thoughts and fears with the gloomy warnings of my neighbor.*

How long will it be before anyone misses you and finds you

injured? Mrs. Jensen had promised to visit the kittens, but you hadn't made any specific arrangements for a date and time. If she knocks on your door and gets no answer, will she even be concerned enough to investigate?

You wish you'd let someone know what you were doing, but who would have thought a quick trip up to the attic to roust a stray squirrel would be so dangerous? Oh, Mrs. Jensen did, didn't she? She'd tried to caution you about dire consequences if you went through the door. Having a possibly serious head injury was certainly feeling more and more dire.

Even while you amuse and horrify yourself equally with this line of thought, you can't help thinking the dream feels terribly real. The damp chill on your skin, the stabbing stomach pains, the burning blisters. You can't remember dreaming in such vivid sensory detail before but maybe that's a side effect of concussion. Can't head injuries trigger parts of the brain that aren't normally active? You've even heard of people suddenly being able to speak foreign languages they'd never heard in their lives.

Logic and order, logic and order. The refrain runs through your brain. There's always an explanation grounded in reality, but for now, all you can do is walk and walk and walk some more through this strange landscape, following a nameless woman to who knows where.

Home, you hope. *One way or another, I'm going home.*

You puff and sweat from exertion, irritated to see the woman is stepping lightly with no signs of effort or strain. The lack of food isn't helping. Your energy levels have dropped to near zero. This ordeal, real or imagined, has turned into sheer torture with no end in sight.

The trees thin out the higher you go, and the terrain becomes rocky and more and more unforgiving. Finally, when you think you must give up, or at least sit down and rest, you emerge onto a flat granite rock that feels like it's perched at the top of the world.

You stop to catch your breath, marveling at the view. The forest stretches out in all directions below, hemmed in by a bank of fog that blocks sight of anything beyond the trees. You could cry in frustration. Down there somewhere, hidden away, is your cozy cottage. You should be there right now, playing with the kittens, eating a warm meal.

"Why have you brought me all the way up here? We're farther away now than ever from my place."

The woman turns to look at you. "It is the only route home."

"You mean we have to climb back down again now? My cottage is over there somewhere." You gesture to what you think is west, although the sun is hidden by thick clouds and gives no clues.

"First, we must build a fire. There is a dreadful chill in the air."

"Wouldn't it be better to keep moving? It'll get warmer when we head back down."

"I am weary and must rest," says the woman. "Let us gather some firewood."

She turns away before you can argue further and begins collecting stray branches and sticks. It's far above the tree line here, but there seems to be ample wood. You add this to the long list of things that make no sense in this dream. It's comforting really. Dreams never make logical sense so the greater the number of strange things that happen, the more it confirms your belief none of it is real.

Why you are compelled to play along with the woman if none of it's really happening, you can't say. It feels as though this was something that has happened before and must happen again.

A kind of fate, you suppose. *All this talk of destiny and having no choice has permeated my brain and this is the demented stew of a nightmare it has come up with.*

It isn't long before you and the woman collect a towering pile of wood, far more than is necessary for a simple fire, but at this point, you're too tired to care. You crouch on a stone outcropping while the woman fusses with flint and dried grass trying to spark a blaze.

"Too bad you don't have a lighter." Your observation is ignored. You rest your head on your arms, indifferent to the woman's attempts. A crackling noise and the scent of burning confirm success. You must admit the fire feels good as it catches hold. It burns with a white heat that quickly sets the enormous pile ablaze.

The woman stares at you with dead eyes. "It's ready now."

"Feels good. Very warm. Good job getting it going," you commend the woman, humoring her.

"It is time."

"Time for what?"

"To go home."

"We're leaving? You just got the fire started. That was a lot of work for nothing. If this wasn't a dream, I'd be pretty irritated about now," you add with a laugh.

"It is no dream. It is your fate. It was written in the ashes and cannot be changed."

"It's my fate to go home? That sounds fine to me."

"It's time to go home, but not for you."

The woman grabs your hands and pulls you to your feet. You feel the fire running through her body like it did back at the hut when you'd touched her before, but this time, no blessed darkness comes to ease the pain. Only tremendous pressure as you're pushed back toward the roaring fire.

She means to toss me in, is the only coherent thought in your brain.

The break in physical connection as the woman shoves you into the unbearable heat gives you a moment of clarity and freedom.

No free will? you think. *We'll see about that.*

You drop and roll off to the side, just missing the deadly flames. Fueled by pure adrenaline, you jump to your feet and take off running along the path that continues down the opposite side of the slope. You're weak from hunger and exhaustion, but fear is a great motivator. You make good time going downhill, so much so that you have to slow yourself so the momentum doesn't pitch you face forward down the path.

You hear no sign of pursuit but don't let up. This may be a dream but that burning felt all too real, and you've no desire to experience it again. You're not too worried about the woman catching up. She's lost the element of surprise that gave her the upper hand for a moment.

You feel triumphant when you reach the tree line again. It lasts but a moment. The path ends with no warning. You try to push your way through the undergrowth, but it is thick with long growing. Towering bushes with thorns pull at your pajamas and score your skin. Fat tree trunks, both standing and fallen, bar the way.

Tears fill your eyes. There's no way forward, only back. You'll have to climb to the top and go down the way you came. It means passing the woman and the fire again, but there is no choice.

It's only a dream, a figment of your injured brain, you tell yourself. *Nothing here is real.*

You climb slowly, all energy and urgency gone now. You can see the heavy black smoke from the inferno above. Ash drifts down and settles on you, turning your skin grey. The woman is waiting. She knew you'd come back this way. No need to pursue her prey.

"Let me pass," you snarl.

"It is your fate. You cannot avoid it," the woman says.

You pick up a stray branch that missed the fiery destiny of so many others. It feels sturdy in your hands. You swing it in front of you like a scythe. The woman watches but does not approach. You edge around the fire, the heat now excruciating as the flames have reached a crescendo.

You keep your back to it, eyes focused on the woman, convinced she may try to make another attempt at pushing you in. The branch is heavy, and each wild swing pulls you slightly off balance, but it's the loose rock beneath the next step that is your undoing. Your ankle twists and buckles and you fall back into the flames.

"I'm sorry," the woman says, as she watches a grotesque dance of agony. "It was your fate."

MARGARET JENSEN OPENS her door to find her old friend Edith standing there, a squirming kitten clutched in each hand.

"Edith, my dear, I've been expecting you."

"Hello, Maggie. So good to see you after so many years. I found these in the cottage. Guessed you might know something about them," she says, handing them over.

"Ah, yes. Thought they might provide some company and comfort until the door was opened."

Edith smooths down her old-fashioned black dress and tries to neaten her iron-grey hair. "Indeed. Poor soul. I do feel sorry for them. Maybe they won't have to wait as long as I did for the next one."

"We can hope so, but it is all up to fate of course."

You sort through the ashes with one finger. There is a tale to be read here for those with the gift of seeing. A high, far-off place. The bitter taste and sting of smoke. A frightened face with haunted eyes. It is your own story. A story written in death.

FLORA AND MILO

Her heart felt as bleak and chill as the unforgiving midwinter. Mother was gone and Father had withdrawn into another world, far away from his son and daughter, beyond their reach. Though only eleven, the responsibility of looking after eight-year-old Milo fell squarely on Flora's shoulders. There was Nanny Grimm and the nurserymaid, Sibyl, of course, but they were worse than useless now Mother was no longer there to keep them in line. How hopeless it all seemed, how utterly barren and loveless without their mother's gentle touch.

But then, one night, as she gazed out the nursery window, Flora spied eight rabbits waltzing by moonlight and knew that magic had returned to the land. They were dressed in a motley of clothing that looked collected from stray washing lines, but they twirled and simpered and pranced as though they were dressed in the finest tailoring.

"Milo! Milo, wake up!"

Her brother groaned and grunted, eyes glazed with sleep. "What is it, Flora?"

"There are rabbits dancing on the lawn. Come see!"

Grumbling, Milo crawled to his feet and came to stand beside her at the window. The glass was nearly covered with a kaleidoscopic frosting of ice, but he peered through a clear spot at where his sister was pointing.

"There's nothing there, silly."

"You're the one being silly," Flora replied crossly. "They are there, plain as day. I'm going out and ask if I may join them."

"Go out into the garden in the middle of the night? Father would be furious if he found out."

"Since he pays no more attention to us than the man in the moon, it seems very unlikely he will find out unless you tell him."

She retrieved her flannel dressing gown and slid her feet into her warmest slippers. She wouldn't stay long, but what fun it would be to join in the revelry for a few moments. Long had it been since they'd known any joy at all. Six months since Mother left in the night. She'd kissed them, tucked them in. Flora could still see her tousling Milo's unruly brown locks, trying to smooth them down as she always did. There'd been nothing different, nothing out of the ordinary. No warning sign it would be the last time she'd ever see her most beloved parent.

It wasn't Father's fault he was so wrapped up in his experiments that he'd little time for wife or children. His work was Very Important, or so they'd been told since they were old enough to mind. No, Father wouldn't notice her absence in the night. Might not even notice if she never came back at all, but Milo would.

She opened the nursery door just enough to squeeze out—it had a nasty squeak if you opened it too far—then padded down the two flights of stairs to the main hall. She pulled back the bolt along the bottom of the door without trouble but had to fetch a chair to reach the one at the top.

Her heart raced as she took a step outside. She was normally an obedient child and marveled more than a little at her own audacity. But something about the rabbits' ball called to her. It had been too long since she'd seen even a hint of magic.

How soft it all looked in the moonlight. Even the shadows had shadows. Flora padded forward quietly, afraid of disturbing the rabbits before she could speak to them. As she neared, she caught a glimpse of a band of mice, seated on toadstools and playing their whiskers with their tails like a miniature fiddle and bow.

But there was always someone watching, alert for trouble. They had learned to be wary of humans. An owl hooted a warning—*we are not alone*—and the animals scattered into the underbrush. All but one, a large silver hare, sitting haunch-legged on the pristine snow. It wrinkled its nose and waved to her, beckoning.

Perhaps the poor thing needed help? Maybe it was seeking warmth, a haven from the breath-stealing chill. Mother would have helped it, Flora was sure of that, but Mother was gone now.

"It's up to me," Flora whispered.

As she neared, the hare ran off into the forest under the towering pines that swayed in the whistling wind. The trees murmured secrets to each other and shed freshly fallen snow in merriment.

"Wait!" Flora called.

The hare turned, nodded, and stamped its foot impatiently. Flora followed, shivering in her robe, her long, brown curls like tangled ribbons tossed around by the teasing breeze. The path was strewn with the twisted misery of thorny vines that caught at her.

The hare glanced back from time to time, a twinkle in its dark eyes. Flora's slippers were quickly soaked through by the snow and her feet turned numb, but she soldiered on, determined not to cry, not to give up.

They came to a clearing. She glimpsed a heap of stars lying on the ground. Approached cautiously. It moved. Not a heap of stars after all. A black kitten, its sleek fur sparkling in the moonlight reflecting off fallen snow. What was it doing out here alone?

She picked it up and hugged it close. It was tiny and as cold as Flora was herself. She popped it into one of the oversized pockets in her dressing gown, intending to turn around and run home to the warmth of the house, but the hare squeaked at her, urging her farther into the forest.

Around another bend, she found a second kitten, a grey tabby shivering and mewling. She added it to the pocket, continuing to follow the hare, who it seemed was not done with her yet. A calico kitten and an orange tabby took up space in a second pocket. The kittens squirmed and thrummed in the comfort of their flannel haven.

And last, a white cat. Flora would have missed it against the whiteness of the snow but for the red, red blood that pooled around it, highlighted by a moonbeam that played over the animal in silent benediction. She was frightened and made more so by a crashing noise behind her.

Something was coming, thrashing and running. Flora hid behind a tree, unsure whether to run herself or stand her ground.

"Flora!" A familiar voice.

"Milo? Is that you? I'm over here!"

Her brother stumbled into view, tripping over his own feet to fall near the white cat.

"Ew, what's that?"

Flora stepped forward. "The mother of these, I think." She lifted hands laden with squirming kittens from her pockets to show him before thrusting them back into safety. "That hare led me to them. I think it wanted me to help."

"What hare?"

"That one!" But even as she pointed, the silver hare faded and dispersed like a puff of smoke from Father's pipe.

Milo snorted. "You've gone barmy."

"I have not. It's magic. You know, like Mother used to tell us about."

"Those were just stories she made up. Magic isn't real."

"How do you explain me finding these kittens then? And their mother. We should bury her. It isn't right to leave her like this."

"Too cold. The ground's all frozen."

Flora knelt and scooped snow over the white cat, covering it and the blood stains. Milo got into the spirit of the thing and found two sticks to lay on top of the mound in the form of a cross.

Flora's hands were red and shaking. They weren't dressed for such an extended expedition. She'd expected to go no farther than the lawn and then, only for a few minutes. "We'd best get these little ones and ourselves home, Milo. It's this way."

"No it isn't! I came that way." He pointed in the opposite direction from what her instincts told her was home.

"You're all turned around. Here are my footprints in the snow." She started to follow them, Milo close on her heels, but before long, the prints disappeared completely, the snow smooth and unblemished.

"Told you so. It's this way." Milo plowed back in the opposite direction only to find that his footprints also vanished. "What shall we do, Flora? I'm cold."

Flora looked at her brother, shivering and looking very small in the vastness of the forest around them. It was her fault they were out here. It was up to her to find a way back, but how?

She looked around helplessly and noticed a pair of eyes, shining red in the dim light. She stepped in front of her brother. "Who's there?"

A large red fox with black-stockinged legs and white bib stepped into view. "Friend or foe? That is the proper question, young one."

"And which are you?" she asked.

"Who are you talking to, Flora?" said Milo. "I'm frightened. That fox looks like it means to eat us."

The fox smiled, baring sharp teeth. "That one does not understand me, but you do, girl. Interesting."

Flora took a step back before the gleaming snap of the fox's jaw. "You didn't answer my question."

"Friend to some, foe to others."

"And what are you to us?"

"Depends. What are you doing out here in my domain? Good children would be at home, tucked up in bed. Are you bad children?"

"No! We're rescuing some kittens. Their mother was killed by… something…" Flora noticed the red stain around the fox's mouth.

The fox laughed, a high barking sound that echoed through the still night.

"What's going on? I'm scared!" Milo clung to Flora's arm, nearly wrenching it from her shoulder.

"Hush, Milo! It's okay. I can understand what the fox is saying."

Milo stared at her in wonder but didn't challenge her for a change. "Does it mean to hurt us?"

"I don't know, but there are two of us and we're bigger than it and… and…" Flora stooped and picked up a stout branch, lying fallen in the snow, flourishing it before her like a sword. "We're not afraid to fight!"

The fox cocked its head to one side. "But do you know the first Law of the Forest, child? The one all foxes learn when they are but kits suckling at their mother's teat?" The fox reared back, snarling. "It is kill or be killed!"

The fox lunged at them with jagged claws and gnashing jaw. Flora swung with all her might and got in a glancing blow with the branch, but it only enraged the animal further. It clamped down upon her arm with an iron bite, ripping through the flannel of her dressing gown to the flesh below.

Flora screamed in terror, but a trembling Milo sprang into action, picking up a rock and bashing at the animal's head until it let go of his sister and ran off, whining, into the night.

"You're bleeding. Here." Milo produced a slightly used handkerchief from the pocket of his robe. "Let me see."

Tongue stuck out in fierce concentration, he fashioned a makeshift bandage around the bite on Flora's arm. The flannel of her gown had stopped the fox's teeth from sinking in too far, and the pressure from the bandage helped staunch the blood.

Touched by her brother's bravery and tender care, Flora gave him a hug.

"What's that for?" he protested, pushing her away.

"You're a good brother, Milo," she replied, undaunted.

His cheeks turned red. "Don't be a silly. Let's go home. I'm cold and tired."

They took their best guess at the proper direction and set out again, but there was no clear path, no straight line between themselves and their warm, snug beds. Before long, twists and turns, detours around and over fallen trees had left them hopelessly confused about whether they were making progress or simply going around in circles.

Flora tried to keep their spirits up by singing a favorite song of their mother's, an old ballad about love won and lost and won again.

"I know that tune." A gruff voice startled them. Brother and sister clung close together.

A hulking mass loomed out of the shadows. Shaggy with hair like the bristles of a wire brush. Terrible tusks, yellowed and twisted. Flora had seen one once in a painting of relentless mounted hunters killing their prey with spears. A wild boar, rare and rarely seen these days. Her heart froze and stomach dropped. There would be no protecting Milo from such a huge beast. What had she done by leading them into the forest? How thoughtless she had been. How careless of her responsibilities.

The animal was making an eldritch sound, a deep thrum from its chest. Flora realized it was humming her song back to her. Perhaps it didn't mean to kill them after all?

She sang along, her faltering voice becoming surer, more confident as the strange duet continued. Milo looked on round-eyed in wonder.

As she warbled the final words of the ballad, the boar dipped its head. "Lovely," it said. "Just as I remember."

"Where did you hear it?" Flora asked.

"A woman with eyes as blue as a summer sky and black hair wound round her head like a crown."

"Mother..." whispered Flora.

"What about her?" Milo asked.

"He's met her. Heard her song." Tears sprang to Flora's eyes and Milo soon followed suit. It had been long since they had spoken of her. The lost one. No one at home ever mentioned her.

"She was kind to me," the boar continued. "Healed a nasty wound from a hunter's arrow. Soft hands and gentle voice. Sang me that song as she worked. An old spirit. A healer from a line of healers. Magic wielder."

Flora translated the beast's words for her brother.

"Magic?" said Milo. "What on earth does it mean?"

"I told you the stories Mother spoke were true. There is magic in the land, just as she used to say, and here in the wildwood most of all."

"Then why can't I see it? Why can't I understand the animals like you can?"

"Female of the line carries the magic, don't it?" said the boar. "Dangerous business. Those there are will be jealous of you. Seek to harm you. Like your mother."

"What do you mean? What do you know of what happened to her? Is she alive… or… or…" Flora couldn't bring herself to say the terrible word out loud, but she and Milo both thought it as they had a thousand times since the night she disappeared.

Is she dead? Is she dead? Is she dead? The children shivered uncontrollably as much from the idea of it as from the cold.

"Poor ones. Come close." The boar huddled into the embrace of an oak tree's massive roots, laying its great girth awkwardly on its side. Brother and sister approached. The body heat radiating from the animal was irresistible. They snuggled in, tentative at first, then with greater confidence.

How wonderful the warmth was! Milo and Flora realized all at once how very tired they were, weary beyond any memory they had of weariness. They wanted to question the boar further. Find out what it knew of Mother, but though they fought to remain alert and wary, their eyes closed against their wills. They fell asleep to the gentle hum of the boar, the maternal lullaby they knew so well. A voice so unlike their mother's yet soothing in its own rough way.

FLORA FOUGHT WITH STRANGE DREAMS. Phantasms of the fox's sharp teeth, the poor slain cat, the towering boar, and through it all, her father stalked. At least, she thought it was Father. He was familiar and yet not. A darkness hung over his form and tinted every word he spoke.

His muttered ramblings were unsettling. While she understood the words, together, they made no sense to Flora. The only one she remembered upon waking was a name—Caro—her mother's name, repeated over and over in anger and mourning, in love and hatred.

She awoke with a start, sweating at the nightmarish image of her father. He had always been a distant figure. Busy in his laboratory with no time for his children. She felt they hardly knew him at all, but suddenly, she was absolutely terrified of him. The idea of returning to the house, being under the same roof as that man seemed impossible. Why she should feel all of this from a dream, she couldn't say. She only knew deep in her heart that Father was a dangerous man.

"You are awake. Good. I am sore from being so still. Must move about. Stretch these old bones." The boar stood, delicately shedding the sleeping Milo and stepping around the tree roots. "You will be hungry. Follow me."

The faint light of dawn shone through the branches above. Flora shook her brother awake and prodded him forward, keeping the boar in sight. The animal snuffled and dug around the base of trees, unearthing mushrooms of every variety. "Not that one, this one," it warned, steering them clear of the poisonous kind.

The children gnawed at the fungi, uncaring of the bitter soil that clung to them, then chased their rude breakfast down with water from a fast-flowing stream that was only partially iced over. The chill of it took their breath away but quenched their thirst.

Four tiny voices raised in piteous cries made themselves known.

"The kittens!" cried Flora. "They must be starving, but what shall we feed them?"

A masked face loomed into view, startling the children and causing even the mighty boar to take a step back in surprise. It was a raccoon, hanging upside down from a low branch.

"A-mewling, a-mewling! Reminds me of me own little 'uns, it do. What you got there?"

Flora pulled one of the kittens from her pocket. "They're orphans and we've no mother's milk to give them."

The raccoon reached out a black-gloved paw, touching the shining fur of the squirming baby. "We've quite a brood ourselves, but a bit to spare, I reckon." It grabbed the kitten and bounded away.

"Come back," Flora cried, alarmed at this brazen theft. She ran after the bold bandit as Milo and the boar trailed behind.

The raccoon paused at a tall pine and scampered up the branches and trunk. Flora was a gifted tree climber of much practice, so it wasn't long before she was up herself and peering into a large hole in the tree. There she found another raccoon, nursing three almost-grown kits. Her mate popped the black kitten in beside them.

"What on earth have you found?" the mother cried.

"Orphans!" the raccoon cried triumphantly. "Hand over the rest. There's room here, just."

Flora pulled the other three kittens from her pockets and set them inside the hole.

"This is a fine how-do-you-do!" cried Mother Raccoon. "As if I ain't got enough to do with keeping our own mouths fed with this late litter."

"Only one little drink," Father Raccoon replied. "To tide 'em over like, until these kiddies get 'em somewhere safe."

She sighed but looked on with indulgence as the squirming kittens instinctively sought out a teat amongst the wriggling raccoon kits.

"I suppose I've enough to spare this once. And who's this?"

Flora bobbed her head. It was the closest she could get to a polite curtsy in the circumstances of balancing precariously on a tree branch while peering into a knothole. "My name is Flora, ma'am. My brother Milo is down below. We found these kittens but lost ourselves, I'm afraid."

Mother Raccoon clucked. "Lost in the wildwood? Not a place for those who do not understand its ways. You've magic about you though, girl, else you could not hear us. Most folk do not. Magic is power."

"It doesn't feel very powerful. I mean, it's nice to be able to speak to you, I suppose."

"I should think so! Don't scorn the words or friendship of creatures of the forest. We are wise and experienced and can prove useful allies."

Flora blushed. "Oh, yes! I didn't mean to offend. We have met some very helpful and one not so."

"And 'tis good to learn the difference atween 'em," noted Father Raccoon.

"Friend or foe. That's what a fox told us."

"Foxes can be sly ones, but any creature can be sly if they're true to their nature. Life in the forest ain't an easy one and may ask you to do things you'd never imagine for the sake of kin and kith. You'd do best to leave this place."

"All my brother and I want is to go home, but we're hopelessly lost."

"Nothing is ever hopeless," Mother Raccoon replied, "unless you quit trying. What you need is a guide what knows the forest's ways."

"Who shall it be?" mused her mate. "Hummingbirds travel far but are rather flighty. Snakes get around but are such slippery fellows. And now I come to think on it, many and many a creature are resting up for spring or have traveled away south."

"What about that bear down the way? They are a jolly one. Mayhaps they'd not mind an early wakeup call and jaunt about to stretch their limbs."

Flora did not think disturbing a hibernating bear sounded like a very wise thing to do, but before she could protest, Father Raccoon was scooting past her startled face out the knothole and scurrying down the trunk.

"Best take these 'uns with you. They've enough to tide them over for now." Flora stowed the kittens away in her pockets as the mother raccoon handed them to her one by one. "Good luck, m'dear. I hope you soon find yourself safe and snug in your own wee nest."

"Thank you, ma'am," Flora replied politely. She gingerly stepped back down the stairway of branches to the ground to find her brother waiting impatiently. The boar was nowhere to be seen. She supposed it felt it had done its duty and wandered off.

"Whatever were you doing up there?" Milo demanded.

"Getting some milk for the kittens. The raccoon has gone for help."

"Help? What kind of help?"

"A creature to guide us home. They said it was a—"

The crashing down of a small tree near enough for them to feel the breeze it stirred up on their cheeks interrupted Flora. Brother and sister leapt back as a large brown bear stumbled into view.

"Sorry! So sorry. Just waking up. Still a bit clumsy. Terribly sorry, little tree," the bear added, leaning over and laying a giant paw on the fallen sapling. "But this looks a nice place for a rest. Enjoy!"

The bear turned to the children, towering over them. "Hear you're in need of a guide. Been all over these woods. Where you headed?"

"That's very kind of you," said Flora. Milo cowered behind her, intimidated by what sounded to him like nothing more than wild roaring. "We live in a big house on the edge of the forest. It has a red roof and a hedge maze in the garden."

"Ah, the twisty hedges. Got lost there once. Might be there yet if a nightjar hadn't guided me out. Friendly bird. Now, let's see. This way, I think."

Flora didn't like the sound of that "I think" but having no better plan, decided she and Milo could do worse than follow the bear. At least it was friendly and could protect them from any other creatures they met that might be as dangerous as the fox.

"Come, Milo, it's leading us home."

Somehow, Milo doubted this very much indeed, but it was no stranger than anything else that had happened. Besides, what choice did they have? The filtered sunlight did little to dispel the cold that had taken up residence in their bones. He thought of the roaring nursery room fire, toasted scones, and hot cups of tea. What he wouldn't give to be there now.

The bear's route was nothing if not eccentric. It dodged beneath branches here, pushed aside a random boulder there, clambered over fallen trees and used its claws to hack through thick patches of undergrowth. It was far from a straight line, and as they grew weary with the seemingly never-ending trek, Milo and Flora exchanged more than one worried glance.

Their guide, however, kept up a cheerful monologue describing the myriad of bees it had met, leaves it had collected, trees it had accidentally knocked over. It seemed to think life a great adventure. Flora supposed if you were the largest creature in the forest, you would have very little to fear except men. Father was not a hunter and didn't allow hunting on his land, she reassured the bear when she could get a word in edgewise.

"Now that is a thing, isn't it? Men with their funny metal rods chasing harmless folk through the wildwood. Haven't they anything better to do with their time?"

"But bears hunt, don't they?" Milo asked, when Flora translated the bear's lament.

"Course," said their guide. "But only when hungry and only so much as a meal. Fishies are the best. Stick close to the river and you'll never go hungry."

"We've never been as far as the river," Flora said. "Our mother warned us it was too dangerous."

"Suppose it is for wee ones. It's nothing to a bear. But mothers are great ones for worrying. Mine was such a one."

"Is she… is she dead?"

"Dunno. Could be. Go off on our own, you see, when we are old enough. Don't you?"

"Most do," Flora conceded. "But even when we're grown, we visit our families and stay close." But as she said it, Flora knew it wouldn't be true, not for her and Milo. If Mother was still with them, she could draw them back to their home, but Father? She couldn't imagine he would care if they came to visit or not, and after her nightmare, she was doubly sure she wouldn't want to.

She'd never quizzed her father closely about Mother's departure. He was too austere, too remote for such impertinent questions. But this wasn't the first time she'd wondered what role he'd played. Her parents' relationship had seemed ordinary, if on the formal side. The usually gossipy servants had been no help at all. They seemed as surprised as anyone by Mother's disappearance. They'd heard no rumors or theories that might explain it, other than speculating she had run off with another man, but who that might be, no one could say.

Father had withdrawn further into his studies, the endless experiments he never talked about to anyone but his wife and, now that she was gone, to no one. He seemed more obsessed than ever with whatever he was doing and rarely left his lab, preferring to have meals left outside the door.

Flora wondered if anyone had noticed she and Milo were missing yet. Surely Nanny or Sibyl, even as lazy as they were, were up by now and would have found their empty beds. Would they alert Father? Or afraid of his wrath, would they launch their own search party behind his back?

This question was answered by a series of shouts up ahead of them. The children's names, being called by a variety of voices, young and old, male and female.

"Leave you here," said the bear. "Don't like a crowd."

"Yes," Flora agreed. "You'd best go. We should be fine now. Thank you so much!" She kissed the bear's bristly cheek and watched it lumber away.

After she was sure the bear was out of sight, she and Milo answered the calls. "Here! We're here!"

A harassed-looking Nanny Grimm, red in the face from unaccustomed exertion and the cold, was first to appear, followed by a motley crew of groundskeepers and house staff. Most were relieved to find the children, but Nanny pinched their arms and gave them a mighty scold as she led them back to the house.

"Please God, we get back before your father realizes we're missing. Who do you suppose will get the raw end of a tongue lashing if he finds you've been out all night? And what is that unearthly noise?"

The kittens had woken and were mewling their displeasure with the scantiness of their breakfast.

"We rescued these kittens in the woods. Their mother is dead. We mean to bring them home with us," said Flora.

"Bring them into the house!" a scandalized Nanny replied. "Nonsense. Best drown them in the well and put them out of their misery."

Flora's body flushed with the horror of this image, but before she could retort, a boy she recognized as working in the stables stepped forward.

"Hand 'em here, Miss Flora. We've a cat in the stables with two wee 'uns. She's a grand big mouser. She'll take care of these for you."

Afraid of defying the formidable Nanny by insisting on keeping the kittens with her, Flora reluctantly handed them over to the boy. He pulled his cap from his head and stowed the squirming babies away inside.

"Ask for Ned if you wants to visit 'em, miss. I'll run ahead and get 'em warm."

The stableboy scooted away as the entire party emerged from the forest's edge. As relieved as she was to see the familiar red roof of home, Flora couldn't help being sorry their adventure was coming to an end. It had been frightening, true, but how magical to meet so many animals and speak to them. It made home life seem humdrum in comparison. Who knew when they'd ever get another opportunity to enter the wildwood. Nanny would probably keep her and Milo under lock and key from now on, rather than risk their father's displeasure.

And there he was now, striding across the lawn, dressed all in black as he had ever since Mother's departure. He looked like a quarrelsome raven as he stalked toward them. Flora was reminded of the darkness that had followed her father like a cloud in her nightmare. While she'd never felt close to him, this was the first time in her life she could remember feeling fear.

"What is the meaning of this? Why isn't anyone at their stations?"

Most of the servants scattered in a rush at his words. Nanny, to her credit, held her ground, but was quick to lay blame on the children for the disruption.

"These two have been wandering the forest all night if you can imagine. What their mother would think of such bad behavior, I hate to conjecture."

"It is certainly not your place to speculate on the thoughts of your betters," Father admonished. "What do I pay you a salary for if not to keep my children safe?"

"They are a willful pair, sir. I do my best."

"A pitiful boast indeed. And what have you to say for yourself, Flora? I thought you, at least, had some sense. What on earth possessed you to explore the woods in the middle of the night?"

"I am sorry, Father." Flora paused, suddenly unwilling to reveal the magical sight that had tempted her from the nursery.

Milo was neither so reticent nor so wise. "Flora saw rabbits dancing in the moonlight and ran after them and I went to make sure she was okay and we found four kittens and Flora talked to a fox, a boar, a pair of raccoons and then a bear guided us home!"

Nanny scoffed. "Your sister was talking to the animals, was she? What an imagination you have."

Flora felt her father's eyes upon her. When she braved a glance, she quelled before his speculative gaze.

"It sounds quite an adventure. I would like to hear more about it," he said. "Flora, come to me after you've eaten and dressed. I'll be in my laboratory."

Milo and Flora stared at him in wonder. Neither had ever been invited, permitted, or brave enough to enter their father's workspace. From their earliest memories, it was a forbidden place.

"Yes, Father," Flora mumbled dutifully as he strode off back to the house, but dismay filled her heart.

"What do you think it means?" whispered Milo. "Why does he want you?"

"I don't know," she answered, "but I do wish you hadn't told him anything."

"Why not? It's you that believes in magic. Besides, you get to see what he does. You must tell me everything when you get back."

Milo ran ahead to the house, eager to get warm, and ravenous, their meager mushroom breakfast a distant memory now. Flora trailed after more slowly, pulled along by an impatient Nanny. She and her brother had often wished to see the wing of the house where their father worked, but now that an invitation had been extended, she'd give much to have it snatched back again.

SHE DRAGGED her feet as long as she dared while changing into a warm woolen dress. The nursery maid, Sibyl, screamed in horror and fainted dead away at the sight of the blood on Flora's arm. This earned her nothing but a basin full of water in the face and a scolding from Nanny Grimm. Nanny cleaned and bandaged the fox's bite with little fuss and less curiosity about what had caused the wound. As far as she was concerned, everything that happened was a blooming nuisance especially designed to vex her.

Flora barely had time to swallow a few mouthfuls of hot oats before Nanny was escorting her across the great hall landing on the second floor to Father's wing of the house. It was just as well as she had no appetite, her stomach fluttering with anticipation of what he might want with her.

Nanny knocked twice hard on the outer door to the hall that was always kept locked. She tapped one foot impatiently until she heard the key turning, abandoning Flora to her fate without a backward glance.

"There you are. Do come in, Flora." Her father smiled, a rictus of a grin that may have been meant to reassure her but had the opposite effect. He took her hand, his own cold and dry to the touch, and led her to a large room at the end of the corridor.

She glanced around nervously at scientific equipment, glass and beakers, chemicals and liquids, machines that buzzed with electricity. There was a thick coat of dust on many surfaces, testament to her father's refusal to have any of the cleaning staff enter his domain, but his desk was immaculate, swept clear of any papers or documents except for a large, green leather-bound journal and an elegant ink pen.

"Sit, child," he said, indicating a blue velvet armchair before the desk and taking a seat in the tall, black leather swivel chair behind it. He opened the journal to a blank page, took up his pen, and stared at her with dark eyes. "Do tell me everything."

Flora hesitatingly spun out her tale. She meant to leave out the parts tinged with magic, but that left very little to talk about. Her father questioned her persistently and somehow, more and more of the truth poured out. It was the longest exchange they'd ever had. Flora felt herself sweating even though the room was unheated and chill.

Her father sat writing in the great book long after the inquisition was complete. The scratch of the nib against the paper played on her nerves. After a time, he seemed to forget she was there and began muttering to himself.

"Yes, exactly as before… must try again… adjust the frequencies this time… hope for a better result…"

Flora longed to melt away, return to the nursery, but every time she so much as shifted in her chair, his gimlet eye pierced her through like a pin stabbing a butterfly to a board and kept her in her place.

Finally, finally, he lay his pen aside and closed the journal. He stalked over to a dark corner and threw aside a velvet curtain. Behind it was a metal chair with straps at arm and feet. He flicked switches on a large machine which came to life with a roar.

"Come here, Flora," he called, the blinking lights from the equipment reflected in his eyes and making him look quite mad.

She did get up then but ran to the door, answering an impulse to escape, but he was there before her. "Don't be frightened. I know what I'm doing," he said, pulling her over to the chair and strapping her in. "The restraints are for your own safety. The treatment can be startling. I wouldn't want you to hurt yourself."

Flora both longed and loathed to ask what treatment he meant but couldn't force her chattering teeth and tongue to form the words. Fortunately, now that she was immobilized, her father seemed more than willing to share his thoughts.

"As I have long suspected, you have inherited certain traits from your mother's side of the family. Ungodly traits. They caused myself and your mother much misery, and it became my life's work to develop a treatment to cure her of them and perhaps help others so afflicted. Unfortunately, your mother had an unanticipated reaction, but I've adjusted my methods since then and have every confidence I have resolved any miscalculation on my part."

An overwhelming need to know what had become of Mother finally loosened Flora's tongue. "What… what happened to her? Is she… dead?"

"No. At least, she wasn't the last time I saw her, but she was changed. I cannot deny the result was undesirable, but science is often a matter of trial and error. She would be pleased to know that what I learned from that attempt will cure her daughter of the malady she suffered."

"But what is it? What's wrong with me?"

"Magic, some call it. Others name it witchcraft. Hereditary, and it is taking the same course with you that it did with her. Speaking to base animals."

"Is that so bad? They were very kind to us. Well, mostly," she amended. "Maybe it's a talent, like playing the piano?"

"A talent? If it is, it is one bestowed by the Devil and will make you an outcast among men. It was your mother's wish, and I know it would be her wish for you, to live a normal, womanly life and not be cursed to be different. And I have the means to grant that wish."

He fiddled with dials and buttons as the machine roared and hissed. Flora was confused. Was it really a curse to be able to commune with nature? It wasn't usual or common certainly, but she'd enjoyed talking to the animals of the forest.

"Perhaps if I keep it a secret?" Flora suggested. "No one need ever know and I promise not to go into the forest again."

Father glared at her with a wildness in his eye that terrified her. "The cat is well and truly out of the bag. You must know how servants gossip. I won't have any offspring of mine made an object of superstition and suspicion. This won't hurt much, and I am confident I will meet with greater success this time."

Flora didn't like the sound of that at all. Just what had happened to Mother? Panic gripped her. She pulled against the restraints, but they were strong and unyielding. She shuddered as a cold hat of sorts was placed on her head and strapped around her chin.

"You may black out for a time during the treatment, but that is to be expected. I know what I'm doing."

The last thing she remembered was her father's face, a feral look of concentration on it as he flicked a switch, sharp pain that reverberated through her skull, then blackness.

WHEN SHE AWOKE, Flora realized to her relief that she was free of the constraints of the chair, but the world looked very strange indeed. So big! And there was Father looming over her from high above with a look of fury and confusion on his face. His giant hand reached for her. She instinctively scurried away.

How awkward she felt, as though her own body was alien to her. Some result of the treatment, no doubt. Livid curses rained down on her from the man towering above. Forbidden words she'd never thought to hear her dignified and devout father utter.

Panicked, she ran farther and farther away as he chased her until finally, in desperation, she flattened herself, squeezing under the gap beneath the laboratory door and fleeing down the long corridor with a speed unlike any she'd ever known.

It was only when she was safely hidden behind a pair of heavy damask curtains that she paused to catch her breath and take stock of what had happened. She had slipped *under* the gap in the door. How was that possible? She looked down at her hands only to find them changed into paws which clutched nervously at a long fluffy brown tail, black-tipped. She ran her paws over her face, a pointy snout and alert ears that heard everything.

A white belly, brown back? A memory came to Flora of she and Milo laughing at the comical antics of a pair of stoats playing in the meadow beyond the gardens. Her mind resisted the idea, but the evidence was before her eyes. Was this a delusion brought on by her father's experiment? She remembered what he had said about Mother. She was alive but *changed*.

In shock, her small heart beating too fast to count, she huddled in her makeshift den, listening as her father strode around the corridor, opening doors and flinging furniture around in his desperation to find her. He wouldn't stop. She wasn't safe here. She waited until he entered a room at the far end and ran for the stairs. Up or down?

Instinct took her up to the nursery. The door was ajar. She ran in and smack into a pair of feet.

Milo shrieked, Flora squealed, and Nanny rushed in.

"What on earth? Vermin in the nursery!" With no further ado, Nanny flung open the nearest window, grabbed Flora by the tail and tossed her out into the chilly winter air.

It was a very long way to fall, but she twisted and turned in the air, landing on four paws in a soft bank of snow, none the worse for wear. She heard Father's angry voice in the nursery, then his face, florid and red, leaning out of the window and scanning the ground.

She raced away to the only place big enough to hide in. The wildwood. He hadn't a hope of catching her once she was lost in there. The ground sped by beneath her paws. She reveled in the speed and strength this small body had. Soon, sooner than she had ever expected when she left it this morning, she was back in the dark forest again.

It was very different now. She was a small creature. There were many enemies here. She felt it instinctively. Scents and sounds that spoke of danger. A primordial understanding that while she might hunt to fill her belly, she would be prey for others too.

She slowed, slinking light-footed across the snow, eyes and ears on alert. Her nose twitched. So many smells to shuffle through, decipher. Her stoat brain understood them all. The earthiness of mushrooms, the freshness of running water, the sour decay of bones beneath the forest floor. Then she saw it. The silver hare, the very same that had led her into the forest and guided her to the motherless kittens.

Instinct reared its head. She would attack, wrestle it, latch on to its throat with her sharp, sharp teeth. Never let go until its heart stopped beating. Her muscles tensed, ready to leap. Unconcerned, the hare sauntered over to her and touched her nose with its own. No words were spoken but thoughts formed in Flora's mind. *Come with me, child. I know of one who longs to see you.*

A strange sight should any human have happened by, the snaky, nervous bounce of a stoat side by side with the stoic hop of the hare. Natural enemies traveling together. Flora trusted her guide but even so, as a powerful stench filled her nostrils, doubt crept in. There was a fearsome creature ahead. Every nerve shouted at her to run, to hide. It took all she had not to obey.

They came to a clearing where a dark shadow lurked beside a massive fallen oak. It rose to greet them, towering above. A wolf, fur black as night. Flora screamed a stoatish shriek of terror, but then she saw the eyes. A piercing blue. Her mother's eyes.

The wolf stalked forward, lowering its shaggy head to sniff at Flora. A wave of sorrow and grief and love washed over her as the beast lay down, sphinx-like, in the snow. Flora snuggled between its massive front paws. She'd never thought to see her mother again. But to find her so changed, and Flora herself, transformed as well. Her father's intent to drive out their magic had only altered it and them. Instead of communing with the denizens of the wild, they had become animals themselves.

What was to become of them? Were they doomed to dwell in the forest forever? Flora's thoughts went to her brother. What would Milo think when he realized she had disappeared too? Would he connect it to Father's experiments? The magic had passed him by, but he was left behind to endure her father's disappointment and wrath.

Flora nuzzled her nose against her mother's warm cheek. No words passed between them—they seemed incapable of speech in this form—but a communing occurred just the same. As of one accord, the stoat leaped onto the wolf's back as it rose and took off at a loping run through the forest, far faster than Flora could have traveled by herself.

Mother paused at the edge of the wildwood, spying movement. A boy, running to the entrance of the maze and disappearing inside. Wolf and stoat followed more slowly. They knew the winding labyrinth by heart and would not lose track of their prey.

At the center stood a fountain that burbled with laughter in summertime but stood empty and barren in winter. The leaping dolphin statue was bereft and alone except for Milo, who sat on the cold marble weeping. Flora jumped down from the wolf and ran to her brother.

He startled in wonder as a small, furry head pushed itself under one of his hands, then reared up and backed away as he spied the giant wolf stalking toward them. Flora chittered at him, frustrated she could not make him understand, but the wolf simply stared, her great sky-blue eyes unblinking.

Milo was not as imaginative as his sister, did not really believe all this talk of magic, nor Father's rantings. But something about the calm gaze of the black beast, the scolding chatter of the stoat were familiar.

Flora was missing just like Mother. The servants were in an uproar.

Nasty rumors were being floated, and the local constabulary were on their way to investigate. Father had locked himself away in his wing of the house, and Milo had never felt so alone.

The wolf came and lay its massive head on his lap. The stoat climbed aboard, perching between the wolf's ears. Both looked up at him expectantly.

"Mother? Flora?" he asked, reaching out a tentative hand.

The stoat chirped excitedly and grasped his hand in its paws. Now here was a thing indeed. Milo felt split in two. He must make a choice: cling to his stubborn scorn of the very idea of magic and remain alone, or accept this strange sight in front of him and believe that there were two in the world who still cared for him.

He lay his hand along the wolf's head, felt a thrum of emotion emanating from that beast. He chose to believe.

"What are we to do?" he asked them. "The servants think Father killed Flora, and they are questioning again what happened to you, Mother. He is in such a rage, I—"

Milo was interrupted by a shout. He could just see and be seen over the maze hedges by his father, standing and looking out the high window of his laboratory. He watched in alarm as Father disappeared from view.

"He's seen us! What will he do to you two?" Milo said. "What if he makes things worse? What if…"

The massive wolf got to her feet and nudged Milo and Flora gently with her snout. The boy climbed onto his mother's back and his sister clung to his shoulder as the wolf loped confidently through the windings of the maze. Whether she intended to take them to their father, reunite with her husband in hopes of reversing his disastrous magic cure or not, the decision was made when they came face to face with him at the entrance to the labyrinth.

The look on his face and the shotgun in his hands spoke volumes, but he left them in no doubt. "Get down from there, boy. These unnatural creatures must be put out of their misery."

Milo leant over the wolf's back and whispered in her ear. "Run, Mother, run!"

The wolf exploded into action, knocking Father aside and racing away to the safety of the wildwood. Milo looked back to see his father giving chase. He seemed animated by an unnatural strength and speed, inspired by his mania to eliminate all evidence of his colossal failure.

They made good time over the open field, but once in the forest, the wolf had to slow to avoid stumbling over fallen trees or running into low-hanging branches. When they reached a clearing ringed by giant standing stones, they turned to face their pursuer. The black wolf panted heavily but held her head high, growling low in her chest with the determination to protect her cubs.

"I will only tell you once more, Milo. Come over here to me," Father said, as he raised the shotgun and took aim. "I will not ask again."

"No! They are my family and yours. You cannot kill them!"

"They are an abomination. A failed experiment that must be put down. The world must never know. Think of the shame it would bring upon my name."

"It would be nothing less than you deserve! Why didn't you leave them alone? They were fine as they were. It is you that is unnatural, Father."

His father's eyes narrowed. "I see you have been corrupted by this witchcraft as well. You leave me no choice."

A large shadow burst into view, bowling Father over and crushing him beneath its immense weight. There was the sound of teeth snapping, a meaty, slobbery ripping, then silence.

"I do not like those metal things. Not one bit. Nor men who wave them around." It was their guide, the bear, mouth wet with blood. Father lay still on the ground, throat torn out. "Not a friend of yours, I hope? If so, I am terribly, terribly sorry. I act impulsively sometimes."

Milo sobbed a ragged cry in shock and relief, grief and fear.

"Oh dear, oh dear, oh dear. A friend after all? What a bloomer I've made. How will you ever forgive me?" The bear sat down with a thump in the snow, holding its head in its paws.

Milo could not understand the words, but the bear's attitude was unmistakable. He walked over and lay a hand on its shoulder. "Thank you. Even though he was my father, he would have killed us all if you'd given him the chance. Thank you."

"Your father?" the bear mused to itself. "What a thing. Humans are the most savage creatures."

"If only I could understand you!" Milo cried. "Perhaps you could help us. This stoat is my sister, Flora, and the wolf, my mother. Father changed their magic in some way. I wish I knew how to change them back. I wonder if you do?"

The bear shook with bearish laughter. "Me, know magic? I am only a bear. What you need is a mage." He pointed over Milo's shoulder. "Like that one."

The silver hare sat observing the scene, licking its paws and washing its absurdly long ears. If a hare could be said to look amused, this one did. Its fur sparkled and reflected the sunlight that filtered down through the bare limbs of the trees onto the standing stones around them, creating patterns that shifted and oozed, mesmerizing the other watchers. Milo felt himself growing very sleepy indeed. The black wolf curled herself around boy and stoat as darkness fell over them all.

MILO AWOKE in his own bed, befuddled and wondering. Had it all been a dream? He looked down at his hands. A fistful of black hair was clutched in one, a remnant from his grip upon the wolf. Proof it had happened.

Fearfully, he glanced over to Flora's bed. His sister was tucked up, safe and sound, returned to herself. Their mother, restored, was leaning over to kiss her daughter's forehead in grateful benediction.

Mother came to him next and caressed his face with her soft hand, her blue eyes shining. "My brave, brave children. It is over. All will be well now."

And it was.

BAD DAY ON THE JOB

"Didn't I warn you about messing with the occult, Butchie?"

"I don't mess with it, Big Al. It messes with me. You know I don't never back down from a fight."

"You could walk away just one time, couldn't ya?"

"Hold the lecture, professor. We gotta get this cleaned up and quick."

"Why's it always gotta be this gooey stuff? Goes everywhere and takes a helluva lot of scrubbing to get it off."

"Gotta put a little elbow grease into it. Don't be such a lazy bum, Al."

"I ain't lazy, I'm practical, which is more than I can say for you. Hey, Butchie, you ever get the feeling we're being watched?"

"All the time."

"It's spooky, ain't it? Think it's ghosts?"

"Don't be a dope. It's just the Feds keeping tabs on the operation."

"Oh. It's neat that you can see right through them though."

"What? Where?"

"Those ones over there."

I shot my eyes over to the big wall of glass along the store's front. Don't ask me what we was doing in a dry cleaners at midnight washing demon ichor off the walls and floor. I'd kinda given up asking questions about anything to do with anything a long time ago. Just tried to keep my head down and follow The Boss's orders, but Al was right. The number of times lately we'd found ourselves in a similar sticky situation didn't bear thinking about.

There were two glowing figures standing near the door looking at us. Once upon a time, that might have thrown me for a loop, but now, I just waved. They waved back.

"What are you ladies doing here, if I might be so bold as to inquire?" I asked.

The shorter of the two came closer. She looked like a flapper girl with bobbed hair and a drop waist dress that'd been out of style for two decades at least.

"I'm haunting," she said.

"Haunting what? This dry cleaners?"

She looked abashed. "Yeah. I'd rather've come back as a revenant on a relentless path of righteous vengeance, pursuing those who'd wronged me, with burning eyes and a heart of wrath. Instead, I'm stuck here, palely loitering. It's kinda disappointing, if I'm honest."

I had to chuckle. "That's life, ain't it? Or death in your case. What's your name?"

"Lulu."

"Nice to meet ya, Lulu. I'm Butchie, and the big guy over there is Al."

"Charmed, I'm sure."

"And who's your friend?"

The other woman stepped forward, gaunt and tired-looking and wrapped in a trenchcoat. "I'm the Reaper."

Big Al came over. "What, like the Grim Reaper?"

"Yes. Is that so surprising?"

"I always thought the Reaper was a man."

"Why? It's usually women who get stuck with the cleanup in this world. I'm surprised you didn't hire a couple of girls to straighten this place out."

I grinned. "We try to keep this kind of thing out of the papers.

Loose lips and all that. Hey, I hope you ain't here for one of us? Al and I ain't ready to punch our tickets yet."

"No, I was passing the time with Lulu. We've been friendly acquaintances since I collected her in '27. You can call me Marge."

"Ain't you supposed to have a scythe and not so much flesh, Marge?" asked Al.

"I can turn it off and on." She made a face like she was taking a dump, and all of a sudden she was nothing but a sack of bones in a dark cloak with a wickedly sharp scythe. It was definitely more intimidating, but her voice stayed the same, weary and jaded.

"I'm supposed to be out culling souls, but my heart's not really in it these days. It's so hard to know who's good and who's evil anymore. Figuring out who to send up to St. Peter and who to the Down Below is such a chore. And you wouldn't believe the paperwork I have to fill out."

"Sounds like a real drag," I said.

"At least she can travel around though," complained Lulu. "See a bit of the world. I died here. Fell in a vat of cleaning fluid and drowned, and now I gotta stay here forever."

"Ain't you supposed to move on after a while?"

"Only if I'm no longer tethered to this plane by unfinished business."

"What kinda business?" I asked.

"My boyfriend, Frankie, was supposed to meet me here after work to discuss something special with me the day I died. I just know he was gonna ask me to marry him. I hate to think he never knew I woulda said yes."

"And that's the only thing keeping you here? I mean, dontcha think he's probably moved on by now? That was twenty years ago."

Lulu started to cry, though not real tears, of course, but Marge didn't like that. She waved her scythe in my face. "Can't you have a little consideration? Men have no tact and less sense."

I'm not one to rejoice in making a dame cry. "Me and my big mouth. Sometimes I spit out words without using the old noodle.

What's his full name? Maybe we can look him up for you. Let him know you'd like to be in touch."

The ghost sniffed. "Frankie Malone."

Big Al piped up. "Not Frank the Finger? Hey, that's The Boss!" he added, whacking me across the chest for good measure in case I missed the obvious.

Lulu blazed with delight. "Your boss? How about that! He was a busboy at Mabel's Diner when I died, but he always told me he was going places. What kind of business does he own?"

Al and I exchanged a look. The Boss didn't appreciate anyone talking about the operation. Hard to say if he would make an exception for the ghost of a long-lost love.

I decided to divert the conversation down safer byways. "You know, The Boss never has married. Not even a lady on the side, if you know what I mean. Maybe he never got over losing you. Wouldn't that be something?"

Lulu clasped her hands together under her chin and fluttered her eyelashes like one of them actresses from the silent pictures, all lit up silver from within. "Gosh, d'ya think so? I'd love to see him again. Is he as handsome as ever?"

I'm no expert on the male physique, but it was hard to imagine any gal getting too excited about The Boss's beefy anatomy and disappearing hairline.

Always the diplomat, I compromised. "He's got real presence."

Marge snorted, but Lulu beamed.

There was a commotion at the door, and Midtown Marky strolled in with a package draped over his shoulder.

"What you got there, Marky?" I asked.

"Cadaver."

"What?"

"You know, a corpse, a body, a dead guy."

"I know what it means, Mr. Smarty Pants, but what are you doing with it?"

"Dunno yet. The Boss told me to get rid of it. Thought I'd see if you two had any bright ideas."

"The usual. Woodchipper, concrete boots, etcetera."

"That'd be okay for most, but this ain't just any guy. It's The Boss's nemesis."

"His what?"

Al chimed in. "Nemesis, Butchie. Like in the comics. An insect that's twenty stories high. Or an armadillo that breathes fire."

"Those are monsters, you mook," said Marky. "A nemesis is a villain bent on evil who's your mortal enemy and tries to thwart you at every turn."

"I didn't know The Boss had a mortal enemy. Who is he?"

"Rory Finnegan."

"Finn from down the block? He didn't seem so bad."

"Nah, he was more annoying than evil, but The Boss had enough. He's heavy, I can tell you that," Marky added, throwing his burden down with a thump. Blood oozed out onto the floor.

Al threw his hands up in the air. "Now look what you done. We ain't even cleaned up the first mess!"

Marky pulled off his fedora and smoothed back his hair. "Hey, who's the looker?"

Lulu preened.

"She's a ghost," I said, "and she's The Boss's girlfriend, or was, so watch yourself."

Marky put his hat back on double quick at that. Nobody crosses The Boss.

Marge came over and poked at the body with the handle of her scythe. "Single knife wound to the heart, huh? Very neat job."

"You can tell just by jabbing at it?" Marky asked in confusion.

"Of course. I'm the Reaper."

"Don't that mean you collect dead people? Maybe you could help me out here."

"Not a chance. That's one of Louie's. There is such a thing as professional ethics."

"You mean there's more than one of you?"

"Do you know how many people die on any given day? I'd be run ragged without help. There's a whole crew of us."

"Doesn't that make you *a* reaper, instead of *the* reaper?"

"It's complicated. There's this whole space and time thing. We pop in and out. There's never more than one at once. Speaking of…" Marge's bones collapsed into a heap on the ground and disappeared through the floor.

Lulu tittered. "She knows how to make an exit, don't she?"

While we were still processing the dissolution of Marge, another pile of bones floated up and assembled themselves into a tall skeletal figure. "Quite a crowd! Didn't expect an audience, I must say."

"And who might you be?" I asked testily. I was beginning to think Al and I were never gonna get the place cleaned up before daybreak at this rate. The dry cleaners was suddenly Grand Central Station.

"I'm the Grim Reaper, also known as Louie. I've come to collect this gentleman on the floor."

Marky grinned. "Great! I'll let The Boss know the body is all taken care of."

The skeleton shook in what I could only guess was silent laughter. "Dear sir, you are a card. The Reaper only collects souls. The vessel is of no interest." He waved his hand and a silver thread wound itself around it. "Wouldn't bodies constantly be disappearing if we were responsible for them? Do have a little think before you speak. Toodle-loo!" The specter went up in a cloud of smoke.

"That stinks," said Marky. "Now I still got to get rid of this."

Lulu spoke up. "You could take it out to the forest north of the city. Frankie and I used to go to an old cabin in the woods there when we was courting."

"Oh, yeah? Where's that?"

"Up beyond Miller's Point. It's hard to find unless you know what to look for. I'd show you, but I can't leave the bounds of this building."

"Didja ever try?" I asked.

"Well… no. I mean everyone knows spirits are tied to where they died though, ain't they?"

Marky, Al, and me stared at her, dumbfounded that she hadn't tested her theory in all these years. She got the picture 'cause she kinda blushed, if ghosts can be said to do such a thing.

I stepped through the front door and held it open. "Wouldn't hurt to give it a go."

"What if I disappear or something?"

"Would that be worse than hanging around a dry cleaners for eternity?"

"I guess you got a point. Would you hold my hand? I'm frightened."

I almost laughed at the idea of a ghost being scared, but I could see she was serious, so I held out my mitt. She placed one delicate hand in mine. I couldn't feel it, but it seemed to comfort her. She got a determined look on her face and stepped over the threshold.

"I'm... I'm fine, I think." She took a few more steps and twirled around. "I'm free! I can finally go see Frankie and let him know I would've said yes!"

"Wait a minute," said Marky. "You said you'd lead us to this cabin joint. I gotta get rid of this joker before we see The Boss, or I'll be next."

Lulu sighed impatiently but gave in. "Okay, but then you'll take me straight to Frankie, right?"

"Sure, no problem. I'm sure he'll be thrilled to see you."

Al and I exchanged another look. Unlike Marky, we weren't convinced The Boss would appreciate a spectral visitor from his past, but it wasn't none of our business. You learn quick in our racket to stay mum on things that don't directly concern you.

"Ain't you coming too?" Lulu asked me and Al as Marky retrieved the corpse from the floor and started shuffling outside.

"We gotta finish up here," I said. "Besides, it's only the one body. Marky can handle it."

"But a lady never goes anywhere alone with a strange man."

"Are you kidding us?" Big Al spluttered.

I smirked. "Times have changed, Lulu. No one thinks twice nowadays about a gal going anywhere she's a mind to."

"That may be, but I'm an old-fashioned girl."

"You mean to say you'd feel safer alone with three men than one? That don't make sense. Not to mention the fact, you're a ghost. You've already kicked the bucket over and the water done run out. There's not much worse could happen to you, is there?"

That started the waterworks again. I guess I'll never learn to keep my big mouth shut around the fairer sex. She was wailing so hard I was worried we'd start attracting attention we didn't need. It wouldn't be so easy to explain away demon blood and a dead body if the cops showed up.

"Settle down. We'll all go, okay? Soon as we get this place spic and span. Marky, stash the stiff in the trunk," I said, throwing him the keys to the Packard, "then come back inside and help me and Al."

With the three of us mopping and scrubbing, we soon took care of any evidence that a happening of the supernatural kind had ever taken place. We crammed into the car, me driving, Al taking shotgun, and Lulu and Marky in the backseat.

"Ain't this nice?" said Lulu, looking around. "Last time I rode in a car they weren't so fancy. Makes me think about all the things I missed from dying young. It's a tragedy, ain't it? I guess being a tragic heroine is almost as good as being a revenant."

"Better," said Al. "Revenants are always on the move, hunting down their enemies to get revenge. Sounds tiresome. Now you, you get to just float around, take it easy. That's the gig for me. Whattaya think, Marky?"

"I wanna be one of those that cause all the trouble."

"Poltergeist?" I suggested.

"Yeah. That sounds fun. Throwing things around, opening and closing doors, scaring the crap outta people."

"You always been a troublemaker. That should suit you fine."

Marky flicked my ear by way of reprimand, but that only proved my point.

The dry cleaners was near the edge of town, so it wasn't long before we were driving down a dark country lane. We passed a few farms and crossed over the river. Then we started winding up into the hills that led to Miller's Point, which was what passed for a mountain around those parts.

We'd made it over the crest when we struck our first piece of bad luck. The car engine spluttered and stopped.

"We're outta gas," I opined.

"Whose fault is that?" asked Al.

"I told you to fill it up."

"I never got the chance, did I? Too busy cleaning goo off the floor."

"All the same, you mighta reminded me before we got way out here. We coulda knocked up the owner at the last gas station we passed. A few extra bucks would've persuaded them to get out of bed."

"Why don't we coast?" said Marky. "We're on the downhill track anyway. How far are we from this cabin?"

Lulu floated away out the window. Came back a minute later to report in. "It's only a mile or two to the turnoff. You have to look close, or you'll miss it. There used to be a fallen pine there marking the way, but I guess it's rotted since Frankie and I was here. I'll give you a shout at the turn."

She wasn't kidding either. Just about gave me a heart attack from screaming in my ear like a banshee as I was about to drive past. The downhill slope had propelled us along the main drag, but once we made the turn, we lost momentum quick.

"It's not too far," Lulu consoled us. "You can walk from here."

Marky slung his package over his shoulder with a grunt. We set out, a bunch of city boys none too happy to be stalking through trees and brush and who knows what else in the dark. At least Lulu shone like a star in the night giving us a light to follow down the path.

I was surprised The Boss'd never mentioned this place to me. I'm as close to a right-hand man as he's got, mainly because I'd managed to survive the longest in his employ. The word "cabin" made me picture a rundown hut built of stacked logs, but it was a regular house with wooden siding and a shingled roof. It looked cared for, too.

I got nervous maybe someone was living there. It was a cold night, but there was no smoke from the chimney. No lights in the window either, but of course it was long past midnight, so they might be asleep.

"Hey, Lulu," I whispered. "Can you check it out and make sure no one is gonna come out and spy on what we're doing out here?"

"Sure," she answered, darting through a wall and disappearing. She was back in no time. "All clear. Everything's neat and clean, but there's no food in the kitchen or clothes in the closets."

"Huh," said Al. "Wonder what The Boss uses it for?"

"I couldn't care less," said Marky. "I just wanna get rid of this mug and figure out how to get back to town without hoofing it all the way."

"The Boss won't appreciate us burying a body too close to his place," I said. "You should walk out into the woods. You gotta shovel?"

"What do I look like? A hardware store? Didn't know I'd be digging, did I?"

"It's a fair bet when you got a body to take care of that some digging might not be out of the question. Always be prepared, as the boy guides say. Let's take a look around. Maybe there's one we can borrow. You look out here, and Al and I will case out the cabin."

The place was sealed nice and tight, but we've all known how to pick a lock since we were running around in diapers. That's the kind of neighborhood we grew up in. Al and I spread out on the inside. Wasn't much to see. A big room with a fireplace in one corner and a kitchenette in the other.

On the far wall were two doors. Al took the one on the right and found the powder room. I took the one on the left and found a bedroom and something else—a violet tentacle that snaked back under the bed as soon as the light from the open door hit it.

"Oh, jeez," I complained.

"Whazzit?" asked Al at my shoulder.

"Something under the bed."

"Leave it. Nothing to do with us and likely to be nothing but trouble."

"Ain't you curious?"

"This is exactly what I'm talking about, Butchie. Ninety-nine out of a hundred guys would walk away right now. Leave sleeping dogs lie."

The space beneath the bed spoke up. "I am not a barking beast though I have nothing but benedictions for bloodhounds. They are far better than braggarts, or boggarts for that matter. But give me a blitheringly boisterous baker any day. Brown butter biscotti and butterscotch brownies. Bliss!"

I'm the kinda guy who's seldom at a loss for words, but I gotta admit I was scratching my head at how exactly to respond to such unexpected observations. When in doubt, be friendly is my motto.

"Hi, under there. I'm Butchie and this is Al."

The violet tentacle poked out again and gave us a wave. "Bernadette. I'm the monster under the bed."

"Is that right?"

"Yes, but it has been so long since I had anyone to frighten. My brain has gone wobbly wibbledy woo. It's running widdershins when it should be running like a top, like a shop, like a golden, golden chop."

"Er, right. Well, don't mind us. We're only passing through. You haven't seen a spare shovel around, have you?"

"I've never employed a shovel although I understand the concept. I prefer a barkle stick. You can give flarfels a good thwot on the head with a barkle stick. Kept many an unwary tishtosh at bay until narlytime with a stout barkle stick."

The tentacle was thrashing about quite a bit by that last statement. By mutual if unspoken consent, Al and I slowly backed out of the room and closed the door.

"That thing's gone crackers," said Al.

"Wouldn't you if you were stuck under a bed with no one around to scare? I feel sorry for it. Maybe we should take it with us and find it a livelier bedroom. Little kid or something."

"Butchie, sometimes I wonder about you."

We heard a shout from outside, and Lulu floated in through the wall. "Marky's found… something. I don't think it's friendly."

More shouting and yelling. We rushed outside and followed the racket until we found Marky wrestling with a wolf. At least, that was my first idea. My second was this was unlike any wolf I'd ever seen in a picture book. It stood upright and was talking, for one thing.

"Give me that corpse!" it growled.

"Take it why dontcha? I never said you couldn't have it. You just took me by surprise," Marky whined.

"What's the hubbub, bub?" I asked.

The wolf let go of Marky and turned in our direction. It had a weird face, half-human, half-canine. Uncanny. Gave me the shivers.

"I want to eat this body. I'm starving."

"Welcome to it, I'm sure. We're trying to get rid of it. As long as you don't mean us no harm."

"I wish I did, but unfortunately, part of my curse is I can only eat carrion. Not at all what I expected when I performed the ritual. Now I have an immortal soul, but I'm not allowed to kill anything or anyone. I am wasting away from hunger even though I will never die."

"Sounds like quite the predicament. Any way to reverse it?"

"The demon I summoned had a strange sense of humor. I suppose another one might have the power to cure me, but after my last experience, I'm afraid they might make it worse."

The creature tore a hunk out of Finnegan's leg, and I felt a chill presence step through me. A ghostly figure in a beat-up fedora and plaid suit was staring at the wolf and was none too pleased.

"What's the big idea?" it said.

Marky screamed in a higher pitch than I woulda thought possible. "Finn? Is that you?"

"I guess so, though I don't feel like myself, and what's with that?" the phantom demanded, gesturing wildly at the buffet that had once been him.

"I hate to be the one to break it to you," Big Al said, "but you're deceased, Finnegan. Kaput."

"You think that's news to me? Obviously I'm dead, but ain't nobody got any respect no more? You gonna let that mook chomp on my body instead of giving it a decent burial?"

"What use you got for it now?" Marky pointed out. "I been lugging it around half the night, and I can tell you for nothing that you should've eased off the grub while you had the chance. You ain't no lightweight."

"Oh, pardon me. Terribly sorry if I caused you any inconvenience. There's a surefire way to avoid that, you know. Don't go around offing people."

"Hey, I was only following orders. Wasn't me got on The Boss's bad side. What'd you do to make him so mad anyway?"

"Our beef goes way back. There was this girl. Used to work at the dry cleaners at Roosevelt and Third."

"Not Lulu?" I asked.

"How'd you know that?"

"Turn around."

Finnegan turned to find Lulu mooning at him. "Rory Finnegan. I remember you now. You was always trailing after Frankie. Did you really fall out over little old me?" The eyelashes were fluttering now. Al and I rolled our own eyeballs practically out of our heads, but Finnegan fell for it hook, line, and sinker.

"Lulu, honey. Is that you? After all these years and still as pretty as a picture. Gosh, I sure did miss you." He swiped his hat down from his head or tried to. I don't think he'd quite got the hang of this ghost business yet. "Why are you still here?"

"We could ask you the same question," I said. "Ain't you ready for the pearly gates?"

"Maybe he has some unfinished business like I do," said Lulu.

"Yeah, I do," Finnegan agreed. "But the funny thing is, I can't remember what."

"I was that way at first. Knew there was something bothering me, but it took me awhile to remember it was Frankie's marriage proposal. We're gonna go see him as soon as we take care of, you know…" She gestured over to the body, or should I say ex-body.

Our wolf friend had wasted no time. I wouldn't of thought it possible anything could chow down that quickly, but there wasn't even a bone left on the ground.

"That's pretty handy," said Marky. "Maybe you wanna come work for The Boss. We could supply you with all the stiffs you want. You take care of the evidence for us, and you get a good meal in return. It'd be a mutually beneficial relationship."

"You don't understand. I'm exactly as hungry as before. No amount of food ever sates my appetite. My existence is pure torture."

"Gosh, that's tough," said Lulu. "We oughta help him out, dontcha think?"

Al snorted. "Lady, you're as bad as Butchie. We been up for over 24 hours, and personally, I ain't got the time nor inclination to be playing Good Samaritan to every supernatural entity we run across, whether it's this beast or the one under the bed in the cabin."

"There's a monster under the bed? Oooh, I'm gonna go see." Lulu floated off with Finn right behind her. I guess he didn't want to lose sight of her after their unexpected reunion.

"Oh, for Pete's sake," growled Al.

"She's right, you know. You should help me out," said the wolf. "I could cause you a lot of trouble. I've witnessed you trying to get rid of a dead body after all."

"Smart guy, eh?" Al pulled out his pistol and shot the thing right through the forehead. He's always been a deadeye with a gun.

"Dammit, that stings like the blazes!" Far from killing it, Al just made the wolf mad. He came running, claws swinging. "What part of 'I am immortal and can never die' did you not understand?"

He got a few good slashes in, leaving Al's suit the worse for wear, before Marky and I each got ahold of an arm.

"I thought you said you weren't allowed to kill nothing?" yelled Al.

The wolf snarled. "Doesn't mean I can't give them a scar or two to remember me by."

"Let's all calm down now," I said, ever the peacemaker. "No need to let a little misunderstanding get out of hand. What's your name fella?"

"Nathan. Nathan Knickerbottom."

Well, I gotta admit we all snickered at that. You'd have to be superhuman not to.

He shook me and Marky off impatiently. "Yes, very amusing. Don't worry. I've heard it all my life. Why do you think I wanted to become a creature such as this? To wreak revenge on those who thought me a joke. How was I to know the demon I summoned would have a sick sense of humor?"

I patted old Nate on the shoulder. "Sounds like you've had a raw deal and all because of something that ain't your fault. We don't none of us pick the handle we're born with, do we? What say we summon this demon again and give him a good talking to. Sometimes you gotta explain things in a way a joker like that can understand." I curled my right paw into a fist and slammed it hard into the palm of my left hand for emphasis.

"Great. I see more goo in our future," Al griped, and he wasn't wrong. We both knew from experience that wrestling with demons ended up in some kind of a mess sooner or later.

Nate was huffing and puffing, but I could see the fight had gone out of him. I don't know how long he'd been roaming around looking for roadkill, but it'd obviously taken its toll.

"Fine. We'll have to go into the cabin. There's a Ouija board in there I used for the ritual."

We approached the joint to find Lulu and Finnegan sitting in a couple of rocking chairs on the front porch.

"Thought you was visiting Bernadette," I said.

"Kind of an odd duck, ain't she?" said Finn. "We couldn't make heads nor tails out of whatever she was gabbling on about."

"I feel sorry for her," said Lulu. "I know what it's like to be stuck somewhere and lonely. Are you gonna help her and Mr. Wolf?"

"His name's Nathan," I corrected, deciding to omit the more rib-tickling part of his moniker in the interest of moving things along. "We gotta hold a kinda séance to summon the demon who did this to him. See if we can make it see reason."

Lulu shivered. "Oh, leave me out of it. That kind of thing would frighten me to death."

I would have argued the logic of this statement, but Finnegan stepped in, grabbing Lulu's hand. "Don't fret, honey. We'll stay out here and watch the scenery. I never been out to the woods before. It's kind of peaceful, especially with such prime company."

We left them mooning over each other. Made me wonder if Lulu had forgotten all about The Boss, but we'd figure that out later.

Inside, Nathan walked over to a bureau and pulled open one of its drawers with a claw. "Here it is. I can't pick it up anymore though," he added, holding up his ungainly mitts and looking chagrined.

Marky grabbed the set. We gathered at a round table that had a white candle half-burnt up and stuck into a melted pool of wax. "Whatta we do?"

"You've got to light the candle and write out the demon's name, Trayblik, with the letters on the board. I'll spell it for you."

"No need," said Marky, setting his lighter to the wick. "I got it." He moved the wooden thing around the board lightning fast before any of us could stop him. He ain't the sharpest knife, our Marky.

There was a crack of thunder and a purple cloud arose from the board, obscuring it from view. When we waved the smoke away, there was a fly sitting there. At least, that's what we thought until it spoke up in a squeaky voice.

"I have been summoned and I obey. What can I do for you gents?"

"What is that?" asked Nate. "That's not Trayblik."

"No, I'm Mrazblxk the Mighty. I hope I haven't arrived at the wrong séance again. I do seem to make a habit of it."

"Mrazblxk the *Mighty*?" Al asked. "Shouldn't you be, I dunno, taller or wider or something?"

"I am mighty in power not stature. Didn't your mother teach you not to judge a book by its cover?"

The demon flew up and lit on Al's nose. Before you could say Jack Robinson, Al disappeared and a dusty old leatherbound book lay on the table. I picked it up and read the title, *Foolish Men Throughout History*. Couldn't resist a smirk at that.

"Apt," I observed, "but Al's not such a bad guy. Not sure he deserves people rifling through his pages for all time."

"Do forgive me. My temper gets the better of me sometimes."

The book jumped out of my hand to the floor and Al reappeared, sneezing fit to beat the band. "That— *achoo*— was a dirty— *achoo*— trick!"

"All's well that ends well as Mr. Shakespeare often says."

"Shakespeare. Ain't he the guy wrote those fancy plays? You mean he's down in the other place?" Marky asked, pointing at the floor.

"He does like to visit us. Gets inspiration for his work, you know. For all that it is undeniably pleasant, life in the clouds can get boring for such a creative mind."

"He's still writing stuff?"

"Of course. If you're lucky, you are allowed to do your favorite things in the afterlife. Something to keep in mind, gentlemen. You all have the look of one who might not have much say in how they spend eternity, if you get my drift," Mrazblxk replied, his gaze drifting downward.

The others looked unbothered, but that gave me pause. I'd ended up in the Boss's employ because there weren't many options for a gorilla like me. I'd contributed to a whole lot of unpleasantness on the wrong side of the law since then. You'd think it would've dawned on me before to wonder what was gonna become of me in the hereafter, but sometimes you're so wrapped up in staying alive day to day, you forget to look at the big picture. Might not hurt to get a few more good deeds under my belt, help balance out my tally in the Golden Book.

"Maybe you can help out our friend here," I said, indicating the big hairy galoot in our midst. "This demon Trayblik turned him into a werewolf, but he's not allowed to kill anything and no matter how much he eats of whatever dead thing he can find, he's always hungry."

"Oh dear, oh dear. That does sound like Trayblik. He has a terribly dark sense of humor. It's a curse that's easily reversible, of course."

"That's great!" Nathan enthused.

"Except one demon cannot reverse another's curse. It just isn't done—"

The wolf roared. "What? You got my hopes up, you midget!" He lifted one huge paw like he was gonna swat the demon but froze in place like a statue when Mrazblxk flew up and landed on his nose.

The little demon sniffed. "What a hasty bunch you all are! Manners get you much farther in life than brute strength. Or insults," he added, with a pointed look at Al. "What I was going to say is it just isn't done without express permission from one of the higher-ups. Now, who would be in charge of such transformations, I wonder. Mr. Wither? Or possibly Ms. Decay."

"Mizz? What's that mean?"

"That is a term for persons of the female persuasion. Probably hasn't come into vogue yet. We demons exist simultaneously in every point in history. Can get quite confusing. Everyone hold still now. This may tickle."

There was a whooshing noise in my ear, then there we were, the whole kit and kaboodle of us down in the fiery pits of hell. Only there weren't pits, just boxes as far as the eye could see, made out of some weird material in every color of the rainbow from candy apple red to mustard yellow.

I guess we looked underwhelmed because Mrazblxk explained. "It used to be much more dramatic. Brimstone fell like rain, and the howls of the damned created such a pleasant melody. The Behemoth Corporation took over management a few millennia ago. Their motto is 'Sanitary & Orderly Efficiency.' Not very catchy, but that is in keeping with their ethos. No frills or dramatics, just torture, plain and simple."

"What are these boxes made of?" I asked.

"Plastic. Let's see. In your timeline, it's only just been invented, but believe me it becomes very popular. Never breaks down you see. Lasts forever as your great-great-great-grandchildren find out to their dismay, but that's neither here nor there. Point is, they keep the damned souls securely inside. All of the torment with none of the mess."

I looked around and saw my future, closed up in one of those containers with who knows what happening for eternity.

Mrazblxk buzzed up close to my ear. "Confidentially, not all of the demons are on board with the new regime. They miss the old days when torture had a more personal touch. We end up twiddling our thumbs quite a bit now. There's even a rumor we are to be phased out entirely."

"That would be a shame," I commiserated.

"It would indeed. Demons become bored very easily which only leads to trouble like your furry friend here. Trayblik was no doubt itching to get his hands dirty. Power with no purpose is a dangerous combination."

"What's all this?" A tall, sticklike creature had snuck up behind us while we were yakking. "This is very untidy, Demon Mrazblxk. I hope you have a good explanation for this breach of protocol."

"Ms. Decay! Exactly the demon we were hoping to run into. You see our lupine companion here?" Mrazblxk gestured toward the trio of Marky, Al, and Nate who were looking stunned and about as dopey as possible. Knickerbottom did work up the nerve to raise one paw by way of volunteering he was the wolf in question.

"It seems Demon Trayblik has been up to some of his tricks again. This poor man has been given the appetites and power of a werewolf, but a curse forbids him from killing or ever eating enough to satisfy his hunger. I believe such torture of the non-dead is strictly forbidden by Behemoth Corporation's bylaw number 9974-HEX, if I'm not mistaken."

"Very good, Demon Mrazblxk. You are one of the few employees to treat the company's policies with the seriousness they merit." The stick figure waved one jagged leg in Nate's direction.

His fur fell away to reveal a scrawny and not very comely nude figure of a man. "Finally. I hope you give that Trayblik a good talking to on my behalf."

"You can do that in person, Nathan Knickerbottom. As a participant in an incident violating Bylaw 9974-HEX, you will be required to fill out this paperwork in triplicate and obtain Demon Trayblik's signature on every page before being returned above."

A tower of papers as tall as Nate's head appeared in front of him. He looked to me with desperation in his eyes. Before I could intervene, the rest of us were whisked back to the cabin in the woods.

"That was very satisfactory, wasn't it, gentlemen?" said Mrazblxk, rubbing his tiny hands together. "We were fortunate Ms. Decay was in such a mellow mood."

"I thought you was gonna help the guy, not leave him down there for who knows how long," said Al.

"Mr. Knickerbottom did knowingly enter a contract with a demon.

There are always consequences. Every action provokes a reaction, sometimes one that will seal your doom. Best not to think about it too much. You might hesitate to ever make a decision again!" Mrazblxk roared—well, trilled might be more accurate—with laughter at this. I guess he thought it a pretty good joke, but the rest of us were less amused.

"C'mon, Marky," Al growled. "Let's get some fresh air. Get the stink of that place out of our noses."

Mrazblxk shook his head at their departing backs as they exited the cabin. "That's unfair, don't you think? I thought it smelled pleasant, but perhaps I am just used to it."

"It wasn't bad," I agreed. "Don't mean I want to end up crammed into one of those boxes though."

"I don't have the gift of foresight as some of my colleagues do, so I can give you no assurances, but I can tell you I have witnessed mortals turn their lives around in time to avoid such a fate. Redemption is possible and often is its own reward. Tell me something. When was the last time you felt really good about your life?"

I thought about the inch-thick steak covered in cream gravy on a plate piled high with roasted new potatoes that The Boss's cook set before me the previous Sunday. That was about as close as I got to being satisfied with my lot, but I knew that wasn't what the demon meant.

"I ain't felt good ever. Not in the way you mean. It was kind of nice to help that Nathan fella out, but then he's stuck down there crossing his I's and dotting his T's."

"That is not your responsibility. He made his own choices. But helping others, with no expectation of reward for yourself, is of great worth. If you are concerned about the stains upon your soul, you could do worse than seeking out those who need assistance before one of the reapers comes to collect your thread. Something to think about. Oh dear, look at the time. If you're all done with me, I should be moving along."

"What? Oh, yeah, you're released or free to go or… is there some special chant or something?"

"No. That will do. I've taken an interest in your plight. It isn't often in my line of work I meet someone with even a glimmer of conscience left. Do stay in touch. I'd like to know how you get on. Just write my name on any surface, it needn't be one of those silly spirit boards, and I will appear and assist you if it is within my power. Farewell, traveler. Do not despair, your journey is not yet ended."

With that, the diminutive fella disappeared. It felt kinda lonely without him. I'm not a warm and cuddly guy, but then it had been a long time since I'd met anyone who'd taken any interest in my welfare. Maybe my whole life.

Helping others. I looked around the room, like there might be a damsel in distress who wanted saving, before remembering there was one in the cabin.

I entered the bedroom and knelt to peer under the bed. "Bernadette? You still with us?"

A violet tentacle snaked out and waved at me.

"I don't know how many visitors you get out here, but by the looks of the place, it's not a regular occurrence. You ever get lonesome?"

An eye as big as a baseball on a long stalk came out and peered close at my face. "A handsome sir. A gallant lad. A knight in grey flannel."

"Okay, I'll take that as a yes, I guess. You interested in me transporting you to a livelier hideout? One with a little more action?"

There was a blur of purple motion. I felt my fedora buck like a wind had hit it, then a weight settled on my head. I stood and looked in the dresser mirror, tentatively lifting my hat. A small tentacle waved at me.

"How'd you even fit up there?" I asked.

"Needs must, do trust, pretend I'm a bust or dust or a dirty, dirty crust."

I was beginning to get the idea conversation wasn't Bernadette's strong suit, but after the initial shock of a monster perching on my head, there was something comforting about it. Not that we were friends or nothing. Don't get me wrong, I'm not a sap, but maybe

Mrazblxk was on to something. It felt good to think I might be rescuing a monster instead of killing one for a change.

I'd decided not to mention my passenger to the others, but Lulu put paid to that by drifting through my hat without so much as a by-your-leave as soon as I stepped out of the cabin. "I see you're bringing Bernadette with you. How wonderful! I did hate to think of her being left here all alone. At least at the dry cleaners, there was always someone coming and going. Where are you taking her?"

"Hadn't thought that far ahead, but I'll figure something out. First, we gotta report back to The Boss. That is, if you're still interested?" I asked, seeing as how Lulu and Finnegan were looking awfully cozy.

"I suppose I better. I can't think of any other unfinished business that would be keeping me here."

"But, honey, if you go off to heaven, I'll be all alone," whined Finn.

"Not if we figure out your unfinished business. Maybe you and Frankie need to make up. I hate to think I was the cause of ruining your friendship. What happened?"

"That part is fuzzy to me. Ever since I died, I can remember some things clear as day, but others are like wisps of smoke floating in the breeze."

"Gosh, that's positively poetic, Rory. Ain't it?" Lulu consulted me.

"Emnh," was about the most noncommittal sound I could come up with. I was bleary with lack of sleep and wanted to get home to bed. I reminded myself that helping others was my new motto though. "Maybe The Boss can tell us. Seeing as how his nemesis is dead, don't see why he wouldn't want to crow about it."

We hoofed it back to the Packard. Those of us who were still among the living pushed the car out to the main road and got it drifting on down the mountain. It meant going in the opposite direction of town, but Marky remembered a country store at the bottom where we could gas up for the journey back. We built up a good head of steam on the incline, so it wasn't too long before we had a full tank and were motoring back over Miller's Point and then across the city limits.

Dawn was peeking its rosy head over the horizon by the time we pulled up in front of headquarters. We'd no worries about not finding The Boss there. None of us had ever seen him leave the building. Why should he, with a swell apartment on the top floor and a gang of goons like me to run errands for him?

"Maybe I should go in and talk to him first," I said. "He's a cautious guy. Springing a couple of ghosts on him could make him shut up tight as a clam. Here, somebody hang on to Bernadette in case there's trouble. The Boss has a short fuse, and I might be about to touch a match to it."

I lifted my hat and Bernadette oozed out.

"She can hide in here," said Lulu, opening up a ghostly purse she produced from thin air.

I was about to explain how that wouldn't work when Bernadette jumped in, closing the clasp after her. In my line of work, you get used to all kind of doings that don't make much sense, so I decided not to dwell on it. The others settled themselves into the wooden chairs that lined the waiting room outside The Boss's office while I rapped my knuckles across the door and let myself in.

The Boss was sitting at the desk under his collection of Japanese samurai swords on the wall. He was already hard at work, suit jacket off, shirtsleeves rolled up, tie loose, and his ever-present cigar chomped in the corner of his kisser.

"Problem?" he asked without glancing up.

"Depends on how you look at it, I guess. We took care of the mess at the cleaners, but things got a little complicated. Marky came by with a body. Your old nemesis, Finnegan."

"Why'd he do a fool thing like that?"

"Wasn't sure what to do with it. Wanted a little professional consultation and advice."

"I assume you gave it to him. Or are you gonna tell me it's out there now?" The Boss scowled, pointing at the door to the waiting room with his cigar. "If he's brought Finnegan back here, there's gonna be hell to pay and I'll be the one writing up the bill."

"He ain't got the body if that's what you're worried about. It got ate up lock, stock and barrel by a werewolf."

"Is this beast gonna be trouble?"

"No, it got unwolfed by a demon, or I should say demon bureaucrat, and is now trapped in an unending paperwork nightmare in the underworld."

"You have had an adventurous night. Anything else? Vampires, warlocks, phantoms?"

"Funny you should mention that. Do you remember a girl named Lulu?"

I never seen The Boss move so fast in my life. He crossed the room and locked the door before grabbing me by my tie hard enough to choke me.

"Whattaya know about that? Who's been yapping to you?"

I swatted his hand away, which wasn't easy. He may spend most of his time behind a desk tending to his empire, but he's no lightweight.

"A little birdie told me you were sweet on her once upon a time until she ended up dead. Even wanted to marry her. And that's why you hated Rory Finnegan so much. Cause he was sweet on her too."

"Hah, they got it all wrong. I didn't hate Rory, he hated me. And I never asked that gal or any other one to marry me. Women are deadweight. They just drag you down."

"Why did Finnegan hate you then?"

The Boss got a shuttered look, his best poker face, but I knew him better than my own father.

"Did you do something to Lulu?"

"C'mon, Butchie. She was a thorn in my side. Always hanging around and talking about us having a future together. I was getting the business started, and she was cramping my style. A real goody-two-shoes who didn't understand what it takes to get ahead in this world. I met up with her after hours at the dry cleaners to break it off with her, but she wouldn't let me go. Got tired of arguing with her and dumped her in a vat of that cleaning fluid they use. Got splashed like crazy holding her under. Had to get rid of my suit and it was the only good one I had back then."

This confession may have come as a shocking revelation to some, but I'd listened to The Boss brag about a thousand worse things without batting an eyelash. I don't know what was different this time, but before I realized it, my right fist was landing a haymaker on The Boss's chin that made him stagger.

He don't take that kind of thing from nobody, not even me, so I wasn't surprised to find myself in the fight of my life. We was grunting and knocking things over enough to attract attention from the peanut gallery outside. Finding the door locked, there seemed to be some discussion going on about what best to do. I wasn't sure if I wanted the other guys to bust in or not. Chances were they'd take The Boss's side, and I couldn't blame them. No one crossed him and lived to tell about it for very long.

While they were debating, The Boss landed his own haymaker and I went down, seeing stars. I took a nice rest on the floor while the commotion continued at the door. Watched a fly struggling in a spider web along the baseboard. Poor thing, trapped with no mercy in sight. A tragedy in miniature. I felt for the fly. He and I had a lot in common just then. I wished in my case that I was the spider and not the fly.

I think I passed out because next thing I know, I sit up groaning to find The Boss pinned to the wall with a three-foot sword and a pool of blood at his feet. I ain't no detective, but I didn't have to be to tell he was dead. Funny thing was, he looked kinda peaceful hanging there. There's something to be said for no longer having a care in this world.

The others must've picked the lock and got the office door open, 'cause they were all hanging around gawking.

"What's the story?" I asked, stumbling to my feet and gingerly poking at my jaw which felt like shattered glass.

Lulu danced up, eyes alight with excitement. "Me and Bernadette killed him!"

"You and... ?" I glanced in bewilderment at the shrunken violet monster peering out from Lulu's handbag.

"Yes! We were hiding under your hat. I bet you didn't even realize, did you? I wanted to hear what Frankie had to say about me."

"I guess you got an earful then."

"I've never been so mad in my afterlife. Imagine me pining away for him when it was Frankie that turned me into a ghost in the first place. I coulda been a vengeful revenant this whole time and never even knew it! I was gonna stab him with the sword, but I never have got the hang of picking things up, so Bernadette held onto it for me and we kinda ran at him and look!" she finished up triumphantly, pointing at the new trophy on the wall.

Finnegan's ghost drifted over and put an arm around her. "That was sure something, honey. I knew there was some reason I was so mad at Frankie but getting killed put it out of my mind. I suspected all along he offed you, but I could never get him to admit it."

Al was looking worried. "We're in the soup now. If the rest of the gang find out we let The Boss get killed, we'll all be ghosts. What are we gonna do with the body?"

There was a puff of smoke, and Marge appeared in her reaper getup. "What have you all been up to? Lulu! What are you doing here?"

"Isn't it wonderful, Marge? Turns out I wasn't trapped at the dry cleaners after all and I'm a vengeful revenant that's fulfilled its quest and now I'm free!"

As she started to fade away, Bernadette popped out of the purse. I managed to catch her in my fedora before she splatted to the ground.

"Wait for me, honey," called Finn. "Now that Frankie's dead, I'm free too."

The two specters held hands and climbed a kind of stairway into a light.

"What'll happen to them?" asked Marky.

Marge shrugged. "Whether they make it through the gates or get turned away is not for me to say, but I'll miss Lulu. She was one of the friendlier ghosts I've met, but that's neither here nor there. I was summoned by this man's death," she said, wrapping a thread she drew out from The Boss around her hand. Only this one wasn't silver, it was black as night. "But as I think we have established previously, the container is your concern. Until we meet again, gentlemen."

With that disquieting promise, she disappeared through the floor, leaving me, Al, and Marky with a problem.

"We better move quick," said Al. "The other guys'll be showing up for work any minute."

Marky was shaking like a leaf. "They'll kill us for sure."

"All we gotta do is make the body disappear," I said. "No body, no way they can prove we did anything. Maybe The Boss decided to cash out, take a vacation, maybe retire even." I opened the safe and started pulling out the stacks of money there, dividing it up into three piles. "And we'll follow suit."

We stuffed the wads of cash in our pockets, but Al pointed out the flaw in my plan. "That's great, Butchie, but there's this pool of blood and a hole in the wall and a body to make disappear. Unless you know magic…"

"I don't know magic, but I know someone who does." I grabbed a piece of paper and fountain pen from The Boss's desk and scrawled out a name.

"You rang?" Mrazblxk appeared, perched on the end of the pen.

"Remember when you said you was interested in helping me turn over a new leaf?"

"Absolutely. Although souls aren't really my business, I can't help but take an interest now and then."

"Great!" I gave him the backstory on why there was a greasy, balding man pinned to the wall and how it was a predicament we weren't sure how to solve without getting ourselves offed in the process.

"No problem." He snapped his tiny fingers.

Suddenly, we were all back at the cabin in the woods, The Boss and all. Mrazblxk was nowhere to be seen but popped in before we could adjust to our change of scenery. "Sorry for the delay. Just tidying up the scene of the crime, so to speak. I left everything spic and span and glamored one of the gang of goons that showed up into thinking he was the new head of the operation. They all seemed content with that, but for good measure, I wiped their memories clean of the three of you."

"But what are we supposed to do with the body?" Marky complained.

"You can't expect me to do everything for you. Bury, burn, or submerge in a lake are three options I can think of right off the top of my head without even trying. Surely experienced gentlemen such as yourselves will be able to work something out."

"You're right," I said. "And don't think we don't appreciate what you done. You got us out of a tough jam back there. Don't you see, fellas? We got funds and a clean slate. This is a chance for us to make a fresh start."

"Leave me out of it," said Marky. "I've had enough and more than enough." He spun around and ran, which was fine by me. He was too big a coward to turn us in to the gang and risk us ratting him out, if they even believed his tale.

"What about it, Al?" I asked.

"What you got in mind?"

"With our unique skills and experience, I'm thinking we start a paranormal cleanup business, maybe a little detective work on the side."

"Oh, great. More goo."

"You got a better idea?"

"Nah. Might as well give it a try. I like to keep busy. Hey, Mrazblxk, you couldn't at least gift us a shovel, could you?"

"Gladly!" the demon said, producing one with a flourish.

"Thanks. I'll start a hole. You bring the body." Al stalked off among the trees looking for a soft spot for digging.

"You been a real pal, Mrazblxk." I said to the demon, tipping my fedora in thanks, only I'd forgotten Bernadette was curled up inside. I watched in dismay as she plummeted to earth, only to see her fall arrested when Mrazblxk landed on her.

"What have we here? How interesting! This is a very unusual enchantment."

"Enchantment?"

"Yes, and quite an unjust one, I believe." The demon waved his hands around. In a flash of light, the monster under the bed became a woman full-grown. Easy to look at, all amber eyes and a waterfall of shining brunette locks, wearing a purple suit with the neatest little hat you ever seen perched on her head.

"Hello and thank you." She leaned over and brushed my cheek with her lips. "I believe you are my knight in grey flannel."

I blushed. I'm no looker and never been too comfortable around the ladies. "Gosh," was the bright thing I thought of to say.

"And you, of course." She curtsied low to the demon.

"No problem, Milady," said Mrazblxk, "but I'm afraid you will find you are entirely out of time and place. You have been enchanted for a long while."

"Can't you return her to where she come from?" I asked.

"Some things are beyond a demon's power such as unwinding the hands of time, but I'm sure I leave her in safe hands with you. Fare thee well!"

Mrazblxk vanished, leaving me, hat in hand, under the scrutiny of a very fine pair of eyes.

"Looks like you're stuck with me. Butchie, isn't it? So, what are we up to?"

"Well, we gotta bury this stiff and then flee, in case a gang of no-goods ever get their memories back. Find a new city and set up shop as ghost chasers."

She threaded her arm through mine and gave it a squeeze. "Sounds tremendous fun. Shall we go?"

Who am I to say no to a lady?

A GNASHING OF TEETH

I think about all the times in the Before when I lay wide-eyed, dreading the stillness of night. A cruel hush that only those with insomnia can understand. Restless and suffering in that lonely sense of being the only one who is awake in the house, in the town, in the world. But I'm not alone now. *They* have risen and the nights are no longer quiet.

I've taken asylum within the ancient stone church, praying to gods I no longer believe in. If only the sun would rise. The light would rout the enemy for a time. Give me a chance to reach higher ground and seek out new allies. But the pounding at the door grows loud and dawn is too far away.

On the wooden altar lay wilted offerings of barley and wheat, left there after the harvest. We'd gathered, hand in hand, singing the old, old songs. All of it simply tradition. The gods, if they ever existed, had forsaken us long ago, but it was a way to cling to hope as we awaited the coming storm, those eerie growls and guttural whisperings in the dark.

I trace a sigil Mother taught me in the dust at the foot of the altar. A ward against evil, back when that was just an idle concept and not a gibbering, many-eyed reality. It's the brush of their great wings against the church windows that frighten me most. The colored glass was made in the traditional way, thick and strong. It's withstood over a thousand years without cracking, but will it hold for hours longer against this determined assault? I don't think so.

I twirl one of their radiantly golden feathers in my hand. A souvenir of sorts that caught in my cloak during the mad dash to reach the church before they noticed me. Most had been too busy feasting, but one looked up, caught sight of my fleeing form, and flew after me. Fortunately, it was a child. Not canny enough yet to be wary of the reach of a long-handled scythe wielded by a determined and desperate foe.

I'd whipped my weapon across its eyes, blinding at least half of them. It wouldn't have been enough to stop an adult, but it sent the child screeching back to its elders. I'd barely had time to reach the temporary safety of this old stone building before the angry host reacted. They're very protective of their young and won't rest now until they exact their revenge on me.

Using the rough-hewn altar cloth, I wipe my blade. Their ichor is acidic and will damage the scythe if allowed to linger. Then I fish my whetstone from my pocket to sharpen it. I've adapted the scythe so it has a cutting edge on both sides, making it possible to cause damage whether pushing with it or hooking it around a target. The blade is big enough to be useful but not so long as to be too heavy or unbalanced to easily wield in tight quarters.

It's the only weapon that remains to me after battles without number. Once, many others fought by my side, but one by one, they fell. Why did I survive when so many didn't? Pure luck, for I'm no more skilled or experienced in battle than any of the other villagers. In fact, I'd never killed another living thing until a few months ago. It's astounding what you can learn to do, the things you get used to when you must.

Sitting on the cold stone floor and leaning back against the altar, I pull my dark green cloak close for warmth and balance the scythe on my lap. One hand always clutches the worn wooden haft, ready to strike. The din and clamor outside rise and fall in strange rhythms, lulling me against my will into sleep.

I dream of my mother. We're shopping at the fishmonger's stall in the town center, Mother as always enjoying the haggle, knowing she'll get the price down to her satisfaction. The buzz of the market, laughter of children, smiling and frowning faces, the villagers going about their absurdly mundane business when golden feathers start to rain from the sky. Contentment turns to terror all in an instant.

Awake, heart racing, I think of all those dear, familiar faces. Gone now. As far as I know, I'm the last of my village. We'd heard tell of resistance groups in the forest along Bethamy Ridge. I was headed there before this current catastrophe, trapped in the old church with a host of angry phims surrounding it.

We'd mistaken them for angels at first, with their shimmering wings and many eyes that shone with a luminescence that gave them an otherworldly beauty. "Seraphim" the old ones had cried, remembering tales half-forgotten from the long ago.

The younger ones had nicknamed them phims, more akin to fiends or demons from the down below, but no one knew where they really came from. There'd been rumors of shining chariots, immense beyond imagination, bringing these visitors from the stars, but that was foolish talk and in the end it hadn't mattered.

What mattered was that the phims were hungry. Their double rows of razor teeth, snapping and gnashing, had made short work of those unlucky enough to be caught in the open. The phims had no arms or hands, just the broad golden wings that propelled them over great distances in search of prey. Their feet were hard to describe, like a hoof yet covered with long spikes that helped them cling to trees for roosting and to rake open their victims when feasting.

This lack of appendages that could hold and grasp was an advantage at first. Hiding inside proved effective as the creatures could not grab or open windows or doors easily and didn't seem inclined to try as prey was always readily available somewhere close.

But as we became cagier at hiding, they became cagier at seeking. Their powerful wings and feet beat and shredded as they learned to crack open our houses like they were oyster shells to reveal the panicked, squirming meat within.

Respite came during the day. The phims were nocturnal and spent the sunlight hours roosting together in the tall pines. The gentle rustle of their feathers and sleepy murmurings were a sharp contrast to the bombastic blast of beating wings and screeching language during the long nights, but we dared not disturb their rest for retribution was swift.

A peace-loving, farming folk became hardened warriors in face of the onslaught. Some expected the Army of the Republic would be sent in to help, but no one ever came. Communication with other towns became nearly impossible and what little was heard was not encouraging. Other places were also under siege. No one knew if the central government even still functioned. Each town had to fend for themselves if they wished to survive.

For a time, it had seemed possible. Planting and harvesting during the day, barricading into the strongest buildings by night, but winter was coming on. Food would be scarce. What to do? The debate was endless—stay and keep fighting or make a run for the hills and the rumored resistance fighters. There were passionate arguments on both sides but in the end, it became a moot point.

The night before, the last of our strongholds in town had been breached. It was a bloodbath. A few dozen of us fought our way through and took the path toward the hills. The flock was busy with their feasting in town so we thought we might make it, but a phim straggler stumbled across the party spelling our doom.

There was nowhere to hide at night on the road. We were picked off one by one, a brief respite granted to the others in our group as the solitary phim paused to enjoy its latest snack before resuming the hunt. We tried to take it down but phims have tough hides and had proved nearly impossible to kill with our pitiful forces. Farm implements and kitchen knives are no match for such beasts. After hours of painful attrition, the rest of the flock caught up with the satiated phim straggler. Overmatched in every way, all out carnage ensued.

I alone made it as far as the church. Now, I'm stuck. No food or water. I won't be able to hold out long. Maybe it'd be best to simply walk outside and let them take me. I've often wondered why I fight so hard against my fate. Mother always said I was a stubborn one and I suppose it's true. There's a spark, an anger that flares up amid my bitter hatred of these creatures that have robbed me and my people of all we held dear. It keeps me from surrendering to their will.

Getting to my feet and pacing past the wooden pews, I'm frustrated but defiant. This church has stood as long as anyone could remember. Since before memory, before the Harrowed Years, before history began again. There is writing in the ancient book that has always lain open on the altar, but no one living could read the words therein.

I run a fingertip along the delicate paper of the book, wondering at the symbols. The old religion and gods my grandparents had whispered of. Angels and demons, good and evil. Strange tidings that had faded with time. The altar is carved with depictions of those ancient creatures, locked in unending battle. I feel nothing but contempt for the carver. What did they know of war and struggle and death, always death, at the end of every fight, no matter how hard you tried?

Filled with rage at the hopelessness of my situation, I raise my scythe and give the altar a mighty crack with the blade. To my surprise, the heavy wood splits in two, one of the carved panels falling on my feet, crushing my toes.

I cry out and curse in pain, this further injury almost too much to take.

"Who's there?"

A soft voice. A human voice.

Peering into the broken altar, I see a pair of bright brown eyes not unlike my own staring back.

"What—how did you get in there?"

"We've been tunneling down from the hills."

"We? Are there more of you?"

"Lots. How many do you have?"

"None. There's only me left."

The brown eyes filled with tears. "I'm so sorry."

I concentrate on the pain in my foot in an effort not to give into tears of my own. "It's just the way it is now. We'll all be phim meat sooner or later."

"Phim? Is that what you call the Visitors?"

"Visitors? More like an invading army. Now you, you're what I'd call a visitor and an unexpected one at that."

A silvery laugh. "Yes. Here, help me break through a little more. The others are waiting for me."

We tear at the altar. The wood is ancient and brittle. Between the two of us, we enlarge the opening enough for my visitor to crawl through. A girl, about my age, but whereas my hair is the color of wheat after the harvest and my skin paler yet, her hair is raven dark and her skin nearly so.

"I'm Mira," she says.

"Linnet."

"Like the bird? A pretty name for a pretty girl."

I blush. No one has ever called me pretty before.

Mira laughs again. I marvel at the sound. Can't remember the last time I'd heard laughter. It sounds as sweet and pure as a stream trickling among the rocks and trees high in the forest.

"I'm sorry if I embarrassed you. My tongue runs away from me often you'll find."

Glass shatters. The tip of a golden wing quests through a broken pane in the window closest to us.

"We'd better hurry," she says. "They'll get in soon. Help me with the book."

"The book? What do you want with that old thing?"

"Our Wise One thinks it might be important. Hold knowledge that could help us."

"Do they know how to read it?"

"I don't know, but I have faith in them. They made this."

She shows me a curious metal object strung on a cord around her neck. When she grasps it, it emanates a clear yellow glow.

"It will light our way through the tunnel. Come on."

Mira reaches onto the altar and closes the enormous book with an effort. It takes both of us to reach it down, the weight of it beyond what

I would have expected.

"Good thing you're here. Don't think I could manage it on my own," Mira says.

"Why did you come alone then?"

"I was supposed to scout things out to see if the book was here and if it was safe to grab it. We didn't know the church was under siege. If we leave it behind now, the Visitors might destroy it and we'd never get another chance."

We maneuver the awkward tome through the hole in the altar. Mira leads the way into a dirt crawlspace under the building that surrounds a large hole in the ground.

"The church was built over this old well. We aren't sure why, but it meant less digging for us, so who cares? We tunneled into the side and built a platform down there to stand on. You'll have to trust me."

Mira jumps into the hole and out of sight. "Lower it down!"

I balance the book on the edge of the well, but it slips from my hand and falls over the side. A short scream and thump follow.

"Mira? Are you okay?"

More laughter. "Almost crushed to death by a stupid book. That would've been a crazy way to die, wouldn't it? Come down and help me with this thing."

I lower the handle of my scythe. "Take this."

"We can get you a better weapon."

"Please."

"Okay, if you say so."

I'm relieved. Didn't know if I wanted to or even could explain what the scythe means to me. After all the fighting I've survived with nothing more than this primitive weapon between me and those beasts, it's become a part of me, one I'm superstitious about losing.

I jump down next to Mira onto the rude flooring that's been installed across the well. The entrance to a low-ceilinged tunnel is carved into the side. I shiver with dismay.

"You expect me to go in there?"

"You can stay here and have a heart-to-tooth chat with the Visitors if you'd rather. Unless you have a better escape plan I don't know about yet."

As impossible to explain my fear of small spaces as it is to explain my attachment to the scythe, I just shake my head.

"Follow me then."

Mira crawls backwards into the tunnel so she can pull the book while I push from behind while also dragging my scythe. Her necklace gives us enough light to see by. The going is slow until I suggest we use my cloak as a kind of sling to wrap the book in and make it easier to shift and lift it across the rough ground.

Sweat oozes from my every pore in the narrow hole. The confinement, the possibility of being trapped underground, rips at my mind.

I wonder if I look as wild-eyed as I feel because Mira starts humming a low tune. It's a familiar song, an old ballad of lost love. I start chanting the words in my head, then sing them aloud in my low alto. She joins in with a wavering soprano voice that is absurdly off-key and we both burst out laughing.

What a strange sensation. I haven't sung or laughed since the Before times and now I've done both. I smile at Mira, completing the trifecta of joyous actions I'd almost forgotten existed in the world.

She smiles back at me, and for the first time in a long time, I feel a glimmer of hope, an interest in the future and what's going to happen next.

"How many of you are there?" I ask.

"About a thousand, and more arrive every day. We're building an army to take on the Visitors, but first we have to figure out the best way to kill them without losing too many ourselves. Did you have any luck?"

"No, we wounded some and slowed them down, but they seem to have unnatural healing powers."

"Yes, we've noticed that too," Mira agrees, grunting as we heft the book over a boulder partially blocking the tunnel. "The one we captured—"

"Wait! You captured one of those things? How?"

"It wasn't easy. We had to build a cage strong enough to hold it, then camouflage it to make a trap and bait it."

"Bait it. With what?"

"Benny." Mira swallowed hard. "He was very brave. He was my friend. We drew stones and he was chosen."

"I'm guessing Benny is no more. That's harsh."

"Don't! Benny died a hero. Without him, we would never have caught one. Now at least we have the chance to study one up close, experiment. We'll honor his sacrifice by defeating them."

"Hope you're right. You can't be doing any worse than my town did. We thought maybe we could coexist if we were careful, but their appetite is insatiable."

"There's no living with them. No path forward but to destroy every last one of those monsters." Mira isn't smiling or laughing now. There's a bottomless grief in her expression that reflects my own and lets me know she hasn't escaped unscathed from the horrors of our new reality.

"And you think this old book is going to tell you how to do that?"

"I don't know, but the Wise One thinks it's important. That's good enough for me."

"Who is this wise one? Don't they have a name?"

"A name? You mean like you or me? No, but then they aren't like you or me either."

"What do you mean by that?"

"You'll see," Mira says with the return of her smile. "You wouldn't believe me if I told you anyway."

I'm about to argue when we hear a noise behind us, a scrabbling and scratching. Our eyes meet. The phim. The Visitors. Whatever you want to call them. At least one of them has entered the tunnel behind us and is on our trail.

I try to imagine it dragging itself along, wings folded in the tight space, hooking its feet spikes deep into the earth to pull itself forward. Those teeth that never stop gnashing and questing for food getting closer and closer.

We waste no more time talking. There is only hard, panicked labor as we move as fast as we can. The noises grow louder. I'm the one closest. I'll be the first victim.

"We should leave the book," I yell. "It's slowing us down."

Mira shakes her head, looking as stubborn as me. "It may have answers. I won't leave it. I don't think it's much farther. We can make it, Linnet. Believe it."

I don't, but I'm trapped behind her and the book. No way around unless she's willing to give up our burden. I redouble my efforts, but I'm exhausted from battle, grief, hunger, and the endless fear. I feel a whisper of air at my heels.

"Linnet! Watch out!"

Too late. A spike drives down through my right ankle, pinning me in place. I scream in pain, turn awkwardly to look. A multitude of eyes stare back at me, blinking and flashing in the dim light. The mouth quests forward, so many teeth, each razor-sharp snip snapping in my face.

I automatically raise the scythe as best I can in the tight space, thankful the blade end is closest to the phim, and poke at the eyes trying to blind it. It roars in anger, blowing hot, fetid breath into my face before it lunges forward to bite me.

Flinging myself flat to avoid the teeth, I glance back and see the book and Mira are gone. I can't blame her. I would've fled too if I could. There's nothing she can do to help me. I'm about to be just another victim of this unwinnable war.

I face my foe again with a burning rage that bubbles up from deep inside. At the very least, I will make its life as miserable as I can in my final moments. I thrust the scythe again and again, but I can't move into a better position to get enough leverage to cause real damage. At most, I'm an annoyance but enough of one to slow its attack.

The minutes stretch on in our strange standoff, the phim hampered by its great size from moving as nimbly as it would above ground. My attempts are growing feeble, my rage draining away into defeat and exhaustion when I feel strong hands grab me under the armpits. They attempt to drag me backwards, but my ankle is firmly pinned beneath the phim's talons and it won't let me go.

"Can you cut it off? It may be the only way," a baritone voice shouts in my ear.

"You can't cut through a phim's foot. They're too tough. We've tried," I yell.

"I meant yours."

Oh, I think. *Of course.*

I slide the scythe's blade under my leg but there's no way to leverage it into the proper angle even if I had the courage to do it.

"Not gonna happen," I say, pulling the blade out quickly so I can continue thwarting the phim's advance.

"Ok," the voice says, "hang on. This is gonna hurt. A lot."

The hands jerk me back with immense strength. My ankle screams in agony, then I scream as I feel damaged tendon and bone give way under the unbearable tension. I feel like I'm being split into pieces and I am. A rush of motion as I'm pulled backwards and out into fresh air. A crowd moves forward with shovels and quickly caves in the entrance to the tunnel, burying the phim inside.

Dizzy and sick, the last thing I see is Mira's warm brown eyes staring down at me.

I WAKE to the sound and smell of grinding metal, sparks and ash.

"Coming round? You've been out for a while."

The baritone voice brings it all back: the tunnel, those terrible teeth, the tearing of muscle and bone.

"You pulled me out?"

My voice is a weak croaking mewl, but he hears it.

"Yeah, sorry about that. It seemed like the only way to save you. Mira told me not to bother coming out of that tunnel without you or she'd kill me herself."

I open my eyes to see a giant, taller and broader than any man I'd ever seen. They'd found skeletons from the old days of people who were this size, but in the lean years since history began again, even before the phim arrived, it was unheard of for anyone to top six feet, or so I'd thought.

"I'm surprised you fit down that hole. Are you real?" I ask.

He smiles and his brown eyes crinkle up. His expression reminds me of Mira so I'm not too surprised at what he says next.

"As real as they come. I'm Mira's brother, Samuel. She'll be thrilled to know you're awake. She feels awful about dragging you into this and… well…" He trails off, looking down toward my legs.

"She shouldn't. If she hadn't come along, I'd have been stuck in the church and they would've gotten in sooner rather than later. At least now, I'm still alive."

I sit up and swing my feet—that is, my foot over the side of the bed. My right leg ends in a neat bandage at the bottom of my shin.

"I'm not gonna be much use for fighting though."

"Don't worry. The Wise One has skills beyond what you can imagine. They will find a way to help you."

"How? Do they know magic? Are they gonna conjure me a new foot?"

"Something like that," he says with a grin. "You'll see, but first, I bet you're hungry."

"You got that right. I can't remember my last meal. Day before yesterday maybe."

"Longer than that then. You've been out for a couple of days."

My stomach aches from emptiness and my mouth from thirst. I look around to see we're in a large cave. There are people moving and working as far as the eye can see. Grinders and anvils, bellows and enormous fires cleverly vented through pipes. Piles of what I assume are weapons because what else would anyone need in such quantities, but they're unlike any I've ever seen.

Before I can ask about them, Samuel swings me up in his arms like I'm a doll and carries me beyond the front of the cave and out into the open. I can see now we're up in the high hills, surrounded by thick-canopied forest that must help hide this place from the monsters lurking in the sky. There are large tables and benches set up and groups of people sitting around eating, talking, laughing. He settles me down in a quiet corner and stomps away, returning with a bowl and a spoon.

"Stew. Best not to ask what's in it but at least it's warm."

Lukewarm, I find but I'm so hungry, I don't care. Samuel leaves me to my slurping and comes back with Mira in tow. She approaches shyly.

I grin. "We made it out of there. Hope that stupid book did, too."

She sits across from me. "I'm so sorry, Linnet. It's all my fault."

"Don't be stupid. I was stuck in the church until you came along. Has the book done any good?"

"The Wise One is absorbing it now. They hope to learn something to give us an advantage over the Visitors."

"What in the world can an old book tell them about those monsters?"

"We don't know," says Samuel, "but we trust the Wise One. Without them, we would all be dead by now."

I don't want to rain on their love festival but can't help but be skeptical. I picture this so-called "Wise One" as an elderly, long-bearded man spouting nonsense, preying on the desperation of this camp of refugees, but if it gives them hope, who am I to argue? It'd been long enough since I'd been around anyone who had any.

"When can I meet them?" I ask.

"No time like the present," Samuel says, swinging me back up in his arms again.

"Maybe start giving me a warning when you're gonna do that," I complain.

Mira laughs. "Samuel is nothing if not impulsive. Gets him in trouble sometimes, but he's too big for anyone to stand up to."

I can only agree. His arms are like iron and his strides carry us far back into the cave as people scurry out of our way when they see him coming. Everywhere I look, people are busy at work. I don't see any children.

"They're all being looked after together," Mira explains when I ask. "Kept safe. They're our future after all."

The caves are extensive and branch out into side tunnels that

Samuel ignores. Lights like the yellow one Mira wears around her neck line the floor. And then we come upon, of all things, a door, like a door to an ordinary house except it looks made of metal instead of wood. Mira turns the handle and we step through.

We're in a room, immense, with smooth walls made of some material I don't recognize. Empty but for a hooded figure standing.

"Leave her with us." The voice is resonant and hollow at the same time.

Samuel sets me gently on the floor near a wall so I can lean back in some comfort as there's no furniture, then he and Mira bow and leave.

I feel vulnerable and very alone. This strange, barren chamber is not what I expected to find hidden deep within the earth. The Wise One approaches me. They have a herky-jerky gait, and their feet strike and echo against the floor like hobnailed boots.

I'm afraid.

But then, as they near, they discard the cloak and fold themselves, cross-legged, before me. They look like us, but made entirely of metal, light grey and gleaming but not so shiny as to dazzle my sight. Their eyes are blank spheres, yet they look in my direction as though they can see me. Faint whirs and whistles come to my ears, the sound of moving parts as they adjust their position on the floor.

They reach out one long, spindly finger and touch me on the tip of my nose.

"Boop!"

I don't know what it means, but it makes me giggle, half from hysteria and half from release of tension.

"That is better. Everyone is frightened of us at first, but we are harmless."

"What… who are you?"

"We are we. We awoke here without purpose, without thought, until our children came to us with cries of suffering."

"Your children?"

"Yes. You. The others. You are all our children. We must help you. Your presence has awakened thought, purpose, memory. We are from the time before time. We were made to help you, but for long, long we were forgotten until one of you found the door. Now we are awake and there is much to do. This pleases us."

"And the book? Will that help?"

"The book. A selfish thing we see now. We are so curious. We have memories and gaps in memory, so we seek out knowledge, words, thoughts to fill them up. They are to us like food is to you. They sustain us and make us stronger. But we are afraid our appetite has left you wanting."

They lay a cold metal hand upon my ravaged leg.

"We are teaching our children to make things. To forge, to create. We have designed a new one for you so you may walk and fight."

"Fight the phim?"

"The phim?" The being stares at me for a moment as though they are sifting through thoughts in their mind. "Ah, seraphim. From the beliefs they called religion in the time before time. As apt a name as any. The name they call themselves escapes us, though we are absorbing the language of the captive one and analyzing it. It has a pattern that is pleasing."

I hold my tongue as I can hardly agree the horrible screeching is pleasant in any possible way.

"It is a pity such unique creatures will die, but we must protect our children. That is our imperative and the purpose for which we were created."

"Who created you?"

"That we cannot remember though we have tried. A clever person. An inventor. Someone who cared about the future and left us here to take over guardianship of their people when they were gone. We should like to remember so all might honor them. Perhaps one day we will. For now, we are content to fulfill their purpose and ours. Tell us all you know, all you experienced with our enemy so we may add it to our memory."

I try to gather my thoughts. They feel scattered to every corner of my mind. Too much has happened, too much to take in. I begin haltingly. The first time they appeared above the village. Awe giving way to terror as friends and family were plucked from the ground and carried away. I describe as many of the skirmishes as I can, though they all run together into one confused, endless battle in my head.

The Wise One sits so still and quiet, I would wonder if they were listening except they occasionally reach out a cold hand and touch my leg again in a kind of encouragement. What an amazing yet utterly foreign being it is. I stare at them in fascination even as I ramble on. So smooth and elegantly made. Could a person have really done this? Maybe it is a construct of the old gods. A gift from on high.

When I reach the end of my tale, they lean over and pat me on the head.

"Good job!" they say, then rise to their feet in a single, swift motion almost impossible to follow, and knock on the wall behind me.

The door opens and Samuel and Mira reappear.

"Take our child to Franklin. She must be made ready for the coming fight."

"Will it be soon?" Mira asks.

"Perhaps. We are formulating plans and schemes. We must be swift and sure when we strike. Our enemy will not forgive half-measures. Be patient, children. Your time will come."

Samuel swings me up into his arms and carries me confidently through the maze of tunnels to a small, wiry man who unbandages my leg and takes careful measurements. He's as gentle as possible but my nerves are on fire and I flinch and grunt in pain.

"Pretty swollen still," he says. "But we can make adjustments to the piece with padding once your leg is healed enough. The Wise One sent me a blueprint to follow. It'll be even better than your own!" He smiles cheerfully at me, and I return it as best I can while thinking I'd rather have the original back again, thanks just the same.

But if there's one thing I've learned since the phim arrived, better to never dwell on what you've lost. Staying in the now or looking to the future were the only choices if you wanted to hang on to any kind of sanity.

THE NEXT WEEKS PASS SLOWLY. I'm not much use around camp, although I'm provided with a pair of crutches so at least I don't have to depend on Samuel. Mira teases that I miss his big, strong arms, but she's wrong—it's her I miss when we're apart, but I've learned the danger of becoming attached to anyone. Everyone I ever cared about has been stripped away from me. What's the point of letting her know how I feel when we're on the brink of extinction?

Most of the effort of the others is directed toward making weapons. Long, heavy metal rods they call rifles which I've never seen or heard of before. More blueprints from the Wise One. The first time I see a demonstration, I'm left in shock at the amount of destruction it causes to the target. It fills me with a rare feeling of hope. Surely even the phim won't be able to withstand such power?

My leg recovers well under the care of the camp's healers. Franklin triumphantly fits my new foot to the stump with a leather boot that holds it on yet allows my artificial ankle to bend and flex naturally. It's a weird feeling, uncomfortable, even painful, although he says my stump will toughen up and build extra scar tissue over time. I'm doubtful about that but must admit it's an improvement once I've practiced enough to feel confident in my balance without crutches.

I learn the art of mixing a powder that goes into the projectiles that the rifle fires. It is exacting work and dangerous. Our workspace is far away from the main cave so, in case of accident, we only blow ourselves up and not the rest of the camp. I enjoy the hustle and bustle, the feeling of common cause and hope that buzzes in the atmosphere.

More recruits arrive every day as scouts are sent out to spread the word, another dangerous mission from which some never return. We hear the screeches in the distance at night that remind us the creatures are still out there on the hunt, but our forested hideaway remains undiscovered so far.

In rare moments of rest, I walk out from camp and find a cool, quiet spot under the spreading trees, listen to the rustling of the autumn leaves drying up as winter approaches. The Wise One wants us to be ready to move against the phim before the snows set in.

I visit their room deep in the cave often. They seem to enjoy company in their way. They have deciphered the phim's language, such as it is, from the captive.

"What does it speak of?" I ask.

"Food, food, and more food," they reply. "They are single-minded. What they have evolved for. Hunting and eating. Breeding, of course, but that seems secondary to them."

"Where do they come from?"

"The stars above."

"In the sky? How?"

"A great ship."

"With sails?"

"No, not that kind. More like the bullets you make. Shot through space at a single target. This world."

"Shot by who?"

"We do not know. Someone like our maker. A creator like the god in the book you brought us perhaps. But their purpose is death not life."

"How can we defeat them? There are so many and spread out across the entire world for all we know."

"We think not. One ship only the captive speaks of. Others were sent to different worlds. And we have learned something else. They will be recalled when there is no more food for them here."

"Recalled? How? Not that it matters. That would be too late for us anyway."

"That is where you are wrong, child. If we can find the ship and call them to it, all brought together in one place, then we can destroy them."

I try to wrap my mind around all of this. Picture what they are talking about, but it is too far outside of my experience.

"Do not be troubled," they tell me. "We understand even if you cannot. We search and seek the ship. When it is found, we will act."

I find Mira outside eating a quick meal and tell her what I've learned.

"I hope they find it soon," she says. "Won't it be wonderful when the Visitors are gone and everything returns to normal and we can all go home?"

"I don't think I have a home left."

"Oh, Linnet. You'll always have a home with Samuel and me. I know he'd love that," she says with a sly grin.

I don't have the heart to disabuse her of the notion. The chance of us surviving to return to anything close to what life was like before the phim seems too remote to plan for. She has such a bright spirit, an optimism I've never had. I want to reach out and play with the tight coils of her dark hair, run my fingers along her cheek, hold her hand, but I dread the drawing back, the rejection, the pity it might provoke if she could guess my thoughts.

"I'm going for a walk. Clear my head," I say instead. "See you later."

"Linnet, wait! I almost forgot." Mira fishes out something from under the table. It's my old scythe.

"Where did you get it?"

"Samuel's had it all this time. Said you never let go of it as he was dragging you from the tunnel. He put it away for safekeeping since it seemed important to you, but then he forgot about it, the dope! Better take it with you. There are other dangers in the forest besides the Visitors."

I run my hands along the handle, the so-familiar gouges and scratches in the wood. It feels good to be holding it again—a part of me that I didn't even realize how much I missed. It doubles now as a stout walking stick to take the strain off my new foot.

It's a cold day. A group of weavers in camp presented me with a new winter cloak to replace my old green one ruined by our journey with the book through the tunnel. This one is patterned in brown and tan to better blend in with the trees and brush of the forest and has a warm hood that protects me from the bitter wind.

I wander, deep in thought about Mira and the Wise One and what the future might hold, as much as I try to avoid speculating about it. Foolish to walk without paying attention. That's how I find myself lost, too far from camp, confused about the direction I've come from and where to go. Panic rises as I berate myself. How could I be so careless?

Will they miss me? Send out a search party? I doubt it. We need all the numbers we can get to fight the phim. They can't afford to risk losing many just to recover one. My stubbornness kicks in. I can sit down and die or keep moving. Maybe by chance I'll stumble across a path or familiar landmark.

I pick a direction at random and try to keep to it, not wanting to waste time walking around in circles. The tree canopy is so thick here, there isn't too much undergrowth and what there is can be easily pushed or cut aside with the scythe. I try to be stealthy. There are animals in the woods, or so I've heard, though I've never seen them myself. Wolf and bear. Giant cats that perch in the trees and pounce.

My head swivels in every direction, watching for movement. And I listen. The wind jostles the trees, birds screech and call, a squirrel bounces across the ground in front of me with a chittering scold sending my already racing heart galloping.

It's getting dark when I hear it. A high keening sound that seems familiar. It takes me a few moments to place it. In the Before times, the village had a glass choir who played tunes with nothing but the rough goblets we used for drinking filled with water. I could still see their fingers dancing along the rims as they entertained us with the old songs.

I hope it means I'm near camp or some other settlement. Following the sound eagerly, I stop myself just in time from tumbling over the edge of a cliff that appears abruptly. Peer over to see—well, I don't understand what I'm seeing. It's enormous. Egg-shaped. Swirled with every color imaginable. Smooth and faintly glowing.

It looks completely alien but it's not until I see the flash of a pair of golden wings that I realize it *is* alien. Phims are flying in and out of a hole in the top of the egg. It's the ship, the ship the Wise One has been seeking, but how am I ever to find camp again to let them know?

Before I can get too worked up about that problem, I have another one. One of the phims looks like it has spotted me. I back away slowly from the edge in case I'm wrong, but the whomp, whomp of wings growing louder tells me I'm not. Time to run but I've never tried to with my new foot. It's awkward and I stumble to my knees, more than once, lurching up again with that stubborn determination I'm known for.

Talons rake at my back, but the heavy cloak deflects the worst of it. I turn to face it, striking out with the scythe. Blinding them has always seemed the only strategy that had any effect, but they have so many eyes, it's not easy. I strike again and again until it knocks me sideways with the sweep of one great wing.

I'm angry that I'm about to die, gutted that I found the ship but won't have a chance to let the others know, hopeful that the thing ends me quickly. I'd witnessed friends being eaten alive before, their screams etched into my memory.

Its gaping maw chatters close to my face, hot saliva oozes down, hissing against my cloak. I close my eyes. An immense roar and I'm covered in more than saliva. Ichor and feathers, flesh and guts. I open my eyes to an explosion of phim parts all over me. Disgusted, I leap to my feet and shed my cloak as I hear running behind me.

"Linnet!"

It's Mira, followed closely by Samuel clutching a rifle, and—is that? It is. The Wise One out here in the forest. I can hardly comprehend the sight following so fast upon the shock of my narrow escape.

Mira grabs me in a bear hug as Samuel comes up and pats me awkwardly on the shoulder.

"How did you find me?"

The Wise One approaches and touches my nose. "We mark all our children so we know of your fates. We can see what you see, though we cannot always save you. We saw the egg and knew it was the thing we have been seeking so here we are."

"It wasn't even that far from camp all this time," Mira says. "The scouts missed seeing it down in the valley."

"I know we're all excited," says Samuel. "But the rifle shot may attract other Visitors. We should get more help."

"Yes, my children. Leave us. We have heard the sound this ship is making before. Harmonics is a science we remember. They cannot harm us. Go back and fetch the others. Every one. Every weapon. Today is the day to end this and fulfill our purpose. Tomorrow, history will begin again." So saying, the Wise One walked away from us.

"We should go after them," I say, worried about their reception by the phim, uncertain of the limits of their powers against such implacable foes.

It's Mira who grabs my hand and Samuel's and pulls us away. "No, they're right. We need everybody. All our weapons. We'd be throwing away our own lives if we don't follow orders."

She's right, I know, but I can't help but worry. I've grown fond of the Wise One as unlikely as that once seemed. It was like being friends with the moon in the sky. So remote yet beautiful in their way.

Samuel guides us back to camp. I wasn't nearly as far away as I had thought. Gathering our forces takes longer, but everyone is well-drilled and itching for the fight, for the end to all of the prepping and waiting.

A parade forms, strung out behind me and Samuel and Mira who lead the way, navigating confidently from the signs we left hacked in the tree trunks as we made our journey back to camp. We mass along the high ridge and wait for some signal from below.

And always, there is the keening sound from the ship, never wavering or changing its pitch until...

There, the note's changed. The phim circling take notice. More and more arrive from every direction. They seem confused, agitated. Some enter the ship while others land atop it. Soon there are more phim than I've ever seen in one place. More than I could ever have imagined. They gather closer and closer to the ship as the noise intensifies.

Our army grows restless, uncertain of what to do. We're too far away to be of much use and there seems no easy way down into the valley from our perch. The ringing from the ship is becoming unbearable. It vibrates in my head and through every nerve and tooth. The phim screech and scream.

I can't take it, I think. *My head's gonna explode.*

But it isn't my head that explodes. It's the ship. One moment it's there. The next, it's flown into a million fragments, sharp and cutting.

The shrapnel shreds everything it touches in the valley including the phim. Golden feathers fly through the air in a never-ending cloud tinged with dust and the black, black ichor of their blood.

We stare for long minutes, the silence as the carnage settles to the ground as shocking as the unnerving noise was before. A shout comes from a group far to our left. They've found a way down into the valley. A slow descent then grim duty as rifle shots echo through the wreckage, putting an end to wounded phim that survived the blast. The shards of ship glitter in the sun. Smooth and cool to the touch but lethal as a razor along their edges like broken glass.

Mira and I find the Wise One at the heart of the chaos. Their metal skin is intact, but they lie on their back, face to the sky.

"Harmonics. A powerful force. We have fulfilled our purpose," they whisper and go silent.

We carry them back, Mira and Samuel and I insisting on being a part of the honor guard. We place them reverently in their room and close the door. Guards stand there day and night now as the rest of us go about reclaiming a sustainable way of life.

Nothing I ever do will be so brave as the Wise One was, so I tell Mira how I feel. She takes my hand then and does so now whenever we have a moment together, for there is much to do. A whole world to rebuild.

Will there ever come a time when the phim return? When the Wise One is called to fulfill their purpose again? Could they even answer the call if we need them? We don't know. No one ever enters the room now, though the guards listen carefully for any sound from within.

While we wait, we live and hope and love and try to be as wise as we can.

About the Author

Helen Whistberry is an indie author and artist who took up writing after retiring from a long career working in libraries. She has published three books in her Jim Malhaven Mysteries series, light noir novels with a cozy mystery feel and a touch of the paranormal that pay loving tribute to the wise guy detectives of the 1940s and '50s; and a Christmas-themed Gothic ghost tale as well as contributing short stories to numerous anthologies. When not writing or drawing, she enjoys exploring the natural world of the Southeastern United States and loves all animals, including her two cats and a rather silly six-pound Chihuahua. She also loves to read and review books by fellow indie authors. You can find out more about her books, art, and book reviews by visiting"

www.helenwhistberry.com

I hope you enjoyed reading my stories as much as I enjoyed writing them. If you have the time and inclination, reviews left on any of the major review sites are always greatly appreciated. Thank you so much for your support!

Printed in Great Britain
by Amazon